thirtyninestars
Austin, Texas

DIGGING UP THE DEAD

A Crispin Leads Mystery

by
MEREDITH LEE

Digging Up the Dead: A Crispin Leads Mystery

This book is a work of fiction. To give the work authenticity, the authors use the names of actual historical figures. However, these figures are placed into situations that are the products of the authors' imagination, and do things that they never did in real life. Therefore, even though actual historical figures appear, the reader should consider some of the actions as fictional. Apart from the people, events and locations adapted from history, the entire work is an invention of the authors' and, therefore, any resemblance to actual events or persons, living or dead, is unintended and entirely coincidental. The authors have not been compensated for product placement. The use of actual venues, locations, products, or events stem from the writers' affections and/or attempts at authenticity.

ThirtyNineStars
Austin, TX

ISBN: 9780999223321

Library of Congress Cataloging in Publication Data: 2018906805
1.Title. 2. Fiction. 3. Mystery. 4. Suspense.

Printed in the United States of America
Written by Dixie Lee Evatt and Sue Meredith Cleveland
Cover Design by Elizabeth Mackey
David Aretha, Yellow Bird Editors

DEDICATION

This book is for the men who've loved us:
Chevis R. Cleveland and Gary C. Evatt.

DIGGING UP THE DEAD

Prologue

Valley of the Kings, Egypt, 1923

The boy heard his mother wailing but it came from somewhere far away. Diggers had pulled his broken body out of the limestone rubble and laid him on the hard sand not far from the dead and dying. He knew that soon he too would die. He wanted to tell them what he'd seen: the hand that had pulled down the frame that held the scaffolding in place, causing the cave-in. But his lungs were crushed and couldn't produce sound.

His fading thoughts were of his family and his fate. He strained to recall the teachings of his faith. What happens to murder victims when they face the final judgment, when every act and every desire must be accounted for?

Will the manner of my death erase the stain of my crime? Surely it was a small crime, to accept baksheesh to tell a lie. If I tell my secret now, will I be cleansed of my crime? But his throat was full of dust and his lungs were no longer able to hold air.

Then the water boy, who had become a local celebrity only a year before when he discovered the fateful stairs that led to the extraordinary discovery of the tomb of Tutankhamun, stopped breathing. He disappeared into little more than a footnote in history. His death and his secret would not be noticed again for more than seven decades.

Inna lillahi wa inna ilayhi raji'un.
From God we have come and to God we return.

Chapter One

There is something decidedly off-putting about waking up to the sight of a dog running into your tent with a human hand and forearm dangling out of his mouth. It didn't help that Crispin was suffering from a hangover, having ended the previous night with one too many bootleg Egyptian whiskeys. It was the only thing strong enough to erase the sting from the fight she'd had with her father.

The brindle bulldog dropped his trophy next to where she lay, face down on a camp cot while still dressed in her work clothes from yesterday. The dog yelped and shook his head so hard that the drool slobbering from the side of his mouth splattered Crispin's cheeks. He cocked his head in expectation.

"Seth, pa-lease," she begged just as two Misr field workers, breathless and dusty from the chase, charged in, cursing, before they noticed Crispin and pulled back.

"Sorry, miss, but the dog, he ran away with it," one said, pointing at the amputated limb on the floor.

Crispin pushed herself up onto her elbows and grabbed Seth by the collar. "What's going on?"

"We found a man. Dead. The police are on their way."

Crispin's head started to throb and she felt her stomach pitch and churn. She knew what was in store for her. She reached under her cot to retrieve a leash, attached it to Seth's collar, and handed it to one of the men. "Take him."

She emptied her pillowcase and gave it to the other man, indicating that he should use it to retrieve Seth's disgusting prize. "Get that, too."

When the second man picked up the dismembered arm she flinched and turned her head, but not before noticing a crude tattoo on the back of the hand. It looked like a saber plunged deep into the middle of a wide semicircle. The fingernails of the hand were chipped and crusted with dirt, but the field workers had the thing bagged and were gone with Seth before she could see more.

Standing, Crispin swayed and sat down again, nearly missing the corner of the canvas cot. The foul taste in her mouth reminded her of last night's puke-a-thon that ended with the dry heaves around 3 a.m. Now ascending decibels of a nasty migraine were mixing with an old-fashioned hangover to create a stew of perfect misery. She needed quiet. She needed strong American drugs. She needed a dark place. Only one of those things was available in this desert plateau.

Crispin hunted through her canvas bag for her prescription. She found a tube of Tom's of Maine toothpaste and used her finger to rub the minty paste across her teeth and tongue. She slathered sunscreen on her fair skin, tied her thick auburn hair back with a scarf, put on her darkest sunglasses, and settled a wide-brimmed hat low on her forehead before opening the tent flap to a sunlight so bright it seared through her glasses.

"Heaven help me," she whispered. The intensity of her headache was so strong that she felt the outline of her skull through the skin of her face, the orbs of her eye sockets pulsing with each heartbeat. She ignored everyone she passed as she crossed the dusty path through the busy campsite, making straight for the mess tent where strong Turkish coffee and the restorative promise of caffeine awaited.

Breakfast service was long since over, so the dining area was occupied by only a handful of stragglers. She almost ran to the coffee bar, where she watched while the thick brew of water and coffee, ground nearly to dust and spiced with cardamom, came to a boil in the copper ibrik. She had just sat down and taken her first welcome sip when her brother looked through the tent flap. Although they were twins, Clinton was the one who had inherited their mother's rich olive skin tones and their father's athletic build.

"There you are."

"You have a gift for stating the obvious," she replied, taking a second gulp that scalded the tip of her tongue.

"Bit testy, I see. Can't blame you after what you pulled last night." He eased onto the seat next to her.

Crispin covered her eyes with both hands and leaned on her elbows. "I don't need this right now."

"Okay, so let's talk about something else. Did you hear about the dead man?"

Before she could answer, their father, The Daniel Leads, Ph.D. walked in, accompanied by two men. They sat down at a long table across the way. Ignoring Crispin, their father signaled for Clinton to join them. Crispin decided to disregard the snub and joined her brother.

"Inspector Sabri, this is my son, Clinton," Dr. Leads said. "He's taken time away from his postgraduate studies in geological sciences at Cornell to work on our project. He is a world-class scientist and we are lucky to have him with us. We will miss him when he returns to London. This is my daughter, Crispin."

Before her father could say more, Crispin offered her hand to the middle-aged inspector with a close cut military style haircut and piercing deep set eyes. "My doctoral studies are in the field of burial rituals."

"I think you will find that the Saqqara necropolis offers up its treasurers to those who know how to read the signs," the inspector said. His attention was on Crispin, but his comments were directed to Dr. Leads.

"Then our Crispin is sure to be the one to uncover the next big secret," the portly man next to her father added with unadulterated pride.

"Thank you, Ashraf," Crispin responded, giving her old family friend a kiss on his sun-scarred cheek and sitting down next to him. "When did you get in?"

"Late last night," he said with an impish grin. "Unfortunately, I arrived after the party was over."

"Party?" Inspector Sabri asked.

Dr. Leads explained that a group of lifelong colleagues were celebrating because they had put the finishing touches on a major proposal for an excavation in the Bahariya Oasis. "Our plans must now be submitted to the Egyptian government."

"That's where I come in," Ashraf said, with another full-faced grin and a wink at Crispin.

"We've made a great deal of progress here and want to propose a course to guide future expeditions. But, that is not what you want to discuss, is it, Inspector?" Dr. Leads asked.

"It is all of interest, all of interest. However, you are correct. I am here regarding the matter of a find of more recent origin."

"Was the whole body cut up or just the one arm?" Crispin asked. She relished the shock in the faces of the men.

"What do you know of this case?" the inspector asked.

"Nothing much. Seth, he's the camp hound, woke me up dragging along a man's forearm. Gruesome idea for a gift if you ask me. But then, dogs are that way. Who was it? What happened to him?"

"We are working on identification. The body was discovered in a shallow trench near the midden."

Crispin was struck by the inspector's use of an arcane archeological term for a garbage heap, but didn't comment. She opened a blank page in her leather field journal, a prized possession since it had once belonged to her mother. She hoped that if she focused on note-taking she would be able to tolerate the pain in her head until the meds kicked in. As the men discussed the case, she listened with half of her attention while absentmindedly drawing a rough diagram of the camp.

When she got to the point of placing an "X" where the body was found, she asked, without looking up, "Are all of that fella's parts accounted for?"

"Really, Crispin, is that necessary?" her father asked, his tone sharp and dismissive.

"No. I suppose not," she replied, standing and gathering her journal. "Am I necessary?" she asked, directing her question to the inspector. He shrugged and she turned, leaving without further comment.

Outside, the sun was so intense that she was only able to go a short distance before she had to stop and close her eyes. Even that did little to protect from the pain of the penetrating bright golds and yellows. Ashraf caught up with her.

"I have something for you," he said, creating a blessed shadow when he stepped between her and the sun. He fished into the pockets of his cargo shorts and pulled out a package wrapped in blue cotton cloth and tied with lavender grosgrain ribbons.

"Salma made me promise to put this directly into your hands," he said. "I will be in hot water if I fail in my mission."

"What is it?"

"She didn't tell me. If I know my wife, it is some overpriced bauble she couldn't resist," he replied.

When Crispin reached to take the package she dropped her journal. Ashraf retrieved it and brushed off the dust as he returned it, giving Crispin a fatherly hug.

"Got to run. Be careful, my dear."

Crispin didn't open the gift package from Salma until she reached the privacy of her tent. Nestled in soft cotton batting was an iridescent butterfly brooch. The cunning design of gold was inlaid with semiprecious stones. She'd never seen anything quite like it.

A note in Salma's ornate penmanship accompanied it: "We found this little lovely of Melete's during spring cleaning. I cannot explain how it escaped our notice all these many years, hidden in a crevice in the tile. But, there it is. Your mother would have wanted you to have it. To treasure it, as did she. In my heart and memory, she is forever young. Not a day passes that I don't think of her beauty, her kindness, her voice. Please come to Cairo and we will share time together. All we have is today. Tomorrow is promised to no one. Salma."

Drowsy from the effects of the strong painkiller, Crispin tucked the brooch in her pocket, lay back on the cot, and was soon lost in a deep sleep.

***

She didn't wake up until she heard Clinton's voice calling from what sounded like the top of a mountain.

"You were down for the count, Crisp," he said when she opened her eyes.

"What time is it?"

"A little after five. I came to say goodbye. I'm taking the red-eye back to London."

Crispin stood up and shook her head to clear what felt like boulders rolling around between her ears. "I'm going with you."

"You know you're welcome but, after last night, don't you think you need to make things right with Dad and Laurie first?"

"Ugh. Don't ever mention Ms. Prada Heels to me again. You know, Clint, I can't stand the thought of her living in our house. She's too young for him. He's acting like a lovesick fool."

Clinton had already heard this complaint too many times to want to rehash his sister's insecurities. "It didn't help that you insisted on watching THE movie all the way through."

"It wasn't just me. It was 'The Gang.'" Even as she spoke the words, Crispin knew they rang hollow.

Clinton told her that she had time to get ready while he made arrangements. The drive into Cairo to catch the flight would only take an hour.

"Do you want me to call Sophie to let her know you are coming?" Clinton asked as he left.

"That's great and I'll follow with an email." Sophie Nessim was Crispin's lifelong friend. They'd met as toddlers in Egypt and reunited as schoolgirls at summer camp in Connecticut. Since then they'd shared everything and roomed together at NYU. Sophie, in London for the summer, had been begging Crispin to join her.

After Clinton left, Crispin mentally went back over everything that had gone wrong the night before. It had started so well with the group of family friends that they had known since their father worked in Egypt as a young man. The "Mediterranean Gang," as they liked to call themselves, spent most of the night talking about their successes, making plans for publication of their findings, and agreeing on their next joint expedition in the Bahariya Oasis.

It felt like old times until Dr. Leads stood up, tapping a spoon on the edge of his glass for attention. He had an announcement. A bombshell. There in front of everyone, he told them that Dr. Laurie Pierce, his colleague from Cornell, had agreed to marry him. Their friends cheered. Clinton hugged Laurie. Crispin grabbed a whiskey bottle and took a long drink straight from the bottle. It was the first of many to come.

At some point, one of The Gang pulled out a computer so he could share recently digitized versions of old home movies. Inevitably, the reels got to the last home movie of Crispin and Clinton's mother, filmed just a few days before she'd died in a plane crash on the tarmac in Egypt. Dr. Leads suggested they stop it, but Crispin, now well into her cups, stood up and confronted her father. "No way. That's my mama. I want to see it."

Dr. Leads took Laurie by the arm and excused himself, but Crispin had yelled after him. She couldn't remember exactly what she said, but she did remember that Clinton pulled her away and took her to her tent. She didn't need to watch the movie. She knew it by heart. They'd been in preschool at the time of the accident, and over the years they'd watched the movie time and again. It had helped reinforce childhood memories whenever they faded.

In the film, their father seemed to Crispin's eye to be more distinguished than Ashraf and their friends. She'd always thought it was not just his slightly formal way of dressing or the premature graying around his temples that set Dr. Leads apart. Something in the way he stood and moved made him seem aloof, as if observing, but not fully participating in, the fun. Their mother, Melete, sat as if royalty behind a stone table in the garden. The Gang passed platters weighted down with feta cheese, olives, and pita bread. They poured wine with the abandon of young people who cannot see death's closing shadow.

That movie, so precious to Crispin when she and Clinton were growing up, now seemed sullied, something else ruined by the intrusion of Laurie Pierce into their life.

Upset, embarrassed, gritty, and hot, Crispin decided to shower. Safe in the privacy of the rushing water, she allowed herself to cry. She held her head back, letting the hot water wash over her face and rinse away the tears. Her weeping released some of the tension, but did nothing to salve her hurt.

Back in her tent, as she leaned forward to towel dry her hair, a rainbow of light unexpectedly danced off her face and onto the wall behind her cot, reflecting a pattern that looked familiar. Crispin tried to remain perfectly still lest the reflection disappear. When she turned toward the source of the image, she saw that the light was reflecting off her mother's brooch. She'd left the brooch on the folding table and now it was aligned so that sunlight through a crack in the seam of the tent bounced off the stones and projected a distinctive arc-shaped reflection onto the wall.

"Where have I seen that before?"

The image on the wall flickered as the sunbeam moved through the brooch but then disappeared, robbing the brooch of light. Crispin rubbed her temples, confused by what she'd seen. She realized that she hadn't eaten in hours. She needed fuel. First eat. Then think.

At the mess tent, Crispin filled her plate with ground beef and rice, buttered carrots, beets, and breadsticks. She picked out a corner table and kicked off her sandals, tucking one foot under her. Her other leg dangled off the bench and she began to swing her bare foot as she tried to decipher the meaning behind ancient symbols hidden in heirloom jewelry.

Unseen by Crispin, two hands reached under the tent flap and dumped a small viper from a basket. The asp inched toward Crispin's dangling leg. Finished with her meal, she blindly fiddled around under the table with her foot trying to slip it back into her sandal. As she groped for her shoe, the snake reared up to engage Crispin's foot in a fencing match. The snake lunged. Her foot parried. The snake answered, but her foot was too quick. Just as the snake reared for a final deadly strike, Crispin succeeded in sliding her toes into her sandal and stood up. Oblivious to her near miss, she bussed her table and returned to her tent. She had just enough time to pack before the flight to London.

Chapter Two

Sophie, preparing for Crispin's late-night arrival from Cairo, tucked the pillow under her chin and wrestled it into a fresh pillowcase, causing feathers from the worn ticking to flutter to the floor. She plumped the pillow the way her grandmother had taught her. Crispin didn't need to know it was Sophie's only pillowcase. After all, what did one expect from an economy sublet in London? Multiple sets of thousand-thread-count Egyptian cotton linens? She stooped to pick up the feathers as the phone rang. It was Georgia returning her call.

A Savannah princess, Karen Farris was known by her friends and family as "Georgia." Sophie and Crispin met Georgia as freshmen at NYU, where they became inseparable friends and roommates, sharing secrets and developing a deep trust in the years since.

Georgia picked the Manhattan campus less for its stellar academic reputation than its proximity to her personal Mecca: Saks Fifth Avenue. Besides, she said, the Big Apple was an ideal place to kick around before returning to the predictable, sedate life expected of a Farris woman. After six years in college and almost as many changes in her major, Georgia wasn't the least bit embarrassed that she was still working on an undergraduate degree.

"Ain't no sense rushin' things," she'd say with the languid drawl that even her professors found charming.

Tonight Sophie could hear the whirring of a NYC police siren in the background. Georgia must be standing by an open window at her Midtown apartment. Cupping the receiver between her shoulder and ear, Sophie tied on her running shoes in preparation for her evening workout and waited patiently until Georgia, always breathless, spoke. "Can you hear me, Soph?"

"Crispin is hurting, again," was all Sophie needed to say to get Georgia's undivided attention.

Two years earlier, when Crispin returned wounded from Italy, it had been Georgia who set up a road trip for the three of them. She'd brought a hamper of gourmet food, boxes of colorful tissue, and toe-tapping CDs that begged them to sing along. When they arrived at the remote cabin in the Adirondacks, Georgia told Crispin, "Honey, if you need to howl at the moon, go ahead."

Georgia listened while Sophie told her about the call from Clinton and Crispin's sudden decision to leave Egypt.

"It ain't good," Sophie said. "Some guy was killed and she's playing like it doesn't bother her."

"Holy shit. You want me to come to London?" Georgia asked.

"Not yet. I'll let you know."

"I hear you. Soph, love her for both of us. She doesn't deserve to get pulled back into the undertow."

"I'll try but you know our Crispin. Sometimes I think she's a magnet for trouble."

Chapter Three

Crispin slept fitfully, her mind wandering from semi-conscious thought to near sleep. Eventually, she dream-traveled to her childhood bedroom in Ithaca, New York. She could smell the shape and hear the colors of her favorite things: precious seashells collected from faraway beaches, a goldfish bowl spilling over with movie stubs, stacks of dog-eared crime novels, gaudy souvenir posters of Egyptian gods, and side tables crowded with a hodgepodge of framed family snapshots. The feeling of being there was so right and real and settling that when she opened a tentative eyelid she was disoriented by shadows trapped on an alien wall.

The shift from the soft comfort of her imagination to the sharp reality of Sophie's London flat was a stark rebuke of everything that had gone so terribly wrong in Egypt. Last night Sophie had welcomed her with genuine excitement, full of plans for the two of them. After helping Crispin settle in, Sophie had tucked back into a deep sleep.

Crispin got up, wrapped herself in a throw, and huddled on the sofa as she tried to make sense of the events that had once again torn apart her relationship with her father. For the past two years Crispin had thrown herself into her graduate studies, winning praise for her coup as the first secular academician to publish landmark studies in two high-powered academic journals based on the writings of an obscure monk whose diaries validated centuries-old burial customs.

Although the Vatican's decision to give her access to the diaries made her a bit of a legend in certain academic circles, she learned that success is often accompanied by interdisciplinary jealousy. Some of her colleagues started a whisper campaign that her access to the diaries was the result of an illicit affair with a Roman Catholic priest, a "tit for tat."

When she complained to one of her female advisers at NYU, the senior scholar told her to get used to such petty gossip if she planned to remain in the field. "It's how the men keep us in our place," she said. "It's one of the ways they devalue our achievements. They fight over everything. Parking places. Office assignments. Titles. Invitations to parties." She reminded Crispin of the oft-repeated dictum in academia, "The fights here are vicious because there is so little at stake."

"None of that matters," Crispin told her, nearly reduced to tears.

"That's why you will fail unless you understand how things work," her adviser said. "It's their department. Their rules."

"I can't do that," Crispin said.

"Then don't. Ignore them. Do the work. That's all that matters in the end."

Helpless to defend her reputation, Crispin doubled up on seminars and took summer classes, completing all of her requirements toward her doctorate in record time. She was in the process of putting the finishing touches on her dissertation, rounding out her groundbreaking work on burial rituals and customs. Her work had not only gained her international recognition in her field, but also earned her a prestigious research grant at Cornell University, where her father was a distinguished professor.

Crispin had submitted a formal proposal to be part of the Saqqara team so she could learn more about the region's ancient history of cult burial ceremonies practiced by the middle and lower classes. She was especially thrilled that for the first time she would be working alongside her father as a colleague on an important dig. The near euphoria she'd felt when she joined her father's team melted into disappointment and blinding anger after that hellish fight on the night before she left Egypt.

Crispin was deep into full self-recrimination mode when daylight started creeping through the blinds of the apartment and Sophie began to show signs of life. Sophie slouched past Crispin to the kitchen where she stared at the aluminum percolator as if aliens had left it on the counter during the night. Crispin started to say "Good Morning," but swallowed the words when Sophie growled and gave Crispin a sharp salute with her outstretched palm. She was imposing the Fifteen-Minute Rule.

During their first summer at camp together in Connecticut, Crispin was reduced to tears several mornings in a row by Sophie's bad humor. That's when a mutual friend at the camp, Ellen Sato from Italy, told them about the Fifteen-Minute Rule. It went like this: Sophie and Crispin were to keep their mouths shut for fifteen minutes after waking. Whoever broke the rule would have to make up the other's cot. The rule had saved their friendship and continued to serve them through college.

Crispin could see the entire apartment from where she sat since it was no more than six hundred square feet. What passed for a kitchen was set along one wall behind Masonite folding doors, a space saver like old-fashioned Murphy beds. Mismatched plates, glasses, and mugs were stacked on two shelves lined with scalloped paper that was faded and worn. The living room was just large enough for the sofa and wing-back chair whose chartreuse upholstery had been patched with silver duct tape. Despite the aging plumbing and funky décor, it was a cozy flat.

When coffee was ready, Sophie brought Crispin a chipped mug decorated with a wedding picture of Princess Di and Prince Charles. After some quiet sipping, Sophie broke the silence. "So Clinton tells me that you and the high and mighty Professor Leads are on the outs?"

"I'd rather not go down that road."

"You'll get no argument here. What are your plans?"

"I still have holes to fill in about burial customs for the Average Joe in ancient Egypt. Fortunately, I got a lot done in Egypt before I left, but there are still a few gaps. I'm sure I can find some of what I need at the Egyptian Department of the British Library. How about you?"

"Training." Sophie had finished a graduate degree in economics at Columbia when she was given a chance to train alongside a team in London for the women's 400-meter Olympic trials. It was an offer she couldn't pass up.

Dressing for the day, Crispin was forced to smile at the clothes Sophie loaned her since her Egyptian cottons and sandals would never make it on a frigid March day in London. When it came to fashion, Crispin and Sophie were a study in contrasts. Sophie was almost as tall as Clinton and built like the competitive runner she was. Whereas Crispin was pale, Sophie was proud of the deep chocolate tones of her own skin. If Crispin's clothing sense tended to lag behind current styles, Sophie's was the opposite. Her clothes fused cultural styles from the flashy to the trashy. Unlike Crispin, who often used baggy sweaters to camouflage her shape, Sophie flaunted her sexuality. Crispin used a belt to cinch in the waist of the loaner wool slacks, rolled up the pant legs, and draped a scarf around her neck to compensate for the cleavage-enhancing sweater. "I will definitely have to shop today," she promised herself.

***

Confronted by a barricade of cardboard boxes, Crispin stepped back into the hall to double check the signage.

"Yep," she mumbled to herself. The sign read: Egyptian Department. British Library. She hadn't made a mistake. This was the department that the clerk on the first floor had told her she would find what she was looking for.

Inside, shopworn cartons towered at odd angles and overflowed with yellowed papers and photos. Some of the boxes creaked and shifted as if they were searching for an open space in which to collapse. Those on the bottom were in the worst condition, crushed under the weight of their heavy cousins.

Ahead in the hidden distance, Crispin could hear someone getting a royal dressing down. She surveyed the cardboard blockade and decided to work her way toward the voices by clearing just enough room to step through. She replaced papers behind her as she moved, much in the way a mole digs a tunnel through the earth. It was slow work as she excavated her way toward the voices. When she nudged a dog-eared field journal out of harm's way, she noticed the name of a moving and storage company on the side of a box.

"If this is what happens when you move, I'd fire the movers," Crispin mumbled to herself.

"I could not agree more."

Crispin was startled at the voice coming from the other side of a treacherous looking stack. "Excuse me?"

A wrinkled face peeked around a box. "I was simply agreeing with you," the woman said with the flawless enunciation of the Queen's English. "We should sack the movers."

The woman extended her hand. "Welcome. I'm Ida Fowler."

"Forgive me, Ms. Fowler. I'm Crispin Leads. I didn't realize I was mumbling."

"Don't be, dear. I find that people who spend a great deal of time alone in libraries often vocalize without realizing it."

"The clerk downstairs said I would find someone in this department to assist me," Crispin explained.

Ida motioned for Crispin to follow. "It is easier if you come this way."

Crispin initially thought that Ida was seated. As the old lady squeezed through a narrow opening Crispin saw that she was unusually short. What Ida lacked in height, however, she made up for in girth.

"I fear we are not at our best at the moment," Ida said as they entered her office, interrupting a loud argument between two men. Ida suggested that Crispin find a place to sit. "If you can."

The only place Crispin could see to sit was the chair near Ida's desk. It had the added advantage of being within earshot of the two men's argument. *Okay, so I'm nosey,* she thought.

The older man was short like Ida, but skeletal. The younger man's corduroy slacks hung low upon his hips, and his hair was long overdue for a wash.

The older man prodded the younger, "Go on, Stuart. Tell Miss Fowler."

"But, Mr. Finn…" Stuart started to protest, then sighed and offered a tortured explanation. From what Crispin gathered, he'd been responsible for transporting archive material to the company's warehouse facility, where his team scanned and digitized the documents. He'd just unloaded the mess she'd seen in the hall.

Finn took over the story. "When the morning crew arrived, the door locks were jimmied. They found boxes scattered hither and yon. Most had been torn open and the files dumped on the floor. Paper and notebooks were strewn all about. A frightful mess."

"The unfortunate man. Did you know him well?" Ida said, using both hands to smooth out the strands of silver hair that had escaped left and right from under her hairpins.

"Not really. He was a new man, willing to work nights," Finn said.

"I assume you were the one to make a police report," Ida asked.

Ida noticed the puzzled look on Crispin's face and offered an explanation. "Sorry you have to hear this, my dear. It seems there was an incident overnight. At first we believed it was a case of vandalism. Boxes upended everywhere. A dreadful mess. When the police came to investigate, they found the man under heavy boxes. They believe he had been crushed when the metal shelves collapsed."

"That's terrible. How could that happen?"

"That's just it. No one knows. Such a tragedy," Ida said.

"Yes, Missus," Finn said. "The detectives are at a loss."

"A bad day for us all. An unfortunate soul lost his life and my precious files are in shambles," Ida said. "What will we do?"

Stuart told Ida, obviously not for the first time, that she had no reason to worry about the records since each item had been scanned and now carried a barcode for electronic identification. That's why, he said in a condescending tone, his team had seen no reason to preserve the original order in the first place. "Um, since your system's obsolete, we figured you'd just chuck the mess after we'd be done with it."

"The originals are priceless and they must be preserved. Why, Sir Percy himself…," said Ida.

"Uh-uh, I understand," Finn said in a dismissive way that suggested this was not the first time they'd covered this ground. "I take full responsibility."

"I am confident this is not your fault, Mr. Finn. It is all because the Board saw fit to modernize that these priceless records were put in jeopardy." Ida added in a conspiratorial tone, "I knew that no good would come of it."

"Is that so," came a stern challenge from somewhere behind Crispin.

The voice was as uncompromising and rigid as the woman it came from. Having announced her presence with her formidable vocal weapon, the woman surveyed the mess in silence. It was not the restful silence of a quiet room. It was an uncomfortable rebuke that resonated like a shriek. She looked first at the men and then at Crispin before the full knife edge of her gaze came to rest on Ida.

Just as her neck arched like a goose ready to strike, Crispin intercepted her. Reading her badge, Crispin extended her hand. "Hello, Mrs. Powell, I'm Crispin Leads."

Mr. Finn and Stuart used the interruption as an excuse to bolt.

Without accepting Crispin's extended hand, Mrs. Powell attacked. "Are you responsible for this mess?"

"Me? Oh, no. I've only just arrived," Crispin explained with an unexpected awkwardness. "I'm here in connection with my graduate studies."

"And, you are studying?"

"Ancient burial rituals."

"Mummies and pharaohs? Not particularly original."

"Actually, I find the hoi polloi more interesting than royalty."

"You have certainly come to the right place," Ida said breezily. Then with pride, she added, "You see, dear, we have managed the Egyptian archives since before the last century."

"If you can call this management," Mrs. Powell interjected. "Ms. Fowler, how you could manage to destroy our filing system and subject the Library to a police inquiry is beyond me. Such havoc in the space of one short week while I was on a long-overdue—and may I say, much deserved—holiday."

Ida deflected the sting by turning her attention to Crispin. "What are your access dates, dear?"

"I beg your pardon?"

"Your assigned dates to use the archives. You cannot work here until you get formal authorization from the Director's Office."

"I understood that the archives were open to the public."

Ida motioned for Crispin to follow her. "Used to be, dear, but we had to implement a new policy a month ago. Some things went missing."

Ida produced an internal memorandum from a nearby filing cabinet and began ticking off the requirements. "Let me see. Here is what you need. Just fill out this application form and list the reserve collections you wish to use, along with a photocopy of your passport. Oh, and you will need a letter from a sponsor. One of your professors or someone connected to the Egyptian archives should endorse your request."

Ida wrote a brief note on Library letterhead and handed it to Crispin. "Include this with your application. It might help get you an appointment by the end of the week. That is, assuming the Director's Office is in better order than ours."

"The end of the week?" Crispin asked, unable to hide her disappointment.

A threatening groan came from Mrs. Powell, who had clearly put up with quite enough distraction caused by the problems of an unimportant graduate student.

Crispin concentrated on her breath, trying not to inhale the acrid stench of mildewed cartons and deteriorating paper as she zigzagged her way out of the library to the bus stop. If she couldn't work she decided she could at least do something about her off-season wardrobe.

Marks & Spencer was overheated and crowded. Crispin tried on loose-fitting jeans, button-down shirts, and cable-knit sweaters. She added pajamas, underwear, socks, running shoes, Bass oxblood penny loafers, gloves, and a sturdy wool pea coat to her haul. She'd need more things but the basics would get her through the next few days. Her purchases filled three large shopping bags.

Back at the Drury Lane flat, Crispin warmed her hands around a cup of tea and snuggled onto the couch. Her mind wandered from her erratic exit from Egypt to the disarray at the library. The lack of sleep began to catch up with her because she started counting bodies instead of sheep. "Bodies, bodies everywhere," she hummed. One dismembered corpse in Egypt and one fella crushed under antique Egyptian files.

"Two bodies in two days," she yawned. "Crispin, the mayhem magnet." It wasn't long before her disjointed thoughts gave way to sleep and sleep was overrun by a dream.

In the dream, Crispin wandered through an Egyptian labyrinth, with walls that lofted ten feet above her. The corridors were so tight in places that it was difficult for her to squeeze past without scraping her shoulders on the stones. She was looking for something in the maze, but having trouble concentrating on her ill-defined quest because she was distracted by the hieroglyphics that decorated every surface. Even though she had the sensation that she was underground, there was still sufficient diffused light so that she could make out many of the symbols. They were an unlikely combination of ancient writing and scientific formulas. Some were edged with gold leaf. If she made even the slightest vibration as she passed, the gold would ooze from the walls and pool on the ground. Then, as if it had a will of its own, the gold began to form into shapes of Egyptian statues. As she stooped to touch one, a tattooed hand reached from the shadows and pulled her into a dark chamber.

Crispin woke with a jolt, spilling tea down her front. She realized she was hungry, thirsty, and late.

Chapter Four

Crispin was looking for a strong drink when she found her way into the Pump & Duck. Typical of the hundreds of pubs around the city, the P&D boasted a stone fireplace, a large curved bar that dominated the center of the main room, wooden booths along the wall, and tables squeezed in close to each other. Its most distinguishing feature was the large, etched-glass, mullioned windows that ran the length of the wall that faced the street. She found the heavy tobacco smoke in the bar tantalizing, especially when mingled with the hearty aromas of polished walnut, steamed sausages, and fried fish.

The bartender paused from slicing limes to greet Crispin with an outstretched hand. Her damp gloves were hard to pull off so she was able to avoid his sticky hand without appearing rude.

"Cold one, don't ye think?" he said, in an accent that mixed the strong rolling tones of Cockney with a dialect Crispin couldn't place. "So what'll be then, love?"

"Whiskey, neat."

"American, hey?"

"And you are?"

"Scot by birth. Brit by happenstance," he responded as he handed her a single malt.

As she sipped her drink, Crispin scanned the packed pub.

"Meeting a bloke, then?"

"My brother."

"Come here then. Ye cannae weigh more than seven stone. Now hop up here, and have yerself a look-see," Michael said, stepping out from behind the bar and hoisting Crispin onto it.

Even from her improved vantage, Crispin didn't see Clinton before he spotted her. "Damn, Crispin, what are you doing up there?" Clinton asked.

Clinton had their mother's easy grace and self-confidence, traits Crispin secretly envied. Crispin bore a strong physical resemblance to the oil painting of her paternal great-grandmother that hung in the parlor of her Aunt Tilde's home. The delicate-looking woman in the painting was small-boned, almost fragile, with long auburn hair pulled back in a full chignon that accentuated her long neck, heart-shaped face, and almond eyes. She was holding a baby in her lap, but the way her lips turned at the corner of her mouth—neither a smile nor a grimace—suggested something other than maternal bliss. It was as if the artist had captured an internal struggle that his subject tried, but failed, to hide.

Crispin always paid a visit to the portrait when she stayed with her great-aunt. As a girl, she would climb up on a chair to look closely at the brush strokes. From that vantage, the face disappeared into the paint's texture and brush strokes, shrouding her great-grandmother's fears and doubts that were so clear to her when Crispin stood a few feet from the gilt-framed canvas. On occasion, as she grew from a child to a young woman, Crispin would take a hand mirror to stand below the portrait so that she could search for traces of her foremother in her own face.

While Crispin and Clinton were physically different, there was a tilt to the corner of their smiles and a matching grayish blue shade to their eyes that made it apparent to everyone that this pair was from the same gene pool. Clinton helped his twin off the bar, but she stumbled slightly when he let go of her arm.

"A bit early to be drinking so much, don't you think?" Clinton asked with a critical tone that she'd rarely, if ever, heard him use.

"Not everyone can be perfect," Crispin retorted.

"Now children, don't fuss." The friendly admonition came from Sophie as she joined them. "Guinness for me, Michael," she said to the bartender and then watched as he drew a frothy pint, expertly poured to the Queen's measure on the glass.

"Come on you two, we left the guys by themselves," Sophie said with a nudge to Crispin.

Leery of a set-up, Crispin threaded her way through the crowd. Near the back wall, Crispin saw two attractive men, about her age, at a corner table. The one with broad shoulders and a mop of unruly hair was hunched forward, studying his beer. The second exuded a regal bearing even with his chair tilted back against the wall. He watched the crowd nonchalantly from his perch, his long legs resting comfortably in front of him. He was the first to spot Clinton escorting Crispin and jumped to his feet to pull out a chair for her. The second man moved to match the old-fashioned courtesy of standing as the ladies approached.

Clinton introduced his friends from Cambridge in the order in which they'd stood up: Herbert Van Snyder III and Anthony "Tony" Dexter. Clinton had met Herbert months before when they'd shared a cab from Heathrow to Cambridge on Clinton's first day in London. Herbert later introduced Clinton to Tony, an acquaintance from one of his university seminars.

Herbert was the first to reach for Crispin's extended hand. "How delightful to finally meet Clinton's sister. You are even more lovely than I had expected."

Tony hesitated for only a microsecond before taking Crispin's hand away from Herbert in a handshake. He then pulled her toward him and offered her the chair next to him. The strategic move put Tony between Herbert and Crispin. "Your brother tells me you are here to gather bits of information at the British Library," he said.

Crispin leaned forward in an effort to be heard over the growing din of the pub. "Actually, given the chaos at the Library, I may not be able to gather anything, neither 'bits' nor tomes, from there for quite some time." She described the mess she'd seen earlier in the day at the Egyptian Archives.

"Then there's the man who died at the warehouse. I wonder," Crispin said.

Clinton and Sophie spoke simultaneously.

"Don't you dare...," said Clinton.

"Nip it...," Sophie added.

Since Tony and Herbert looked confused, Sophie explained. "Our Crispin has a way of finding dark mystery in ordinary things."

"It comes from reading too many whodunits," Crispin told them, explaining that the man had died when some shelves fell on him at the warehouse. "I'm afraid that's all I know."

"Ah, a fellow mystery hound!" Herbert said, explaining that he was a member of the Baker Street Irregulars, the long-running fan club of Sherlock Holmes, arguably London's most famous fictitious detective. "Maybe you would like to go with me to one of our informal gatherings?" he asked Crispin.

Before Crispin could answer, a waitress arrived with baskets of crunchy sole and deep-fried potatoes.

"Here's our food," Tony said.

Herbert ordered another round for everyone. As they filled their plates and glasses, the conversation moved on. Crispin hadn't realized just how hungry she was, and asked Sophie to pass the "chips."

"I suppose in England they will forever be called 'chips' and potato 'chips' will remain 'crisps,'" Herbert said as he raised his glass in a mock salute. "Crispin, I will never again think of crisps without thinking of you."

"Hold on, Herb, that nickname is off limits. I'm the only one allowed to call my sister 'Crisp,'" Clinton said, as Crispin popped him with her beer coaster. "And, then only if I am willing to be pummeled."

Relaxing into the comfortable jesting of friends who'd had too much beer and too little sleep, Crispin compared Clinton's friends. One was a playful aristocrat and the other a boyish charmer. If Herbert was Pierce Brosnan in his prime, then Tony was a young Hugh Grant.

Crispin yawned for the second time in a row, and her brother offered to walk her back to Sophie's place.

***

Crispin shivered as the London air, like the vapor off of dry ice, seeped into her clothes. They walked several blocks without talking when Clinton took her hand. Crispin felt a hard knot inside come undone, something she hadn't realized she was holding onto. It was as if she'd been gripping her hands into fists and opened them only to find them empty.

Clinton noticed the change in his sister's mood. "I don't want to fight."

"I know."

"I won't always be able to make things right for you."

"I know."

When they reached her building, Clinton gave her a kiss on the cheek and turned to leave. He was halfway down the block when she ran after him.

"Love you," she said, hugging him.

"Love you more."

Upstairs, Crispin settled into her pajamas and tucked into a comfortable place on the couch. She poured a double shot of single malt whiskey from a bottle she'd stowed under the sink after her shopping expedition. She covered her feet with two pairs of socks and pulled out her journal. She was still writing when Sophie returned.

"Join me?" Crispin asked, indicating the whiskey.

"No, thanks. I've got to train in the morning."

"Well, I don't, thank you very much."

"You know Aunt Tilde always said that it doesn't do any good to try to drown your sorrows because those suckers can swim." Sophie disappeared to change. When she returned, she fixed Crispin a large glass of water and sat down next to her. "Finish this before you tuck in. It'll help with the hangover."

Crispin didn't look up from her writing so Sophie curled up in the wingback. "Do you want to talk about tonight?"

"What part?" Crispin asked, setting her journal aside and picking up her highball glass.

"We could start with you and Clinton. He told me about the brouhaha in Egypt."

"He needs to stay out of my business."

"See, that's just what I'm talking about. I've never seen you that way with him."

"He needs to figure out if he is on Team Laurie Pierce or Team Crispin," she said, taking a large drink from her whiskey and setting it down with a bang.

"I could tell you how unfair that sounds, but you know that, don't you?"

Crispin retrieved her journal and sat silently, doodling on a blank page. "I had a dream this afternoon."

"No shit. You mean a D-R-E-A-M dream?"

The look from Crispin answered Sophie's question without words. Most of Crispin's dreams were the garden variety; the scattered bits of psychological closet cleaning experienced by everyone. Occasionally, however, they were more powerful. Growing up, she pretended that these distinctive dreams were the way her mother communicated with her, to help her, to solve problems or to keep her safe. As an adult, she tried to convince herself that her father was right when he said they were no more than a product of her fertile imagination. Yet, she couldn't ignore the times when the dreams had unlocked riddles and forewarned of dangers.

Crispin described her dream in the Egyptian labyrinth. "I can't help but feel that it has something to do with that corpse they found near a garbage heap in Egypt."

She told Sophie about Seth bringing her the severed arm and Inspector Sabri coming to camp to investigate the gruesome death.

"Let me guess. You're trying to draw a relationship to the body in Egypt and the man killed at the warehouse," Sophie said, shaking her head "I know you too well. You've done this since we were children. You won't let it go until you connect the dots."

"You have to admit that both deaths have an Egypt connection. Maybe that's what triggered the dream."

Sophie sighed, knowing that Crispin wouldn't stop thinking about the D-R-E-A-M until she'd discerned some deep, hidden meaning out of her subconscious or deciphered a confidential message from her muse.

"This one will take some good, old-fashioned cogitating," Sophie said. "Let me know when you get it all worked out."

Crispin tossed a pillow at her.

"Careful or you'll mess up the coif."

Sophie yawned and told her roommate that she planned to leave for the track early the next morning. Crispin said that until she received access to the archives she would spend her days at London museums. The lure of the British Museum, arguably one of the world's most important collections of Egyptian artifacts, was too strong for Crispin to resist, so she would start there. Fortunately, what the Drury Lane flat lacked in creature comforts, it made up for in convenience since it was an easy city walk to the Tube.

As she turned out the lights, Sophie admonished Crispin, in an offhanded way, to be careful. "Watch your back."

Before the day was over, Crispin would recall the warning and regret that she'd hadn't taken it more seriously.

Chapter Five

A typical London downpour had Crispin dodging puddles the next morning. She took refuge under awnings as she walked to the British Museum. Her first stop was the museum's café, where she had a chance to dry out while enjoying an unobstructed view of the full expanse of the Queen Elizabeth II Great Court. The glass roof and sweeping staircases filled the space where once there had been an open-air courtyard cluttered with service buildings.

She warmed herself with coffee and shortbread before taking out her mother's field journal to organize her agenda for the next several days. It was a 1970s-era rich leather journal with a zipper closure. Inside, the right-hand pocket was designed to hold pads of paper. Pockets on the other side were crafted for notecards, pens, and similar material. The front was embossed with her mother's initials.

Crispin had uncovered the forgotten journal while poking around in the attic at home in Ithaca looking for an extra suitcase for her trip to Egypt. She'd spotted a dusty trunk with peeling tape, marked with her mother's name. "Melete" was written in block letters that were almost faded away.

A familiar scent drifted up as she'd lifted the lid of the trunk. It was that faint but unmistakable mixture of fresh magnolias and spring grasses. Although most of the clothes inside were strangers, she buried her face in them, hungry for the sensation deep in her memory triggered by that forgotten, lingering smell that told her that her mother had once worn these clothes. The sense of smell has such a powerful connection to memory. She closed her eyes and for a moment she was certain that the sensation of something caressing her shoulder was the touch of her mother's hand and that the soft movement of air near her ear was her mother's whispered reminder: "Feel deeply with your heart, Little One."

That's when she'd discovered the journal, wrapped in tissue and tucked inside the deep folds of an embroidered jacket. When she went to the kitchen to ask if she could take it with her, she found her father and Ashraf embroiled in loud discussions about plans for the excavation in Saqqara. Locked in an animated debate, she wasn't sure if either man heard her request when she asked her father's permission to take her mother's journal. Since neither man acknowledged her presence, she went upstairs to finish packing.

Now, sitting in London with the journal, she was patting herself on the back for her decision to bring it with her. It had been a useful tool for record-keeping and note-taking while she did field work in Egypt.

In truth, however, the utility of the thing was just a fraction of its genuine appeal. What she treasured were those precious stains on the cover and side, places discolored by human touch. That's where her mother had held it as she'd worked, where she had rested her hands, causing the oils of her skin, over time, to seep into the leather, marking its ownership, embossing it with her touch.

Crispin rested her hands on those same points in an unconscious imitation of her mother's grip. A childish sensation that she'd felt on and off her whole life passed like a shiver through her mind. It was a juvenile stubbornness to reject the certainty and finality of death.

Her sensible, adult self prevailed and returned to mapping out her plans. She knew just where she'd begin. With Roxie. The Roxie Walker Galleries had the best Egyptian funerary pieces in the Museum. Every time she returned to the Roxie, Crispin felt as if she were popping in on long-ago friends who, although they still lived in the old neighborhood, always had fresh stories to tell.

Even though her academic studies of burial customs spanned centuries, continents, and cultures, Crispin was, at heart, an Egyptologist and had been since childhood. Her first love of the ancient culture began with her father's station in Egypt for academic studies when she was a toddler. Later when they moved to Turin, Italy, she spent every spare minute on weekends at the city's Egyptian museum collection, the largest outside Cairo. The Turin holdings, with its Royal Papyrus, Tomb of Kha, sarcophagi, pottery, and ancient burial paraphernalia, held endless fascination for her and helped to shape her lifelong interest in the rituals of death.

"So many mummies, so little time."

"Crispin?"

The man's voice made Crispin realize that she'd been concentrating so hard that she'd spoken out loud. Again, with the nasty habit.

Slowly her sheepish gaze traveled up from her journal, past a vaguely familiar tailored suit and starched collar, to meet Herbert's distinctive green eyes. About the same height as Clinton, Herbert gave the impression of being smaller. Crispin wasn't sure if it was the cut of his Borrelli sport coat and four-button vest, tailored to accentuate his slim waist, or his long fingers, but he brought to mind a racehorse—beautiful, well bred, impeccably groomed, and yet powerful.

"Herbert, what a pleasant surprise. Please join me."

"Perhaps for just a moment," he said, pulling out the chair across from her. "I must say I am surprised to see you. Assumed you'd be hard at work at the Library."

"My request for access is pending. What brings you out on such a cold, wet day?"

"Actually, I am here for a meeting."

"A meeting. What kind of meeting?"

"Family duties. One of my ancestors held a position here. They bring the hereditary trustees in once or twice a year to listen to impressive reports from impressive scholars about impressive findings. Dreadfully dull stuff, really."

Crispin had an odd feeling that she knew the answer before she asked the question. "I see, and who was your fortunate ancestor?"

"My great-great-grandfather. His full name, if you will, was George Edward Stanhope Molyneux Herbert, the Fifth Earl of Carnarvon, former Viscount Porchester. He was 'Porchey' to his friends."

"THE Lord Carnarvon?"

"Indeed, one and the same. I must say that was a long time ago. I'm afraid my own life and work are not nearly so notorious."

"I still can't get over it. Why didn't you say something about your connections last night when I was badmouthing the mess at the Egyptian Archives?"

"Wrong crowd. Wrong place, I suppose," Herbert said with a smile.

"I still don't understand how they let things get in such a mess."

"It's one of those quintessential English stories. The hullabaloo began innocently enough when the wife of Sir Reginald Percy returned from holiday in the United States. Percy is one of the most distinguished members of the Library's Board of Keepers. I think his wife was just trying to tease the old boy with a news clip about a foul-up at the patent office in the States. Seems they'd tossed out original applications from the likes of Thomas Edison and Eli Whitney."

"I remember reading about that," Crispin said.

"Sir Percy almost choked on his Drambuie."

Since the British Library was also on the verge of digitizing its archives, Sir Percy vowed he would make "damn certain" that all of the original historic collections would be preserved intact, even if it meant raising additional funds. True to his word, Sir Percy browbeat the Keepers into agreeing to the value of redundancy. Because of its prominence, the Egyptian Department was one of the first collections to get funds for the file conversion and preservation.

"Let's hear it for redundancy," Crispin said.

Checking his watch, Herbert stood up to leave. "Right then. Sorry I cannot stay longer, but I am obligated to be duly impressed in a few minutes and I would not want to disappoint."

"I'd love to hear more stories sometime."

Given her lifelong interest in all things Egyptian, she would have to ask Clinton why he hadn't mentioned Herbert's connection to the most famous archeological find of the twentieth century. What schoolchild hadn't heard of Lord Carnarvon, who had hired Howard Carter to excavate along the West Bank of the Nile near Luxor? Their persistence was rewarded in 1922 when thirty feet below the surface of the desert Carter faced a sealed door. Beyond it was the tomb of the Blessed of Amun, Tutankhamun. Miraculously, the burial chamber had remained virtually untouched for more than three thousand years until a water boy working for Carter stumbled onto the buried staircase. Tut's tomb was filled with marvelous treasures and relics, including the young king's solid-gold coffin.

Crispin polished off her coffee, wetting her fingers to make sure she picked up every crumb of the buttery shortbread. She headed straight to the north staircase that would take her to Roxie. When she stepped around a corner, orange cone markers left by the cleaning crew warned Crispin that the long marble staircase had just been mopped and might still be slippery. But she had her head down, thinking about her dream, about Herbert, and about the mess in the Egyptian collection. One minute she was stepping off the landing and the next she was stumbling, then falling. She tried to break her fall by grabbing the railing, but the stairs gave no purchase until she finally landed face down, legs splayed at the foot of the staircase.

Before she could stand up, museum patrons offering assistance surrounded her. Two helped her to a nearby bench while an American teen gathered her backpack and jacket where they lay scattered near the top of the staircase. The girl's mother brought bottled water and offered to call an ambulance. Crispin assured them that nothing was broken and begged them not to worry.

"The worst injury is to my dignity," she said with a false bravado and a forced chuckle just as Herbert joined the commotion. "I heard about your fall. How can I help?"

Crispin's knees betrayed her when she tried to stand.

"I have a car. Let me drive you," Herbert said, offering his arm. "Clinton will never forgive me if I fail to take care of his little sister."

"I'll have you know I'm older. A full twenty minutes," Crispin replied, with a smile, glad to have an arm to lean on.

Herbert navigated his Alpha Romero sports car through the crowded London streets with speed and ease, never once dropping even close to the posted speed limit. Ordinarily, Crispin hated reckless driving, but today she was grateful. As they rounded a corner on what felt like two wheels, Crispin gripped the car's leather safety strap, which she secretly nicknamed the "Oh Shit Strap."

He offered to stop at a pharmacy, but she assured him she had plenty of prescription painkillers. At the flat she excused herself to change into comfortable clothes, and when she returned to the living area, she was happy to see Herbert waiting with hot tea. He fluffed up pillows and helped her prop one bruised foot on the ottoman.

"You are really doing too much," she told him. "I'll be a little black and blue, but otherwise I'm none the worse for wear. However, there is something you can do for me."

"Your wish is my command. What do you need?"

"Company. Do you mind sitting for a while?"

"My pleasure," he replied, unbuttoning his jacket and folding it over the back of the couch before taking a seat close to her.

Herbert looked incongruous against the frumpy furniture and shop-worn surroundings of the flat. "If I am going to stay, I'll pour a cup myself."

Relaxed, Crispin began telling him about her plans for the next several days while waiting for her access to be approved.

"If I can help, I ask you to call on me," Herbert offered. "The old family name can still, on occasion, open a door or two."

When he asked questions about her studies, she took his interest as a compliment since so many people her age found her study of death and burial rituals either macabre or depressing. Herbert seemed genuinely interested.

"What I have found in my research is that the rituals can be sad or joyful or both."

"Such as?"

"Take for example Ghana. It is not uncommon for a band to accompany the pallbearers as the entire funeral procession dances its way to the cemetery."

"I had not heard of that."

"Funerals have always been at the heart of Ghanaian culture and social life. It is a time of celebration. There are even customs where a party is thrown a year after the funeral to commemorate the life of the departed."

Crispin said her doctoral thesis was based on the idea that this need to honor and ritualize burial was common from the earliest humans, through time, to touch every culture today. "I find evidence wherever I look."

"So you are a detective, of sorts," he said with a smile.

She said that she thought historians and archeologists were a lot like police detectives. "You begin with a single isolated fact and, then with care, must dig through layers of irrelevancy to find truth."

"We are all sleuths that must keep in mind that what we consider clues may not be what they seem," he replied.

"Ah yes," she laughed, paraphrasing Sherlock Holmes. "But, from a single fact one must then deduce not only the chain of events leading up to it, but what must ultimately come from it."

"So we agree, Britain can claim the best detectives, fictional ones at least."

"Not so fast. I refuse to concede that point without additional evidence. Facts, if you please."

"For pure gore and human suffering, you can't top Dick Francis," Herbert said. "He always delivers a juicy torture scene before all is said and done."

"Spare me, please. Any pedestrian with a modicum of imagination can write torture," Crispin countered. "For the ability to capture the criminal mind, I'll take Dashiell Hammett anytime."

"He is great for period pieces, but it is so much easier, don't you think, when one is writing about one's contemporaries?"

Herbert said. "Appreciate, if you will, the skill needed by a writer such as Ellis Peters to set his sleuth in the twelfth century."

Crispin refused to give ground. "Yes, but Elizabeth Peters does it with greater wit." She yawned. With grogginess overtaking her, she added, "Amelia Peabody is superior to Father Cadfael in both her sophisticated panache and pure gumption."

"To be continued," Herbert said, standing to clear the cups away.

"Thank you for spending time with me," Crispin said.

Herbert slid his arm into the sleeve of his jacket. "I'll ring later to check on you."

Crispin sat nursing bruises in places she didn't like to think about until her painkillers helped her drift off. She didn't nap for long, but just as she woke again, her thoughts returned to the moments before her fall. There was a fleeting silhouette, just on the edge of her peripheral vision. Something she could almost see. A shadow or, perhaps, a hand? Or did she dream it?

Chapter Six

The next morning Crispin stopped in at Ida's office to report that she'd filed her research application and would soon have letters from sponsors.

Ida was dressed much as she had been when she joined the Library staff soon after World War II, in a simple shirtwaist, floral frock. Her thick, orthopedic stockings had seams up the back. The ensemble was completed with sensible high-top, lace-up shoes and a wool cardigan.

"I owe you a great deal of thanks for helping me," Crispin said, pulling up a chair. "How's the filing going?"

"Mercy me, at times I must admit that I feel outmatched," Ida sighed. "Fortunately, some of the files aren't as disorganized as I had feared. It is just a matter of verifying content and putting them in order again. As you can see, I have a system."

Neatly lettered signs were taped to every flat surface in the office. Ida was using them as markers in her first pass at bringing order out of chaos. With the same kind of emotion that a grandmother displays when showing off baby pictures, Ida told Crispin that because she'd developed the original alphanumeric coding scheme, she could quickly sort files by category and date.

"What slows me down is re-boxing and making checklists," Ida said with a whisper, not wanting to be heard by Mrs. Powell, who was across the room.

Just at that moment, Mrs. Powell hung up the phone and joined them, staring pointedly at Crispin. "Don't you have somewhere you need to be?"

"We're working out the details for her research," Ida said, winking at Crispin. "What can I do for you, Mrs. Powell?"

"Miss Fowler, before I leave for the Board meeting I want to remind you that we must submit a detailed cataloguing of every piece we re-file to be sure that nothing was stolen at the warehouse. The Board insists that every document be accounted for."

After Mrs. Powell left, Ida dropped back into her chair. "So much to do," she said, sounding slightly overwhelmed.

"Can't they send you some temporary help?"

"I asked Mrs. Powell, but she says the budget is too tight. You see, I feel a certain responsibility because I recommended Mr. Finn's company for the job."

Crispin hated to see the older woman miserable so she did the only thing that she knew was guaranteed to make an English woman of a certain generation feel better. She offered to make tea.

"What a splendid idea," Ida replied, showing Crispin where to find what she needed: an electric teakettle, serviettes, bone china cups, and silver spoons. Before long the two were enjoying a chat over hot Assam tea and homemade biscuits.

Ida still lived in the house in Wimbledon where she grew up. Her father's political connections meant many of the luminaries of the day were entertained at their home. Ida had actually met some of the scholars and explorers whose work she would later personally index and catalog. She told Crispin that she'd started soon after the war when the library, archives, and curatorial departments were still under one roof.

"At the time, I wasn't much older than you and I had already held a classified position during the war as a driver for one of Sir Churchill's staff."

It was with no small measure of pride that Ida told Crispin that, although she'd been semiretired for a number of years, she still felt indispensable to the Library and had trained Mrs. Powell as her replacement. Ida said she believed that some of the other woman's chronic bad humor was due, in part, to the fact that the Board had insisted that Ida retain an emeritus position.

"Sir Percy calls me a 'living link' with the past," she said, almost giggling like a schoolgirl. "I think he just hates to see things change. Why else would he insist that they keep a bag of bones like me around?"

Crispin offered to tidy up the tea things while Ida tackled the files again. After she washed the cups and put everything away, Crispin saw Ida struggling with a box. "Here, let me get that," she said, easily taking the box from the older woman. "Where do you want it?"

"My dear, you are so strong."

"You should see my roommate."

Crispin decided that a little manual labor would help her work out some of the kinks from her fall. That morning she'd traded her Weejuns for running shoes so that she had better traction on wet streets and suspicious staircases. She rolled up her sleeves and told Ida that she'd be happy to move more of the boxes. That's how, without intention or a preconceived plan, Crispin found herself spending part of each of the next three days helping Ida bring order out of chaos.

Crispin would visit a museum in the morning when crowds were thin. Afternoons were reserved for Ida. The rhythm of the days was made easier because Mrs. Powell was a creature of strict discipline and regular habits who took her midday meal precisely from twelve to one and was frequently called to appointments. Crispin and Ida became adept at working together when Mrs. Powell was away. They delighted in a certain devious pleasure by thinking up creative explanations for Crispin's presence if Mrs. Powell returned sooner than expected.

During tea breaks, Crispin shared information about her studies. "I've postulated that one of the characteristics that have set humans apart, from Cave Man to Space Man, is the need for a ritual to dignify and mark death. I've found the theme across continents, time, and culture."

"Very interesting, dear, I am sure. But, if you don't mind me asking, I would like to know how a lovely young lady such as you became interested in death?" When Ida said the word "death," she lowered her voice to a near-whisper, as though the Grim Reaper would come calling if she said the name too loudly.

"It's not easy to explain," Crispin confessed, her voice softening and her words slowing as she spoke. "Someone I cared about once told me that he thought I chose this field because I never had proper closure after my mother died."

Ida reached out and gave Crispin's hand a gentle squeeze of encouragement.

"It's okay," Crispin said, responding to Ida's gesture. "I've asked myself the same question more than once. I was only five. It was a freak accident. Her plane exploded while landing so we didn't even have ashes to bury."

Ida wisely let the words hang without response. She poured fresh tea for both of them and let the silence fill the void. After a few sips, Crispin was ready to share more.

"So many of my memories from those days are mere snapshots, silly, timeless, things that little girls think are important. Like her caramel lipstick. It left a faint shadow on my cheek when she kissed me goodnight."

Just days after the accident, Crispin said, she'd found a tube of the lipstick in a bathroom drawer and started carrying it with her everywhere she went. She said that she could still picture her five-year-old self, sitting at a mirror trying to imitate her mother's smooth, practiced strokes. But, the lipstick had grown fragile in the Egyptian heat and fell apart into a gooey mess on the bathroom floor. Crispin said she cried for days, clinging to the empty lipstick tube.

"In my mind, that messy tube was her goodnight kiss, something that I would never have again," Crispin said.

"I understand. My own papa is long since gone, but I still have one of his old sweaters in the cupboard because when I touch it to my cheek I can feel his hugs," Ida said.

Crispin imagined Ida at sixty-five, stoically facing the loss of her beloved parent. Even when we grow old, we're still somebody's baby.

"Sometimes the best kiss is the lost kiss, the remembered kiss," Crispin said.

"The never-again kiss, the last kiss," Ida added, drying a tear and taking in a deep breath that seemed to pull her back from memories. Squaring her shoulders, she changed the subject. "Enough of such talk. Tell me about your morning."

Crispin had spent the morning at the Tate Modern Gallery, a remodeled power station that houses contemporary works by the likes of Dali, Picasso, and Warhol. From its high windows that overlook the River Thames, visitors are treated to a panoramic view of the Millennium Footbridge with its ultramodern blade-of-light design that connects the Tate to St. Paul's Cathedral on the opposite bank.

"Silly stuff if you ask me," Ida had huffed. "I am sorry, but there simply is no place for heaps of river rock and, pardon my language, *urinals* in a legitimate museum. Lobsters as telephone receivers. Really?"

"I'll confess, there's a lot of it I can't appreciate," Crispin had admitted. "But, I do like the intensity of Rothko's colors, as if the emotions, the sadness, the anger, and the pain of a lifetime are trapped inside layers and layers of color."

"Perhaps," Ida had said, but conceded little to the younger woman's point. "If they just did not have to go out of their way to make everything so ugly."

After a productive day of cleaning up "Finn's mess," as they came to call it, Crispin was on her way out when she saw a box on the top shelf of the storage room without one of Ida's new index labels. Assuming the box was just turned the wrong way, Crispin tossed her backpack on the floor. She'd failed to zip it completely so some of the contents spilled out. She should have fetched the stepladder, but instead tried to reach the box by standing on a short stool. Holding onto a shelf with one hand and stretching to reach the box with the other, her foot slipped and she pulled the box down on top of her. Loose papers, photos, and files spilled out around her and covered the floor.

Just then she heard Mrs. Powell calling for Ida.

Crispin rushed to pick up the mess, all the while looking over her shoulder, afraid that Mrs. Powell would catch her. She'd only just managed to slip the box back into place as Mrs. Powell came around the corner and found her.

"Miss Leads, this has gone entirely too far. This area is restricted to staff. You have no right to be back here. You must leave immediately!"

Apologizing profusely as she left the room, Crispin gave one last, clandestine glance to see that the box was safe. On the way out, she whispered an invitation to Ida to join her later at a nearby bookstore.

***

The window display of hardbacks by E. M. Forster, Virginia Woolf, and George Bernard Shaw told passers-by that Bloomsbury Books and Basics was dedicated to the works of British and Irish authors. After a lazy half-hour of browsing, Crispin purchased *The Poems of Dylan Thomas* and a British printing of the latest Harry Potter. She was in the store's coffee bar enjoying Rowling's adventure about a boy wizard when Ida joined her.

"This place has been here since I was a girl," Ida said as she settled into a chair. "I fancied it better before they remodeled. As you know, I am not too keen on modern things."

"Ida, I don't think of it as either/or. Sometimes it's just a matter of appreciating what both have to offer. Take the opera *Aida*, for instance."

"I'm not surprised that you are a fan of Verdi." Ida stirred her tea.

"And Elton John." Crispin said she'd seen the pop star's version of *Aida* as a musical on Broadway and loved it.

"But Ida, just because I liked the rock version doesn't mean I won't enjoy the classical version when I see it on Friday," she said, adding that Tony Dexter had tickets for them.

"I thought you were stepping out with young Lord Van Snyder."

"Oh, it's nothing serious. Herbert and I like a lot of the same things. For instance, he's invited me to meet his friends at the Baker Street Irregulars, a group of mystery fanatics, like us. That's all."

"Pity, really."

Crispin remembered to tell Ida about the unlabeled box. "I'm sorry I didn't get a chance to organize the contents for you, but Mrs. Powell lowered the boom."

"No matter, dear, I shall sort it all out since it looks as if going forward you will be busy with your research." With a flourish and a smile, Ida then pulled a letter from her purse and presented it to Crispin. "This arrived for you just as I was leaving the office. Your paperwork cleared in record time. Our archives are officially at your disposal."

"How can I thank you enough?"

"You should thank the young lord. He put in a good word for you."

"Herbert?"

"And, you say he is only a 'friend.' Pity."

She gave Crispin a packet that contained a key to her assigned research carrel, explaining that she'd moved her from the one Mrs. Powell had assigned to one of the newer ones that had been recently remodeled. "You'll like it better," she said with a conspiratorial wink.

Ida said that she could tell that Crispin was impatient to get to work. They walked back to the Library and hugged as they parted, promising to make time again soon for tea and conversation.

Crispin located her assigned study space and was pleased to find a mahogany desk and Victorian lamp that had been rewired to provide modern illumination. She began to settle in by lining up her pens, highlighters, computer disks, and erasers in a neat row. A consummate Virgo, she always insisted on ninety-degree angles and sharp pencil points. She recognized that her care was borderline neurotic, but she couldn't work efficiently unless her space was tidy.

There was a surprise waiting for her when she emptied her backpack, an envelope from the Egyptian Archives. She must have accidentally shoved it into her backpack in the rush to tidy the papers that spilled out of the box in the storeroom. Crispin knew she had to return it, but curiosity got the better of her. "So, I'm a snoop."

Inside the yellowed envelope she found several deteriorating parchment sleeves that protected delicate celluloid negatives. When she held one up to the light, it appeared to be a photograph of a rather humdrum Egyptian artifact. She examined the others, but nothing seemed out of the ordinary until she noticed the file code marker on the corner of the negatives. Crispin had spent enough time with Ida over the last three days to easily decipher the coding system. This material was from the fabled Tomb of King Tut.

Or was it?

The pieces didn't look familiar. Then she saw it.

This can't be right.

The code indicated that the photos were taken in "AII."

Impossible.

Anyone who knew anything about the Tut tomb knew that it consisted of only four chambers: Antechamber (AC), Burial Chamber (BC), Treasury (T), and Annex (A). There was no "AII," or "Second Annex."

Crispin studied the negatives more closely. Each one bore the same code. If she were right, and the wild thumping in her heart told her that she was, she was holding evidence of something new and exciting, something that, perhaps, had never before been made public, let alone published. The adrenaline rush was cut short when the rational voice of her father intruded into her internal dialogue. She could hear him as clearly as if he were standing next to her.

"Crispin, you must learn to control your taste for unsubstantiated assumptions until you have the facts," he barked.

"Point well taken," she admitted to herself. "So let's review the possibilities. Let us begin with the most obvious, she thought, taking out a tablet and writing "(1) Human Error."

This could be no more than a simple case of careless recordkeeping and labeling. There were thousands of objects removed from the tomb and some eighteen hundred photos taken by Harry Burton alone. The full excavation took Carter six years to complete. It defied logic to think that no record-keeping mistakes were made.

Equally plausible was the possibility of simple age-related decomposition, she considered, adding to the list "(2) Age Disintegration." Sometimes when tombs were opened, particularly fragile objects, especially those made of wood, had been known to crumble into dust the first time they were touched. That's why creating a photographic record is the first step in any professional excavation plan. Egyptian archives are full of photographs of objects that no longer exist.

She added one more possibility to the list: "(3) Theft." Both Thomas Hoving, the former director of the Metropolitan Museum in New York, and Britain's own Sean Thurman had documented a number of stolen Tut objects. Although Thurman is the superior Egyptologist, both men had put forth interesting theories.

Looking at the three possibilities on the list, she had to admit her initial excitement was waning. Then she looked again and smiled. None of the first three scenarios—mistake, age, or theft—explained the coding, indicating another previously undocumented location, or fifth chamber, for these items. None explained a "Second Annex."

"How many times have I told you to observe carefully the small fact on which large inferences may depend," she heard her father's subconscious lecture. "Crispin, you must remember that most discovery is slow and meticulous, weaving one thread at a time."

She knew the drill. He'd been telling her to slow down and be careful all her life. Never mind that he had achieved tenure at Cornell largely on the strength of a single spectacular breakthrough in the carbon-dating techniques used for delicate materials such as fabrics. The first step in Project Slow Down would be to return the photographic negatives to Ida, but not before making copies.

Crispin tried to rein in her excitement, realizing that she faced hours of work studying the thousands of pages that had been written about the most famous burial site in Egypt.

Her dissertation would have to wait a little longer. Something wonderful had, quite literally, fallen into her lap. Even as she began mapping a plan of attack for her research, her foot was tapping and a voice inside her head kept repeating, almost singing: "A fifth chamber. You've found evidence of a fifth chamber."

Chapter Seven

Crispin felt the haunt of timelessness as she hopped off a double-decker bus and joined the late evening crowd at Royal Albert Hall. She would not have been surprised to see Lilly Langtry decked out in turn-of-the century finery, signing autographs for fans. At the entrance, the doorman ushered an elderly woman nestled in an ankle-length coat of silver fox out of the queue. "This way, Lady Christine."

La-di-da.

Inside, Crispin spotted Tony searching the crowd. He was nattily dressed in a black suit, periwinkle oxford cloth shirt, and pale yellow tie. Tony was one of those fellows who are more sexy than handsome. A critic might say that his ears protruded, and he had a toothy grin. He wore his hair a tad too long so that it stuck out around his earlobes and, in moments of excitement, escaped and fell over his eyes. When that happened, he would absentmindedly rake his fingers through it in an attempt to control the muddle. Still, there was something about him. Perhaps it was his proper diction and flawless manners. Or, maybe, the attraction was the soft droop in the corner of his large eyes that disarmed her.

Crispin was wearing her new smoky burgundy dress made of a close-weave knit. She'd selected it not only because she knew the color was good with her skin, but her mother's brooch was perfect to hold the cowl neck in place. She'd done her hair up in a ponytail and pulled through tendrils in wisps that accented her long neck. She'd even added a tiny splash of shimmer above her cheekbones.

When Tony helped her off with her coat, his look told her that he found her body-hugging dress more appealing than her usual baggy sweaters and jeans. "Did you wear that just for me?" he asked.

"Of course, because there is nothing a woman likes better than to have a man think that," Crispin replied.

"Point taken."

Once they were seated, Tony presented her with a wrist corsage of white orchids against a tiny spray of gamboge freesia. The last time anyone had given her a corsage was at her high school prom. There was an aw-shucks quality to the unexpected gesture that she found endearing.

Although their seats were in the rear of the hall, they were on the orchestra level. The stage set was a clever amalgam of Egyptian icons, complete with colonnade and backlit views of pyramids. The familiar story held them in its grip from the first aria to the final tragic scene when the tormented lovers, Radamès and Aida, are buried alive as punishment for treason. As the curtain came down and the audience stood to cries of "Bravo!" Crispin shivered with an ill-defined sense of foreboding. Thinking she was overcome by the sorrow of the scene, Tony put his arm around her waist and drew her close.

Crispin and Tony took a cab to the Pump & Duck after the show. Making their way through the crowd of pub regulars, they endured a chorus of catcalls for showing up in theater finery. They found Sophie, Herbert, and Clinton at their regular table in the rear.

"So, Tony, you're the one who has been monopolizing my sister's time," Clinton teased as they pulled up chairs.

"Certainly not," he replied. "Tonight was our first date."

Crispin could sense Tony's discomfort and reached under the table to give his hand a little pat. When he held on to her hand, she decided that she liked it.

"You do clean up good," Clinton said.

Sophie kidded that she was surprised to find her roommate still awake so late into the evening. "I haven't seen her for days. She's been out of the flat before I get up and in bed by the time I get home," Sophie told Tony.

Because she was not yet ready to unveil her suspicions about a fifth chamber in King Tut's tomb, Crispin told them only that she'd left the flat at dawn so she could take an early train to Griffith Institute in Oxford for research.

"Why not use the Web?" Tony asked.

"I prefer to deal with original records."

"There is no telling where you will turn up, Lady Crispin," Herbert said. "First the Library, then the B.M., and now the Griffith. Do tell, what secrets are you chasing?"

"If I tell it won't be a secret," she replied, as a waiter delivered her order of bangers and mash.

"Brilliant," Herbert replied with a good-natured smile.

What Crispin didn't say was that she was personally examining original documents that were only available at the Griffith, including Howard Carter's field cards, daily journal, sketches, conservation notes, photographs, and eyewitness accounts of the first excavation season.

Through hours of reading, Crispin had grown increasingly confident that her find was terra incognito. If she were correct, questions had to be answered about how such an extreme oversight could have gone undetected for so many years. She was a long way from being ready to go public.

Crispin could tell that Sophie's radar was picking up on her underlying excitement, so, Crispin employed a little diversion. "I wish you could have come tonight," she said to Sophie. "I almost cried like a baby."

"I'm surprised you can still be moved by such a blatantly manipulative sop," Sophie joked, sprinkling salt on her shepherd's pie. "Especially since you've seen it more times than I can count."

"My offer of assistance with the red tape still stands," Herbert said, digging into his roast beef, watercress, and horseradish sandwich.

Crispin told him she appreciated the offer but that she'd been fortunate because a family friend from Egypt, Ashraf Rashad, had already written letters of introduction.

"I must say, we Egyptian enthusiasts travel in a small circle," Herbert said. "I have known Ashraf ever since I took up the family duties. We have endured many a dull meeting together."

"He's in town on business," Clinton said to Herbert, adding, "Crispin and I are having dinner with him tomorrow night. You're welcome to join us."

"I would not dream of intruding, but do give the old boy my regards."

***

It was a lovely night and Crispin wanted to stretch her legs after being cramped up inside all day. With Tony by her side, they took their time walking to Drury Lane. The streets of London were always busy, but at night they seemed calmer, as if the city intentionally lowered its voice out of respect for the veil of evening. Contemporary London blended with the traditional cityscape. One minute they were strolling past residential buildings with well-preserved nineteenth century porticos designed by Wedgwood and the next they were dodging late-night joggers listening to music through the latest in miniature headsets.

"Doesn't it bother you that Sir Herbert assumes you need his help?" Tony asked Crispin.

"He's only trying to be friendly."

"Given the way you were raised, I don't think you could possibly understand."

Crispin stiffened. "Try me."

"We British cling to the vestiges of an arcane class system. Even though I am studying business administration at university and will have a good position someday, my colleagues see me as a working-class stiff."

"Surely, you don't include Clinton in that indictment."

"No. He is like you, blind to subtleties of class structure on this side of the pond." After a pause, Tony added, "I think that's why I didn't fully appreciate my father until it was too late."

Crispin listened as Tony told a story about once taking his father on a grand tour at Oxford. "In truth, I was a bit full of myself. Scholarship and all."

He said that he was raised on the "dodgy" side of London, part of a large working-class family. "I am the first Dexter to go to university," he said, with a mixture of pride in his own accomplishment and shame at his family history.

Throughout the tour at Oxford, Tony's father had patiently listened to all of his son's recitations about the history and architecture of each of the fine halls they visited. Tony was confident that he'd impressed his old man until they stopped for sandwiches at a basement coffee shop. Halfway through lunch, his father excused himself to talk to a janitor who was using a large electric buffer to polish the travertine floors. When his father returned to the table he showed his first real excitement of the day, explaining that he'd gotten tips on a cleaning product to use at the office building where he, too, worked as a night janitor.

"I was so young and stupid that I was embarrassed that my father could be so common," Tony sighed. "It was not until his funeral last year that I had matured enough to appreciate how rare was his pride in his simple, honest work."

Tony stopped walking. Crispin stood by him, giving him time to speak. "There was a lot of unfinished business on the table when he died, things unsaid."

Crispin took his hand. "If I've learned anything, it is that there is no promise of tomorrow."

Once they'd arrived at Drury Lane, Crispin checked her watch and calculated the time difference to New York City, explaining to Tony that she needed to call the States before it got any later. She gave him a warm embrace and peck on the cheek before abandoning him on the stoop. He stood there for several minutes, watching from below as the lights came on in her flat before finally turning to leave.

***

Days before, Crispin had run into a roadblock when she first tried to make copies of the Tut negatives from the Second Annex before returning them to Ida. She'd considered scanning them digitally, but they were so fragile that she was afraid of damaging them. Luckily, Georgia was an expert in such matters. The one solid achievement on her college transcript was her photography coursework. Georgia was a natural in the darkroom and a whiz with the digital software that let her enhance and restore even badly damaged prints and negatives. When Crispin asked for her advice, Georgia offered to make high-definition digital reproductions. Unfortunately, she would need to work with the originals. Crispin sent them to Georgia in New York by express mail. The turn-around time would only be a few days so Crispin crossed her figures and hoped they wouldn't be missed.

That's why Crispin was anxious to check in with her friend. She was hoping the negatives were on their way back to her.

***

In New York, Georgia's phone rang just as she was getting ready to leave her apartment. She started to ignore it since she was running late, but the machine answered on the second ring, broadcasting Crispin's voice. "If you're there, please pick up."

Dropping her purse as she dashed to the phone, Georgia caught the call just before Crispin was ready to give up.

"Hi, hon. I'm here," Georgia yelled breathlessly into the receiver. "I was on my way to Barney's for the spring shoe sale."

"More shoes?"

"A girl can never have too many shoes."

"Well, far be it from me to keep you from your hobby. I just wanted to see if you'd had a chance to work on the stuff I sent."

"I finished yesterday, and if I do say so myself, they're lookin' good," Georgia told Crispin, describing how she'd used blue filters to enhance the grainy images.

While chatting away about her technique, Georgia addressed a padded envelope and promised to mail the new prints and the original celluloids back to Crispin right away. Just as Crispin hung up, Georgia's phone rang again. Talking to one of her stable of boyfriends, Georgia stuffed the envelope into her tote. She didn't notice that she'd inadvertently addressed the envelope to Sophie instead of Crispin.

***

Crispin changed for bed. Before settling onto the couch, she poured a double shot of whiskey and retrieved her mother's field journal from her backpack. Though she was intent on spending time organizing her latest research findings, her thoughts kept returning to the pub. She realized how expertly Herbert had steered the conversation toward subjects he wanted to talk about and away from those he didn't. He made it seem effortless, the way he drove his car, planning three turns ahead until he arrived exactly where he wanted to be.

Tony, on the other hand, was less certain and in some ways more endearing. When he shared his regrets about his relationship with his father, it wrenched at a tender place in Crispin. Her face flushed at the memory of her drunken tirade against her father in Egypt.

Sipping on the nightcap, Crispin was reminded of a bit of Georgia wisdom: "Honey pie, there are plenty of men you'd like to go to bed with. The trick is to find one you'd like to wake up with." Crispin wondered, "Which is which?"

Chapter Eight

Crispin was surprised the next evening when she walked into the Basil Street Hotel in the Knightsbridge dining room to see that her brother and Ashraf were not alone. Tony was with them. Ashraf had promised the twins good English prime rib and Yorkshire pudding at one of his favorite London haunts. The small Edwardian-style hotel was almost one hundred years old and had the ambiance of an English country house full of paintings, tapestries, and antiques.

Over the years Ashraf had remained the closest of a group of family friends from the time the Leadses spent in Egypt. When Salma, a cosmopolitan woman of exceptional beauty and the beneficiary of generations of upper-class breeding, married Ashraf, the more cynical among their friends suggested that Ashraf's money and influence were the primary attractions. It certainly wasn't his physique. He enjoyed the pleasures of a well-set table a bit too much so that his middle hung generously over his belt. Ashraf had a full head of glorious, near-white hair, but his face, with its broad nose, complexion that had suffered from too many hours in the sun, and eyes that seemed to be in a perpetual squint, was anything but handsome.

Most of their friends in the Mediterranean Gang were academicians. Ashraf was the exception. Raised in a middle-class home, his political instincts helped him work his way up through the ranks of the Egyptian bureaucracy. His ultimate appointment to a high-ranking position with the Egyptian Supreme Council of Antiquities gave him power, influence, and a generous income. In the end, however, it was his wide-ranging business interests, not his salary as a public servant, that supplied him with sufficient wealth to support Salma's taste for luxury.

"Speaking of butterflies, here's our very own," Ashraf said as he rose to welcome Crispin to the table, tenting her with a hug and pulling out a chair for her.

"Butterflies?" she asked.

"Indirectly," Tony said, explaining the metaphor in chaos theory that suggests that even something as small as the flutter of a butterfly's wings alters the universe to some extent, albeit immeasurably.

"Thus, even small changes may lead to unexpected outcomes," Tony added.

A waiter appeared over Crispin's shoulder to fill her wineglass and take their orders.

"The idea is that chaotic occurrences beyond a system's control can produce ordered structures and patterns on a grander scale. Thus, from order, chaos. From chaos, order." Clinton continued with his narrative that was a blend of chaos theory, politics, and ecology.

It was at times like this that Crispin understood why personal relationships, like academic achievements, came so easily to her brother. He had that rare ability to turn even an obscure theory into intriguing dinner conversation without being either stodgy or condescending. Crispin loved her twin too much to find fault in him but at times she wondered if while they swam around in that amniotic fluid together he'd somehow sucked up more than his share of the good stuff, such as self-esteem, empathy, compassion, and sensitivity, and left her to shape her psyche out of the leftovers traits such as self-doubt, jealousy, and guilt.

Halfway through the meal, Crispin remembered Herbert's request. "By the way, we have a mutual friend," she said to Ashraf. "Herbert Van Snyder III. He asked us to give you his regards."

Crispin detected the slightest look of puzzlement on Ashraf's face before he smiled. "He makes a joke?" Ashraf said, laughing. "We are more than friends. In two days, we return to Egypt on business."

"Speaking of Egypt," Clinton said, "how are things coming along at Saqqara?"

"You know your father. He keeps things moving and puts in more hours than men half his age," Ashraf replied. While he talked, Ashraf kept his gaze fixed on Crispin.

She could read his unspoken question but had no intention of engaging in a discussion involving her father. She signaled the waiter and ordered a B&B. After a drink that left a delicious burning sensation down her throat, Crispin changed the subject. "What about the corpse they found before I left? Have the police made an identification or determined the cause of death?"

"Inspector Sabri is doing what he can, but it is a strange case. No one seems to know how he, or should I say 'his remains,' wound up at the camp, Ashraf replied. "He was a young man from the village. His widow is left with nine-week-old twins and little hope of climbing out of poverty."

Crispin absorbed the reality of the young man's death and wondered if he'd been the cheerful helper who had helped her brush dirt from the shards they'd found. "His name?" she asked.

"Madu. It means 'of the people,'" Ashraf said.

He had been her bright-eyed, passionate helper. Madu, who spoke of honoring his ancestors.

***

Crispin returned to the flat intending on putting in a few hours of work. She wanted to be ready for tomorrow's meeting. Ashraf had used his connections to arrange an appointment for her to visit the famous, retired Egyptologist, Sean Thurman, at his home.

Surrounded by books and papers, she'd curled up in the wingback close to a space heater to work. In spite of her attempts at scholarly discipline, her mind, and her libido, kept replaying her walk home from the Basil Street Hotel. Tony had insisted on escorting her to her door after they said goodbye to Ashraf and Clinton at the restaurant. The deep fog gave a feeling of intimacy as the pair walked slowly through the London night. When Tony pulled her into the deep Edwardian doorway of a closed shop to kiss her, she found herself returning his kiss with a hunger that reminded her just how long it had been. But, when his hands traveled down her back to explore her hips, she pulled away. "Let's walk."

Something subtle and ill defined held her back. Maybe it was the way Tony tried to control her. Instead of strolling together as equals, it sometimes felt as if he were walking her like a pet. She tried to explain away her hesitancy, telling herself that his awkwardness was a remnant of his rough-and-tumble childhood, a start in life that he tried to cover with a thin veneer of good manners and proper speech.

When they arrived at her building, she turned him down when he asked if he could come up. "I have an important appointment in the country tomorrow and I'm not nearly ready," she explained.

He insisted that they make plans for a late dinner at the Pump & Duck, so she agreed on a time and date that she could fit into her work schedule. Before he left, Tony once again pressed Crispin close to him and they shared another kiss, more passionate than the first.

Upstairs, settled into her favorite place, it wasn't long before Crispin's resolve to work into the night was losing the battle with her tired brain. Her eyes closed and she fell back into the labyrinth. In the dream labyrinth she was in the grip of a disembodied hand.

The hand belonged to an Egyptian boy who clawed at her arm. He was dressed much like the workers in archeological digs at the turn of the twentieth century and seemed to be struggling, through pain, to tell her something. His body began to convulse and he opened his mouth as if to scream. Instead of sound, he vomited butterflies, hundreds in every color and shape. The instant the wings of the butterflies touched the air they dissolved into purple smoke. Crispin turned in horror and started to run, but the corridors were turning murky and dirty. She stumbled on, drawn toward a distant, insistent sound. Someone was calling her name.

She realized, half awake and half still dreaming, that the sound was coming from outside her dream. Her fingernails were clawing something real, the arms of the wingback chair, further shredding the worn cloth. The distant voice was Clinton's. He sounded desperate. Stirring to wakefulness, Crispin was choking and her eyes were burning. The room was filled with smoke.

Chapter Nine

Huddled outside on Drury Lane with Clinton and Sophie in the frigid night, Crispin watched as the fire trucks arrived in a wail of sirens and flashing lights. The building was evacuated and someone from the fire team passed around blankets and strong, sweetened tea to the tenants.

"Helps with the shock, love," he explained. "Shock'll be your main concern at the moment."

A fire captain came to Sophie and Crispin with good news. The fire was small and confined to the sitting area of their apartment. His men would use an industrial fan to pull out the smoke and assured them it wouldn't take long. "Mostly smoke but particularly nasty—and potentially lethal."

An hour later as the captain was finishing up, he told them that the initial report would list the cause of fire as of "indeterminate origin."

At last able to return to their apartment, Sophie, Crispin, and Clinton pitched in and began scrubbing smoke from the sitting room walls, furniture, and floor.

"Thank God I left most of the important stuff at the study carrel," Crispin told Sophie as she examined a stack of scorched notebook paper. While straightening out the charred edges of the paper, Crispin began a hacking cough.

"Crisp, just let us finish up," Clinton told her. "You've been through a lot."

"Besides, you could use a bath." Sophie wiped soot from her friend's forehead. "This color only looks good on me."

When Crispin returned to the living room with her freshly washed hair wrapped in a towel, her best friend and her brother had their feet up and were enjoying a glass of wine.

"Much better," Sophie said, as she reached for the bottle of wine and a glass. Crispin waved her off and reached for the whiskey, filling an Old Fashion glass from a bottle of Talisker that was half empty. As she settled cross-legged onto the floor, leaning back against a chair piled high with books and papers, she took a long, slow drink and let the smoky burn warm her mouth and throat.

"Mark Twain had it about right. 'Too much of anything is bad, but too much good whiskey is barely enough.'"

If she'd expected a response from Sophie or Clinton, she didn't get one. Instead, they talked about the fire. None of them could come up with a satisfactory explanation. Their first thought had been the space heater, but it was in good working order and the fire captain insisted it had not been the source.

"Maybe it came out of my dream," Crispin said sheepishly.

"Here we go again," Clinton teased.

She gave Clinton and Sophie a synopsis of the dream and told them that while she'd bathed she'd replayed the dream in her mind. "Some of the images, such as the butterflies, I can understand but, frankly, for most of it, I haven't a clue."

Clinton, who'd organized her handwritten notes and cleaned her computer case, said that since the dream was undoubtedly inspired by her heightened interest in Egyptian tombs, maybe it was no more than an allegory for her latest line of research. "From what I saw there's more there than just burial rituals," he said, indicating her paperwork.

"Yes, but that's a specific case," she said.

"Give it up, Sister. What exactly have you been up to on all those trips to Oxford?" Sophie asked. "You know we'll find out eventually."

Crispin, at first, hesitated, afraid of being shot down. "I may have found something," she finally said. "Actually, that's why I'm going to see Sean Thurman tomorrow."

Clinton and Sophie listened while Crispin walked them through her suspicions of a fifth chamber in the Tut tomb and her ideas about the photographs and documents she'd found.

"Your ideas are sound up to a point," Clinton said.

"Thanks a lot," Crispin shot back.

Clinton forged ahead with his analysis. He said that although her suggested explanations were each valid, the list was incomplete. "You mustn't allow yourself to assume that there are only three possible explanations," Clinton stressed. "You should think of every possibility and eliminate them one by one, until you're left with the one that the evidence best supports."

"Or, as Holmes would say, 'When you have excluded the impossible, whatever remains, however improbable, must be the truth,'" Crispin said with a grin.

"You and your Holmes," Sophie kidded. "I think Herbert has you hooked."

"I thought you were dating Tony," Clinton said.

"Is that why you invited him along tonight?"

"Me? When I saw him in the lobby I just assumed you had."

Sophie broke into a loud laugh. "Clint, why did we ever worry about this woman? She's been in town less than two weeks and she's already got a pair of handsome men sniffing after her."

Sophie's cackling embarrassed Crispin, but her friend poured it on. "Don't you see how it goes?" Sophie continued. "It's Herbert by day and Tony by night."

"Is that right, Crisp? Are you seeing them both?"

"I never explain," Crispin said, intending to stand and strike a statuesque pose. As she stood, the towel on her head toppled over her face. Reaching for it, she got tangled in her robe.

Clinton had to steady her when she wobbled to regain her balance. "Easy does it, Grace."

So much for a grand exit.

"Clearly, I'm done for. It's time to get some sleep. Good night, Brother."

"Ah, 'To sleep, perchance to dream.'"

Crispin gave him a look that said she'd had all the dreaming she wanted for one night.

***

The next day, which had started badly when she uncharacteristically overslept, wasn't getting any better. Late, frustrated, and lost in the hills of the Cotswolds, Crispin pulled over beside a dry-stone wall to once again consult a foldout road map.

That morning she woke up with a jerk at the sound of someone knocking at her door. One look at the alarm clock told her she was in trouble. "You've got to be kidding me. It's 9 a.m."

She was frantic when she let Herbert into the flat. He said he'd heard about the fire and dropped by to check on her.

"I've no time to talk," she stammered. "I have to be in the country by noon."

While she dressed in the bathroom so as not to wake Sophie, Herbert made coffee and toast. He offered to drive her to her appointment, but she refused his help repeatedly until he said he would loan her his car. It made sense from a purely practical standpoint. Not only would she avoid layovers at train stations, but she would also be able to make up lost time once she'd cleared the city.

The two-hour drive from London had been easy, but since turning off the M40 motorway she'd confronted delay upon delay trying to navigate country lanes. Her frustration was now compounded by the infuriating absence of any discernible numbering system or signs for the country roads. "This map is about as helpful as hieroglyphics without the Rosetta Stone," she said, tossing it in the passenger seat in disgust. "What I need now is a friendly face."

She spotted an elderly woman walking a Corgi. After a quick appeal, Crispin was relieved to learn that she was only a couple of turns from her destination. It was, however, in the opposite direction. Doubling back, Crispin found a small, faded marker for the obscure lane that wound to Thurman's white stucco cottage. Bathed in the intermittent sunlight of a cold March day, his house was surrounded by chestnut trees whose bare branches promised summer shade.

The old man was bent over working in the garden. When he spotted Crispin driving up the road, he creaked to a standing position and motioned her to drive on up to the house. He was waiting for her by the front door when she pulled up. In a great rush of adrenaline, Crispin apologized as she opened the car door. "Dr. Thurman, I am sorry to be late, but you see..."

Thurman offered his hand. "Ms. Leads, I presume."

Embarrassed that she had failed to properly introduce herself, Crispin offered her hand. "I'm Ms. Leads and I'm almost never late, but you see..."

The flustered young woman and the old man both found the scene silly and started to laugh.

"Let me start over," Crispin said, relaxing for the first time all day. "I'm Crispin Leads but you must, please, call me Crispin."

"Not to worry. Only the most resolute find their way here the first time. Right then, let's go in, shall we? I've organized a light meal."

Thurman wore his eighty-plus years well. He still boasted a full head of white hair. His back was straight and his calloused hands strong. He reminded Crispin of her maternal grandfather who, like Thurman, often seemed in need of a shave.

He carried their lunch tray laden with freshly picked radishes, sardines, biscuits, cornichons, dark mustard, and Stinking Bishop's cheese from the tiny kitchen to the sitting room so that they could eat near the stone fireplace, darkened by smoke from decades of use. The room had the kind of comfortable clutter that often accumulates in a favorite place. There was a manual typewriter on a small table not far from a desk where a laptop sat open.

Crispin's chair had a pillow embroidered with the fraying cross-stitch of a French slogan, that when translated meant: "The guards die but do not surrender." She moved the pillow to one side.

"Our mutual friend, Ida Fowler, made that for me during the war," Thurman said, pausing for a moment as if memories of another time held onto him. Then he sighed and seemed to remember his duties, handing Crispin a plate before settling into his chair. "When I told her that you were to be my guest for lunch, she was most effusive in her praise."

"I hope you recognize," he said, spreading mustard on a biscuit, "that that is the highest of compliments coming from Miss Fowler. She's known the best of them. I would have expected no less from the daughter of a scholar of the stature of Daniel Leads."

Crispin knew all too well that a stature as imposing as her father's cast a broad shadow. *It sure doesn't let in much light,* she thought.

"When you called, you said that you had been working with the records from the Tut excavation," Thurman said.

"Yes. The Griffith's archives are a treasure trove," Crispin replied, determined to keep her conversation generic until she had a better sense of Thurman's receptiveness to her ideas.

"Nice. You'll find the topic can become an obsession. I've written about Egypt for years and I haven't even scratched the surface. In fact, I'm on to something especially interesting right now," he said, indicating the piles of manuscripts and books stacked along the floor. Many were marked with a forest of yellow Post-it Notes, the telltale sight of a work in progress. Crispin suspected that Thurman could instantly locate anything you asked him for.

Thurman offered Crispin the dish of cornichons. She speared one and bit into the crispy delight.

"As we know from the Temple at Kom-Ombo, ancient Egyptian medical technology was quite sophisticated. What we are just now beginning to appreciate is just how deep the knowledge ran," he said. Dropping his voice to a conspiratorial tone, he asked, "Crispin, can you keep a secret?"

"Always."

He rummaged around on his desk for a few minutes and returned with a manuscript that he said he was finalizing for publication. In it he argued that an Egyptian physician actually conceptualized the existence of germs and viruses as early as the third millennium B.C.

"Imagine what that means," he beamed. "An understanding of the disease transfer mechanism coming that early in human history."

Asking Crispin's indulgence while he smoked a pipe, he scraped the bowl with his pocketknife and then packed in fresh tobacco. He was clearly enjoying her company, talking first about his work and then about his long-ago university career. Before long his discourse rambled into a favorite complaint.

"I find it unfortunate that today's generation of postdoctoral students would rather tear down than build up. They are willing, even eager I would say, to make their reputation at the expense of others," he said. "Besides that, they too often think they can do it all on the Internet. Download and regurgitate, that is what they call research. That is what is behind so much of what they call 'deconstructive scholarship,'" he said, emphasizing the prefix as if it had the bitter taste of Marmite. "They may as well call it what it really is, 'destruction scholarship.'"

Crispin could tell that Thurman might wax on for hours about the faults of modern scholarship so she redirected him by offering to clear away the lunch tray.

"Where are my manners? I have biscuits and cream for dessert. It's in the kitchen."

With Crispin's help they soon had the lunch tray cleared and were back in their cozy chairs enjoying tea, cream, and cookies. It gave Crispin a chance to steer the conversation in a new direction. "I would like to know your opinion of Hoving's work."

Thomas Hoving was one of the most recognized names in the pop-history of the Tut excavation. In the mid-1970s, Hoving led a team that organized the extremely successful, seven-city U.S. tour of the richest artifacts from Tut's tomb. While preparing the exhibition Hoving had, by chance, come across twenty-seven bound volumes of prints, original photos, letters, drawings, and handwritten diaries by Howard Carter and Lord Carnarvon.

"Thomas knew what I know," Thurman replied with a grin. "You have to actually touch something to understand it."

Thurman said it was little wonder that the material that Hoving discovered had been overlooked since it was boxed with piles of what Hoving described as "junk." The junk included reams of yellowed newspaper clippings about the fabled Curse of King Tut. For years after the boy king's tomb was unearthed, tabloid journalists, hungry for stories, had churned out the rumors of mysterious deaths as legitimate news bulletins. It took fifty years before many of the reports were discredited.

"One particularly preposterous report said that when the tomb was opened, the workers found a tablet that said: 'Death will slay with his wings who ever disturbs the peace of the Pharaoh.'" Thurman said, "Never mind that no such inscription existed, the story took on a life of its own when Lord Carnarvon died. Absolute rot."

"The Earl's health had been fading for years," Thurman said. "That didn't keep the press from sensationalizing his 'mysterious' death, purportedly from an innocuous insect bite. Over the years any number of otherwise routine deaths had been attributed to the so-called curse."

Crispin had her notepad on her lap, taking in every word.

"They didn't see the big picture," he said. "It took Hoving to see what everyone else missed."

Hoving had used the long-forgotten journals and photos that he found to build his hypothesis that Carter had not only stolen various objects from the dig, but probably had misled the public about the sequence of events leading up to the first opening of the tomb.

Puffing on his pipe, Thurman said, "I came to similar conclusions, but of course I was working separately, tracing pieces from museums and private collections. I must say that I wasn't particularly popular, because I suspected that the sainted Lord Carnarvon may have been implicated." Tamping his pipe down, Thurman winked at Crispin. "Carter and Carnarvon were undoubtedly gifted archeologists, but they were also human."

"Did you ever publish your suspicions?" asked Crispin.

"Never able to prove it, unequivocally. Besides, the editors of British scholarly journals were not too keen on the topic.

What my critics simply did not fully appreciate was just how chaotic the Tut excavation could be at times."

"The constant parade of visitors made work difficult, I am sure."

Thurman nodded. "While Carter's workers may have been too busy to keep an eye on every piece, Carter was himself meticulous in his methods and records. Had to be, really. In that chaos, it is a wonder that more wasn't overlooked."

"Or lost?"

"To be sure."

Bingo.

***

Driving back to London, Crispin was so intent on replaying the conversation with Thurman that she didn't notice the black van.

It shot out from a side road and rammed full force into the side of the Alfa Romero, sending it spinning out of control. Her car made two complete 360-degree turns before coming to an abrupt stop near the edge of the road. Crispin was rattled, but conscious when she saw the van back up and make another run at her.

Crispin clutched the steering wheel with both hands as the car was forced over the embankment, tumbling hood over wheels twice before landing on its roof in the muddy field below. She was left dangling upside down, her forehead bleeding where she was hit by a book that turned into an airborne missile during the rollover.

Dazed, Crispin watched as a pair of man's highly polished dress shoes walked toward the car. The rest of the man that they belonged to was hidden from her line of sight. She squirmed to free herself but she couldn't reach the seatbelt buckle and her legs were caught in an awkward position against the steering wheel. She thought she heard a female call for help, but in the fuzziness of her final moments of consciousness, she couldn't make out if it was her own voice or some woman yelling down from the road above her. The shoes turned and walked away just as everything faded to black.

Chapter Ten

Crispin's sense of time and place was a mishmash of confusion. Moments merged into minutes of discomfort. A sickening medicinal odor provided the first solid confirmation that she was alive.

At least my nose still works.

She considered opening her eyes, but the effort seemed beyond her strength for the moment. Her swollen eyelids felt unnaturally heavy and sticky, as if glued together. A quick body scan told her that her toes were able to stroke what felt like parchment-thin cotton. Sheets perhaps. When she moved her head, her cheek and chin brushed something unpleasant and stiff, plastic covered in commercial-grade cotton. It crunched and didn't yield the way a pillow should. She elected not to try to adjust her position again since even the slightest turn set off a seismic headache. It was one more sign that she'd survived whatever put her here. Lying still, she concluded that she was in a bed and that someone nearby was talking.

Another good sign. My ears work, too.

"I think she's coming around."

Clinton?

"Crispin, can you hear us?"

Sophie?

Crispin found her voice, but the words that came out were dry and faint. “What’s that awful smell?”

“That’s our girl,” Sophie said with noticeable relief in her voice. “Never could stand the smell of antiseptic.”

“You’re in the hospital,” Clinton explained. “There was an accident.”

“I remember.” But Crispin drifted away before she could finish the thought.

It was hours before she was able to sit up and carry on a sensible conversation. By then Tony had arrived and her friends were tormenting her about her driving.

“What’d you do, forget to drive on the left?” Sophie teased.

Crispin started to explain, but held back. She remembered bits and pieces of the accident. She remembered the van. She remembered rolling over and over. She remembered the shoes. The rest was a blur. She’d need to think things through before bringing her friends in on her suspicions. Besides, her head was throbbing.

“What will you tell Herbert about the car?” Sophie asked.

“Herbert, oh my God, he’ll be so pissed,” Crispin moaned, easing her aching head back on the stiff pillow.

“He should just be thankful that you are not badly injured,” Tony said. “After all, it is just a car.”

“It *was* just a car,” Sophie corrected.

A nurse looked in the room and told the young people that Crispin needed to rest, ordering them to leave. Tony lingered for a few minutes after Sophie left. “I’ll be back tomorrow,” he promised after the now perturbed nurse motioned to him, indicating that visiting hours were over.

Once Tony was gone, Clinton sat down on the edge of Crispin’s bed. “Were you drinking?”

“That’s unfair.”

"Is it? Crisp, we all see it. You've found a new way to hurt yourself."

Clinton's words sliced through the paper-thin mental wall that Crispin used to hide her past. She crossed her arms and slipped her wrists under her armpits. The scars from her childhood addiction to self-mutilation were so faded that they were only visible in her imagination. She'd intended to tell Clinton about the van and the man with the polished shoes, but when he jumped to the conclusion that she'd been drinking, something inside her, a bond with her twin that they'd shared all their life, a bond of trust without conditions, frayed. She needed him to trust her. She needed him to believe in her. She needed him on Team Crispin. The split that had started in Egypt opened a little wider.

"I don't need you to remind me of my many faults and endless imperfections. That's what Dad is for."

"Now who's being unfair?"

"You can go now," she said, sliding under the covers and pulling the thin blanket up to her chin. "Turn off the light when you leave."

Clinton stood up but didn't leave. He turned off the light and pulled a chair next to her bed and sat down. They remained in the dark for a long time. It was Clinton who finally broke the silence.

"You don't get it."

"I'm sure you will enlighten me, Baby Brother."

"I get that you're angry. Never knowing when you might hurt yourself. Do you have any idea what it was like for me? What it's like for me now?"

"For you? It isn't about you," Crispin said, turning her back to him, her eyes moist with emotion.

When he spoke again, his voice was gentle. "It was all of us. Dad felt helpless. For a man like him, helpless is not an option. The more you hurt, the stricter he became. It was as if he believed he could control your impulses, keep you safe, by micro-managing all our lives. Did you know that I lied to my friends about why Dad never attended my lacrosse games? You were the center of our family universe. So frail. So needy."

"Stop it," said Crispin, turning back around and wiping her eyes.

"But it never stops, Crisp. It just never stops. It's as if there isn't enough mother's milk or father's concern or brother's love in the world to make you love yourself as much as the people in your life do."

"I haven't cut myself in years. I've had it under control for 1,730 days."

"Yeah, but now you're drinking whiskey. Self-destruction by another means."

The heart monitor picked up the pace of her quickening heart rate, making it impossible for Crispin to hide the truth she recognized and the guilt she felt.

"I've got it under control."

"Dad doesn't think so. Not after the way you left Egypt. And he's crazy angry and scared about the wreck. He asked me if you were driving drunk and, frankly, I couldn't dodge the question," Clinton said.

"I wish you hadn't called him."

"He deserved to know." Clinton said, running his slender fingers through his hair.

"You are doing that thing you do when you are hiding something. What are you not telling me?"

Clinton stood and stepped back. His face reddened. "Dad caught me off guard when he asked why you were at Thurman's place."

"You didn't!"

"Crisp, it just slipped out."

Crispin wanted to hurl her pillow at her twin. "How much slipped out?"

"The fire." Clinton stuffed his hands in the pockets of his jacket in an attempt to keep calm. "You know that he can read between the lines. He knows how to get the information he wants."

"You ass! You told him about the fifth chamber."

Crispin was petrified that her father would dismiss her ideas as trite or, worst, derivative. Even so, she had to know. "What did he say?"

Clinton shook his head and shrugged.

"He thinks I am chasing unicorns," Crispin spit the words out.

"That's not true."

"You know I'm right. He's always lecturing me about letting my instinct get out in front of my intellect."

"He's concerned about all the accidents." Clinton looked worried. "Frankly, I am, too. I'm going to cancel my trip."

"You are out of your mind."

"I'm needed here."

"Look, Little Brother, you've laid piles of guilt on me tonight. Not to mention, you violated a sacred confidence by telling Dad about my theories. I am in the catbird seat on this one. You owe me, big time. I'm calling in all my chits. You simply must go. It's the chance of a lifetime. Besides, Sophie's here. She always has my back."

Crispin could tell it wouldn't take much persuading. The offer had come a few days back from one of Clinton's professors. He had a chance to be included on a National Geographic expedition to Roatán Island off the northern coast of Honduras after a colleague canceled at the last minute. The work would give Clinton a chance to, as he said, "run with the Big Dogs." He would not get an opportunity like this again.

"I'll think about it. Get some rest." He paused as he opened the door to leave. "Love you."

He waited until Crispin whispered, "Love you more."

Alone, she began to puzzle through everything that had happened since she arrived in London. As much as she hated to admit it, Clinton and her dad had a point about accidents. The fall in the British Museum. The fire. Now the car wreck.

She was glad she didn't tell Clinton about the van or he'd never take the research trip to Honduras. She could dismiss the first two as circumstantial, but the black van was no accident. If it hadn't been for the fire, she might have been able to pass the wreck off as a drunken driver or road rage. Taken together, however, there was no question. She'd been deliberately run off the road.

"That's one too many 'accidents' for them not to be connected," she said out loud. "Someone is out to stop me. But from what exactly?"

She took out a legal pad and began filling pages as she methodically tried to work the problem, connecting people, places, and events. In her notes, she'd interspersed random thoughts and snatches of conversation. In spite of the discipline of the effort, in the end she still had no clear picture why someone was after her.

Frustrated, she leaned over the bedrail to put the pad on the nightstand. Still a bit shaky she missed the mark and dropped it on the floor. Reaching to recover it she saw a plastic hospital storage box under the bed. It was her personal belongings recovered from the wreck. She slipped out of bed and pulled the box over to a nearby chair, each movement a study in slow motion. Inside were her purse, backpack, and several books that Thurman had loaned her. Most of her clothes were too stained from mud and torn to be of any use.

On the bottom was a gift-wrapped package that was somewhat the worse for wear. Thurman had asked her to deliver it to Ida. Curiosity got the best of her and she picked at the torn and mud-stained paper wrapping until she could see what was inside.

"A book. How romantic," she mumbled to herself. "You'll have to do better than that if you are going to win the lady's heart."

Crispin replaced the torn gift wrap as best as she could and decided it was still early enough in the evening to call Ida. Her friend was pleased to hear from her, but distressed to learn of the accident. She offered to come to the hospital, but Crispin told her that she fully expected to be released in the morning. When Crispin told her about the gift from Thurman, Ida was tickled.

"That is just like Sean," she said. "The two of us have been collecting outlandish tales of Egyptian curses for years, the more bizarre the better. He said he'd found a juicy one about Tut that was particularly queer and would send it along for my unofficial archives."

Just as she was going to hang up, Ida casually mentioned that she'd had no luck locating the unmarked box Crispin said she'd seen in the storage room. "When you are feeling better, dear, maybe you can help me look for it. I'll make tea."

Reminded of the box, Crispin felt guilty that she hadn't yet told Ida about the negatives, but took comfort in the fact that they'd soon be back from New York and she could return them in person. After she hung up, Crispin added the mysterious missing box to the notes on her legal pad. Flipping through the pages of random comments, she tossed the tablet down in disgust.

"Even without a headache I couldn't make sense of that," she said, reaching instead for one of the books Thurman had loaned her.

It was a signed, first edition of *Tutankhamen: The Untold Story*, a bestseller by Thomas Hoving, the flamboyant former director of the Metropolitan Museum. It was published around the time that Hoving curated a blockbuster American tour of Tut artifacts. Praised for its breezy writing and gossipy prose, it was criticized by scholars for some of its unsubstantiated bombshells. Hoving accused Carter of clandestine deals, pilfering objects from the tomb, and other shenanigans in violation of the Carnarvon commission with the Egyptian government. Crispin was familiar with Hoving's story about power struggles, scandals, and mysterious deaths surrounding the excavation, but she decided to read it again. Her head still hurt too much for serious concentration so, instead of going cover to cover, she flipped through the book, skimming random selections.

She reread the descriptions of Lord Carnarvon with particular interest since his great-great grandson was now an acquaintance. Hoving said that while Carnarvon appeared superficial, he had a "deadly shrewdness" and was actually a brilliant man, maybe even a genius. In one place, Hoving said that he thought Carnarvon was a classic "disguiser." He defined this as the kind of man who, if discovered with a serious book, would say, "Oh, I just picked it up and, having done *that*, I supposed I should simply turn the pages to the end."

So like Herbert.

Remembering that she hadn't yet called him to explain about the car, she picked up the bedside phone and dialed. The servant who answered offered to take a message. Crispin left her name and the phone number for her hospital room just as the nurse arrived with a dinner tray.

Following a meal that tasted like tepid mush, and another nap, Crispin found herself fully awake at 1 a.m. The hospital routine and painkillers were wreaking havoc with her circadian rhythm. She took a walk around empty, depressing halls. Only the *beep, beep, beep* of monitors and whispers of nurses changing shifts interrupted the quiet. She located a vending machine. Armed with candy and a soda she returned to her room and to her reading.

When Crispin picked up the Hoving book, it fell open to a cross-sectional diagram of the Tut tomb and map indicating its relationship to nearby tombs. It may have been the surge of sugar and caffeine or simply the kind of mental clarity that so often comes in the wee hours of the morning.

What she saw on those facing pages caused her to almost scream out. "There it is!"

Chapter Eleven

On the maps she saw that the Tut tomb was so close to that of Rameses VI they almost seemed connected. The proximity suggested that if there were an undisclosed or forgotten chamber to the Tut tomb it might intersect with one of the chambers of Rameses VI. Many archeologists believed that the reason the Tut tomb had gone undetected by thieves and archeologists through the centuries was because its entrance was buried under the rubble from excavation of the larger, more magnificent Rameses tomb. It was little wonder, since by comparison, the Tut tomb was not much larger than a New York City apartment.

The precedent was legendary. Ancient architects, building the nearby tomb of Rameses III, had accidentally broken through to an older, neighboring tomb of Amenmessu. Today, the only evidence of that long-ago excavation accident is a dead-end passage in the larger tomb. Perhaps another close call, lost in the mists of time, had once joined Tut and Rameses VI, creating another entrance. A back door.

A familiar tingle that started at her hairline worked its way down her spine as Crispin was reminded of the labyrinth in her dream.

Thurman had told her, "You have to actually touch something to understand it."

There was only one way to know. She'd go back to Egypt.

***

When the day shift charge nurse entered Crispin's room she found her patient wide awake, showered, and dressed in the fresh clothes Sophie had brought the night before. "Ready to go, are we?"

"The doctor said if everything checked out I could go home."

After examining Crispin, the nurse seemed satisfied. "Nasty bump that," she said as she gently probed the wound on Crispin's forehead. "The swelling should go down in a day or two."

Before the nurse turned to leave she reminded Crispin, "Best to drive on the proper side of the road from now on."

Crispin closed the door and finished packing up. Her decision to go to Egypt made perfect sense during the night. In the fullness of morning light, she faced reality. The biggest obstacle would be Clinton, who, she knew, would try to stop her. She'd need an ally.

Ashraf!

A call to him, a request, and some speed-packing had her ready for a flight to Cairo by late afternoon.

At Heathrow Ashraf made a fuss over Crispin's bruises, insisting that she let him carry her backpack to the gate. She didn't object since her muscles and joints felt as though they'd been run through a pasta press.

"Your father will be pleased to see you," Ashraf said, as they made their way through Heathrow to their gate.

Crispin stopped at a kiosk and picked up some M&Ms for the flight. It was a ritual that she'd never been able to shake. The first time she tried to board a plane after her mother's fatal plane crash she had a panic attack. Although it had been two years since the accident, fear immobilized her. Clinton saw what was happening, but their father was distracted by check-in procedures and didn't notice. Clinton reached into his carry-on and pulled out a huge bag of M&Ms, his favorite. He divided the candy into two stacks and threw down the gauntlet.

"Bet I can count the colors fastest," he whispered. A full-throated sibling challenge.

The distraction worked. Once they were on the plane, he explained in a way that only a seven-year-old can that M&Ms were magic beans and as long as she traveled with them, nothing bad would ever happen on a plane. He was vague about the source of his fantasy conviction, but she bought the yarn. After that, she never flew without a packet of the candy. Foolish, childish, superstitious, comforting habit that it was, she couldn't shake it.

What if I got on the plane without M&Ms and the plane crashed? It would be my fault. I would have the blood of all of those people on my hands. Can't take the chance.

While Ashraf and Crispin waited on line to pay, she said, "Ashraf, you, as well as anyone, know how things were when I left Egypt. I'm still not ready to see Dad. I don't want to put you in the middle, but would you mind not telling him that I'm in Egypt?"

Ashraf took the candy from Crispin. "Far be it from me to sit in judgment," he said as he paid the cashier.

Even as Crispin assured him that she would eventually work things out with her father, she was fighting a gnawing sense of guilt. She'd had to engage in more than one deception that day. First, she'd dodged Tony, who had arrived at the hospital early for a visit. Something told her that Tony would try to talk her out of her plans and she didn't want the hassle of an argument.

Finally, instead of telling Sophie and Clinton in person about her plans, she'd timed her exit to avoid them and left handwritten notes behind telling them that Ashraf was taking her to Egypt to recuperate. In her note to Clinton she was emphatic: "Now you have no excuse. Go to Honduras. I will be fine."

How many fibs and half-truths does it take to make a liar?

"I swear to you that I will talk to Dad as soon as I'm ready," Crispin promised Ashraf.

"Then we have a deal," Ashraf groaned as he transferred Crispin's backpack to his right shoulder. "What have you got in here? Stones?" he teased Crispin as he adjusted the weight to a more comfortable position.

"Not quite. Extra batteries for my computer."

"A Leads through and through. Always prepared for work."

"Ugh, you make me sound like a drudge. But you do have a point. Working at Saqqara helped but I really need to focus on the final chapters for my dissertation if I'm going to have it ready to defend this fall. At some point I'll need to go back to the Griffith to spend more time with the Theban maps of the Valley."

By phrasing what she really wanted as an afterthought, Crispin knew she was again bordering on deception, but her conscience was assuaged when Ashraf took the bait.

"Of course," Ashraf said with patriotic pride. "The originals are at the National Museum in Cairo and our recent maps are much more detailed."

"I didn't realize there was a difference." Lie. Lie. Lie.

Ashraf launched into an expansive explanation of the time, effort, and expense the Egyptian government had devoted to the new technique of pseudo-holography at the Valley of the Kings. The innovative project avoided the complications of coherent light technology, but produced a three-dimensional schematic map. Egyptian officials had been willing to make the investment in the hope of finding more undisturbed tombs, especially since experts believed that there were at least ten yet-to-be-discovered tombs in the Valley.

Crispin told Ashraf that, if she felt up to it, she would like to access the Egyptian maps.

"Of course. Just say the word and I'll make all the arrangements."

Baited, hooked, and reeled in.

Herbert was waiting for them in the British Airways first class lounge. He insisted on upgrading Crispin's booking so that she could sit with them on the flight. Once onboard, Herbert and Ashraf sat together and Crispin was assigned a seat across the aisle.

Before long the obligatory safety lecture and instructions for stowing luggage were given and tray tables were secured in their upright and locked positions. In flight, Crispin relaxed and accepted a glass of Kendall Jackson Chardonnay from the steward. Whiskey was a no-no while on painkillers. She welcomed the whispers of pears and white roses in the chilled wine that complemented the bruschetta and salt-and-pepper shrimp of the in-flight menu.

The thought of white roses made her wince about the way she had dodged Tony that morning. Crispin had just finished her hospital discharge paperwork when she'd heard his voice in the hall. She begged the nurse to tell Tony that she had already left the hospital. A few minutes later, when Crispin looked out her hospital window, she saw Tony on the street at the bus stop. He was dressed to the nines with high-polished shoes and a coat and tie. In his arms was a huge bouquet of white roses that he held close to his chest in an effort to protect their petals from the wind. He seemed so vulnerable that she had to fight the urge to call out to him.

The memories of his tender gesture made her feel all the more guilty. Worse by far than evading him at the hospital was standing him up for their date at the Pump & Duck. When she'd dropped by the P&D on the way to the airport to leave Tony a note, Michael had become quite agitated. The bartender thought Crispin's facial bruises were the result of a lover's spat, and that the note was a well-deserved "Dear John" letter.

"Ye cannae tell me if that dirty sod laid his grubby mitts on ye."

Crispin told Michael a fictitious story about wrecking the car because she had a hard time driving a stick shift with her left hand.

"Love, ye cannae expect an old shark like Michael to believe ye got in an accident on a country lane without cause."

Crispin had laughed off his scrutiny, but something in her manner alerted Michael and he held her hand a moment longer. "Be safe, now will ye, love?"

The rich airline meal, wine, and painkillers combined to make Crispin groggy. She pulled on her sleep mask, tilted into a full recline, and was soon in a deep, healing sleep. Until she started to dream.

Ida invited Crispin into a parlor for tea. Ida didn't speak, but made her wishes known by gesturing. The table was set with a highly polished, sterling tea set on a tablecloth embroidered in an intricate lattice and ivy pattern. As Ida poured, the tea began to change from a cool brown into brilliant red. It was blood. Crispin tried to pull away in disgust, but found she could not move. She watched in frozen terror as the ivy wound up from the tablecloth and trapped her arms and legs, tying them fast to her chair. Crispin tried to twist free, but the ivy continued to surround her body, making movement impossible. Ida, who was inexplicably transforming into a hideous skeleton, tried to force Crispin to drink the blood while voices clacked in the background. She could even taste the blood.

The taste of blood was real. So were the voices.

Herbert was trying to wake her. She apparently had thrashed around in her sleep trying to free herself from the seatbelt and had bitten her own lip.

"Sorry to disturb," Herbert said as she opened her eyes.

"Was I that loud?"

"Only those close by could hear you," Herbert said, summoning the steward. "Tea for the lady, please." He stepped over her and took the empty window seat next to her.

"No, not tea, anything but tea," Crispin said with such genuine panic in her voice that Herbert immediately changed the order.

"Brandy. Two."

Ashraf seemed to be in a deep sleep, undisturbed by the activity across the aisle.

After they sipped brandy for a few minutes, Herbert asked, "Do you want to talk about it?"

"Not really, not now."

"Then let's talk about my poor battered car," Herbert said, with a sense of mock injury in his tone.

"Oh, my God, I'm so sorry. Do you have insurance? How can I make it up to you?"

The questions poured out of Crispin to the point that she swallowed the wrong way and began to cough. As he patted her back to help clear her airway, Herbert responded. "Yes, I am fully insured and, yes, I think I can find a way for you to make it up to me."

The brandy was doing its job. "Why sir, whatever could a gentleman like you be suggesting?"

"Answer the question," said Ashraf as he roused from his slumber. "I'd like to know what you meant as well."

"Nothing improper I assure you, my friend," Herbert said.

"Well, if a healthy young man like you can't think of something, let me make a few suggestions," Ashraf said, winking at Crispin. "This young lady knows more about death rituals and burial customs than most of us have forgotten."

"So I understand," Herbert said with a wink to Crispin.

Ashraf told Herbert that when Crispin was growing up she benefited not only from her father's expertise, but also from informal instruction from their many friends who lived and worked around the famous burial grounds, mastabas, temples, and tombs along the Nile. By the time Crispin was fifteen she could carry on learned discussions about obscure pharaohs and the mythology of ancient Egyptian gods.

"Herbert doesn't care about all that," Crispin said.

Herbert responded, "There you are wrong. It helps explain your interest in spirituality and death rituals."

"Why don't you use your family connections to arrange a VIP tour of some of the tombs and let her teach you something?" Ashraf asked Herbert.

"Surely, you've seen everything there is to see," Herbert said to Crispin.

"If I returned a hundred times to the same tomb, I would never see all that is there," she replied wistfully. "Do you know the work of the artist Hokusai?"

"Japanese printmaker? Mt. Fuji?"

"The same. In a high school art appreciation class I wrote a term paper on his seminal work, *Thirty-six Views of Mount Fuji*. It seemed to me that he had the right idea. You can study something over and over again and keep finding new angles and perspectives. A different time of day, a different season, a different arrangement, color scheme, light, or composition that tells you something fresh about a thing and its relationship to everything around it. How it is now. How it was then. How it might be someday."

"I told you she was a smart cookie," Ashraf said, motioning the steward to refill his glass.

"I never doubted it," Herbert said.

"Even as an octogenarian, Hokusai returned to the subject of Fuji, trying to penetrate layers of meaning," Crispin said.

"We all do that, don't we?" Herbert said. "Each time that we go back to a place we are someone else, someone who has lived and grown and changed and we bring that experience with us. It is different because we are different."

"So," Ashraf said to Herbert. "You will arrange things in the Valley."

"I'm in," replied Crispin, downing the last sip of brandy.

"But, Ashraf, what about our meetings?" Herbert protested.

"Let me take care of that. You take care of Crispin."

Chapter Twelve

Crispin felt a familiar twinge of guilt when she checked "vacation" under the question: "What is the primary reason for your trip to the Arab Republic of Egypt?"

"Delusions of grandeur" is not exactly one of the options on the form, Crispin thought.

Crispin and Herbert waited in parallel lines to pass through Cairo immigration, but Ashraf moved quickly through the line reserved for citizens and disappeared into the terminal.

At an intellectual level Crispin knew that self-recrimination was a waste of mental capital, so she decided to make productive use of her time in queue by going over some of the problems her research was presenting to her.

One pressing question, she decided, was how anyone associated with the Tut dig could either hide or steal the contents of an entire chamber and then cover up its existence? For that matter, given the tumultuous political climate of the time, how could any huge sell-off be accomplished after the change in antiquities laws in 1922? Egypt had become independent from the United Kingdom that February and the new laws changed the legal provenance of tomb contents. Items discovered after independence were subject to more rigid accountability and a different set of laws than those found before independence.

Another fact Crispin considered crucial was the level of activity in the Valley of the Kings itself. In the early 1900s, the Valley was considered by many experts in the field of archeology to have been tapped out, with no more tombs to be discovered. That meant fewer archeologists prowling around the isolated location so that anyone who had a secret discovery had a good chance of keeping it.

Until Tut.

The discovery of an undisturbed pharaoh's tomb changed everything. Overnight the Valley was swarming with government officials, archeologists, reporters, and tourists. With that kind of scrutiny and worldwide exposure, it would be almost impossible to keep a secret the magnitude of a fifth chamber.

Crispin's intellectual thought process was interrupted when a man behind her nudged her to move since the line was creeping forward.

"Try to keep the order," he said with a distinctive Australian accent.

The word "order" brought Crispin up short.

What if she'd been thinking out of order? The conundrum created by the change in laws and need for secrecy was not really a problem if the order was reversed. It just might have been possible to plunder a secret room slowly and systematically without much risk to the culprit, if it were done prior to the great discovery of the Tutankhamen tomb in November. Otherwise, it just didn't make sense.

Slow down, Nelly, she cautioned herself mentally. *What about the negatives and the designation "Annex II" on the labels?* She was back where she started.

"Next," called the immigration officer.

Next, indeed, she thought.

Crispin handed him her travel documents.

"*Shu esmak*?" he asked.

"*Esmi* Crispin Leads."

"You speak my language?"

"Only a phrase or two."

"How long will you be in Egypt?"

"Just long enough to uncover the truth about eighty-year-old larceny on a grand scale and earn an international reputation," Crispin mumbled to herself in a near-whisper that no one around her could decipher.

"Pardon. Did you say something?" the clerk asked.

"No. No."

Crispin politely answered his routine questions, then joined Herbert and Ashraf at the baggage claim carousel. Both men had their bags, but there was no sign of Crispin's. The subsequent ordeal at the lost luggage department dragged on because the attendant insisted on being helpful by filling out the claim form on Crispin's behalf. Crispin found it tedious to have to spell her name several times and repeat information about her plans and her hotel.

"No matter, Miss. We will see your *shanta* to the hotel."

On her way to customs, Crispin read through the paperwork the airline attendant had filled out on her behalf.

Oh, good grief! Now I'm Cruspin Leans.

It wasn't until the customs officer asked her to open her backpack and purse that Crispin discovered that the canvas case for her zip drives was missing along with two legal pads. "You've got to be kidding me," she said, riffling through her belongings in disbelief.

Exasperated, Crispin pleaded, "I've had my backpack with me since I left the plane. It had to be someone on the flight. If you could just check the bags of the other passengers."

The customs officer was outwardly sympathetic, but he explained that it wasn't practical since most of the passengers had already passed through.

Crispin grew even more frustrated when the customs officer discovered that the name on her lost baggage claim didn't match her passport. She explained what had happened to her since she had landed in Cairo more than an hour earlier. The customs official was determined to play it by the book.

"For our police report, you are Miss Leads or Miss Leans?"

Before she could answer, Inspector Sabri materialized behind the customs official.

"That would be 'Crispin Leads,'" he told the clerk, spelling her name.

"Thank you, Inspector Sabri," Crispin said, offering her hand.

"Glad to be of service. Will you be joining your father in Saqqara?"

"Not this time. I have business in Cairo."

"Let me know if I can be of assistance," he said, handing her his business card.

On the way to the limousine that Ashraf had waiting for them, Crispin's attention was diverted by a German tourist who yelled at a sleepy cab driver while he frantically pointed at his destination written on a piece of paper. Because she was watching the tourist Crispin didn't notice where she was going and bumped into a Middle Eastern man with a large, distinctive port-wine birthmark covering most of his forehead. For a brief moment, Crispin thought he seemed familiar but he disappeared into the crowd.

Chapter Thirteen

"It was magic," Crispin said, the receiver pressed between her ear and shoulder.

Dressed only in a baggy T-shirt that served as her nightgown, Crispin had been on the phone in her hotel room for almost twenty minutes, drinking coffee and entertaining Sophie with a play-by-play of her trip to Cairo. Sophie understood her friend well enough to know that the animated storytelling was in large part to make up for the covert way Crispin had left London.

"So, last night you could say that I ended the day by going from the ridiculous to the sublime," Crispin said.

This final comment capped off Crispin's story about two incidents after she'd arrived at the hotel. The "ridiculous" occurred right after she checked in to the Mena House. She rounded the corner of the hall to her wing in time to see a man enter her room. Given what she'd been through in the past few days, Crispin was in no mood to take chances, so she used a house phone to summon security.

With a flair for the dramatic, the security guards pulled off a simulated SWAT team raid, flanking both sides of Crispin's hotel room door and using their feet to kick it open. With guns drawn at eye level, they took a two-handed bead on the intruder. He turned out to be a senior citizen, naked except for his shoes, standing in the middle of the room, looking sadly confused and lost.

"Apparently he was a bit drunk and had wandered away from his wife, but, to be safe, the guards hauled him off for questioning," Crispin paused. "That only left me with ten minutes before the sublime Light Show, so I hurried."

Crispin had taken a quick shower and dressed in the T-shirt she'd bought at an airport gift shop. The silly gold and lapis design on the front mimicked hieroglyphics. The back gave the English interpretation: "Egypt is for lovers."

She had just enough time to grab a drink from the minibar and station herself on the compact veranda adjacent to her room. That's when *it* happened. The claim to fame for the Mena House, one of the older hotels just outside Cairo, was its location on the edge of the Giza Plateau. Peering into the night sky over the dark courtyard of the hotel, Crispin waited for what was to come.

Then it did. As if by the work of some divine hand, the Great Pyramid of Khufu materialized, washed in light against the inky sky. In less than a breath, the second of the El Ahram, the Pyramid of Khafra with its limestone cap, became visible, rising well above the roof of the hotel. Her father, naturally, disapproved of the way the theatrical "Sound and Light Show" that was staged every night for tourists on the plateau trivialized important historical sites by turning them into carnival sideshows. Crispin secretly loved it. She was able to use it as an excuse to decline Ashraf's offer to stay the night with him and Salma.

"To each her own," he'd said, with a shrug and a kiss on her cheek when they parted.

Describing the show to Sophie, Crispin could feel a residue of the previous night's adrenaline rush. "Soph, the ancients never got to see their work this way. It was magic," Crispin said, just as there was a knock on the door. "Who could it be at this hour?"

Crispin looked through the peephole in the door, but couldn't see anything except an empty hallway. With the security chain still in place she carefully looked through a crack in the door. Sitting near the doorstep was her missing luggage.

"Hallelujah!" she screamed, unlocking the door to pull her bag inside.

Back on the phone, she told Sophie that things were looking up. "Maybe my luck is finally turning around."

"I wouldn't be too sure," Sophie warned. "Your bad luck may have been a stowaway on the plane."

"Please, not that again."

"I'm just saying, be careful who you trust. There are a lot of sickos out there. Jeffery Dahmer looked like a sweetheart too, until they found pickled body parts in his fridge. Now that's an interesting form of burial, frosty fingers..."

"Please, Soph, spare me the graphic details. I haven't had breakfast."

There was another knock on Crispin's door. "Now what? Hold on."

Putting down the phone, Crispin swung open the door without her usual caution. It was Herbert. Conscious that she wasn't wearing panties under her T-shirt, Crispin slammed the door and then reopened it just enough to peek out.

"I'm here for our trip to the Valley," Herbert said, a little uncertain at Crispin's strange welcome.

Crispin apologized, explaining that her luggage had only just arrived. "Can you give me half an hour?"

"Anything for a lady, of course. I'll wait for you at the coffee shop."

In a hurry, Crispin ended the banter by reminding Sophie to send her backup disks and her mother's journal from the

Library study carrel and to deliver the present that Thurman had sent for Ida. "I left the carrel key and book at the apartment."

"I'll do it. I'll do it. You just watch your back," her friend said, invoking the familiar warning.

It didn't take Crispin long to dress and pack a small bag selected from her "tropical wardrobe." The new clothes she'd purchased in London were left at the Drury Lane flat and she was again sporting fabrics fit for the Egyptian climate. As she combed her hair, she was glad to see that the bruising on her forehead was easy to mask under some carefully applied foundation makeup.

The host who greeted guests at the Green Palm coffee shop had a full linguistic repertoire. He welcomed the Japanese couple ahead of Crispin in their native tongue, did the same for her in English, and then turned to the German couple behind her, repeating the performance in *Deutsche.*

She found Herbert waiting for her on a patio. When he spotted her, he rose to hold her chair. "I hope this is satisfactory," he said, indicating an unfettered midmorning view of the Great Pyramids behind the palm-lined courtyard of the hotel.

"It will just have to do," Crispin replied with mock resolution in her voice.

She decided it would make up for lost time if she helped herself to breakfast from the long buffet, choosing falafel with sesame, a selection of cheese wedges, and boiled eggs.

While she ate, Herbert told her that he had booked accommodations for them at the famous Winter Palace Hotel in Luxor and acquired VIP access to the tombs of Nefertari, Sety I, Rameses VI, Hatshepsut, and, of course, Tutankhamun.

His impressive itinerary included some of the most desirable sites in the Valley of the Kings. Crispin was especially glad that they would visit the tombs of Sety I and of Nefertari, who Rameses II honored above all women, calling her "the favorite of Mut." Normally, tourists had to reach the Valley by 6:30 a.m. to wait in line for a small number of admission tickets made available each day for Nefertari's tomb. By limiting access, preservationists hoped to protect the delicate, but still vivid, turquoise, black, gold, and red drawings on the tomb walls.

The tomb of Sety I, although closed to the general public for more than a decade, was one of the most complex and elaborate ever discovered and had been used by Carter as a lab during excavations of Tut. Even in the face of two such rare opportunities, however, Crispin was most excited about the chance to explore Rameses VI since it was linked directly to her ideas about a back door to Tut's tomb.

"The only problem is that we need to get on the road right away since the fellow with the keys to two of the tomb gates is leaving for a symposium the day after tomorrow," Herbert said, downing the last of his coffee.

"You're joking."

"About the road or the key?"

"Both. I've never heard of anyone driving from here to Luxor. Most fly."

"How little you know me. I never joke when I have managed to procure what I deem will enhance and excite the mental sprightliness of a top-notch research sleuth and personal tutor in ancient burial rituals," Herbert said in tone that both teased and flattered.

As preposterous as the proposal was, Crispin saw it as a chance to experience parts of Egypt that she'd never before traveled.

"I lay at your feet a genuine opportunity few are afforded." Herbert held up a ring of keys.

"And, I suppose those are the keys to the tomb?"

"Nay. To our chariot," he said with high spirits that were infectious. By 7 a.m. Herbert and Crispin were climbing into a canvas-top jeep that looked as if it had seen service during World War II.

"Luxor, or as the ancients said, Thebes, is a full-day trip, but we should arrive before dark," Herbert said as he removed a vintage foreign legion pith helmet from a bag on the front seat. A colorful scarf was tied above the brim and flowed down the back.

"You've been busy, my friend," teased Crispin.

"In light of the recent wallop to your head, I thought it best to offer at least a modicum of protection to that valuable brain of yours. I think you will agree that it is a *chapeau* worthy of Amelia Peabody." Herbert added as he started the engine, "Odd to have caught on here since pith helmets were fashioned first from the bark of trees that are indigenous to the tropics."

"I didn't realize you possessed such a wealth of haberdashery knowledge."

"I think you will find that I am full of surprises."

Herbert drove with the same confidence and assurance he'd shown in London; the Cairo streets as familiar to him as those of his hometown. The traffic here, however, was a study in pragmatic chaos that seemed to follow no sense of order. The drivers crawled past each other, ignoring both signage and signal lights. Yield signs might as well have been political posters for all of the attention they received. Cars probed their way into already congested lanes, almost daring the other drivers to hit them.

Yet, for all its mayhem, the atmosphere had a surprisingly friendly overtone. Even the indispensable auto horns seemed to sing, "Can you see me here? I'm coming around." It was in stark contrast to the threats and complaints implicit in American horns that yelled, "Get out of my way."

Before long the city was in their rearview mirror and they were traveling a desert road along an irrigation canal leading to

Memphis and Saqqara. Once outside of Cairo, they shared the road with pedestrians, bicycles, and wooden wagons. Women, draped in black from head to foot, balanced stainless steel pots and baskets of goods effortlessly on their heads. Donkeys pulled overloaded two-wheeled carts, some with bales of elephant garlic and others stacked high with small birds in individual wooden cages, many no bigger than a shoebox.

The road was lined with trees covered with reflective white paint halfway up the trunks to guide night drivers in this world where illumination after sundown came only from the moon and the stars. Scars on the tree trunks bore witness to the occasional failure to keep travelers on the road. If the distant Cairo skyline with its towering minarets and glass skyscrapers hadn't been so modern, one might have mistaken Herbert and Crispin for time travelers as they passed by in their vintage jeep, Crispin's scarf rippling in the wind.

Their initial route out of Cairo followed the Nile past Dahshûr to Beni Hasa. Here the land ached with poverty. Everywhere there was evidence of ancient ways and everyday struggles for survival. Missing or well hidden, however, was even the smallest residue of the once great builders of Egypt's glory days. Structures were ugly, incomplete, or misshaped, often constructed of salvaged materials. Garbage piles and flat-roofed houses, which looked as though at any minute they might collapse, dotted the road's edge and drooped over the drainage ditch as if caught midway in a slide.

By noon, they were hungry so they picnicked near the water's edge from a basket provided by the Mena House. It contained lamb and dill sandwiches on pita bread, soft cheese, a mixture of raisins and nuts, fresh oranges, and chilled tea. The hotel had thoughtfully included packets of moist towelettes and extra bottled water.

Crispin was surprised at the size of her appetite and glad that after the meal, they took the time to visit several local tombs and to stroll through an open-air street market where fast-talking vendors competed for their attention. One particularly insistent old man sat behind rows of carefully mounded spices and colored powders that ran the scale from an incandescent turquoise to more familiar tones of wheat and honey. "Your eyes are rare in color. Blue and green are valued as the most beautiful here," he said to Crispin. "Is this your husband?"

"No," Crispin replied, a little ill at ease, fearing she'd unconsciously sent the wrong signal.

"Ah, a pity. Do not worry. If you come to Misr, I promise you that within one year at least three men will be at your door begging you to marry them."

"Egyptians ask a lot of questions," Herbert said, in an effort to disentangle Crispin from the conversation without appearing rude.

"Unlike the English who ask too few," the ancient spice seller replied and then smiled as if trying to neutralize the sting of his comment. "Forgive me. Perhaps it's better not to think about tomorrow too much. Be like the bird. Eat today. Live today. Tomorrow is, after all, tomorrow."

Crispin was reminded of her father's frequent admonition, "Sufficient unto the day are the troubles thereof." Her Aunt Tilde would correct him by pointing out that the Sermon on the Mount said "evils thereof" not "troubles thereof." He would respectfully concede the point to his aunt but remind Crispin, "Remember, the King James Bible is just an English translation, a human interpretation of an ancient text. It is the underlying sentiment, not the individual words, which matter. It instructs us to keep our eye on the ball. There's plenty to worry about right in front of us. Focus on that and your accomplishments will be worthy."

"Then let us get on with our worthy work," Aunt Tilde would say in a half-mocking, half-loving tone as she took Crispin's hand to escort her to the kitchen to see if the ginger cookies were ready to come out of the oven.

Continuing their drive, Crispin took in the billboards. Coleman stoves, Lipton tea, and Nestlé's chocolate competed for attention in dirt road villages that smelled like a peculiar blend of barnyard dung and exotic spices. The dust-covered people and dilapidated buildings conceded any individuality, blending into the prevailing browns and blacks of the landscape. Defying their gloomy surroundings with color and sound, kingfisher and gallinules birds congregated in the fields and acacia, with their bright orange flower balls, decorated the riverbank and the murky edges of irrigation canals.

Herbert and Crispin stopped frequently along the route to top off their fuel tank, knowing that the availability of gasoline was unreliable in this sparsely populated part of Egypt. After one such stop, Herbert and Crispin noticed an Islamic cemetery. She suggested they go in. When Crispin stepped through the gate her pulse and breath slowed to that familiar and comforting sense of peace that she so often felt when she was in a graveyard. Burial grounds might spook others, but she had always had a deep connection to these resting places and the stories they told. Memories flickered, one after another like a slide show, of some of the cemeteries she'd visited since childhood.

She could see manicured military fields with their identical granite markers, standing square shouldered and plumb lined as if called by their regiment commander to an eternal parade formation, washed in the plaintive sound of "Taps" from a lone bugle just out of sight over the rise: "Day is done. Gone the sun...God is nigh."

She could see the segregated cemeteries of the Old South where the relatives of black descendants carefully preserved these ramshackle yet sacred places, as reminders of days gone by so that their children would not forget the gains that had been made and the struggle still to be waged.

She could see sixteenth century Scottish family burial places where generations of clan history was carved into moss-covered and weatherworn funerary monuments and where genealogies raced against time to decipher and preserve them before all was lost to the mud and wind.

She could see audacious Mexican graveyards crowded with flaming orange, red, and yellow flowers, statues of saints, and painted metal crosses in vibrant colors.

"You seem miles away," Herbert said as he walked up behind her.

Slightly startled, Crispin shook off her wistful thoughts and answered. "I was grave digging."

"What do you mean?"

"It's an expression of my mother's. When I was a toddler we often visited cemeteries and studied the stones and markers. She called it 'digging up the dead.' Of course, she didn't mean it literally. She taught me that by looking for meaning not just in the words but in the unspoken, we could resurrect their story and, through their story, they could live again."

"Has anyone ever told you that when you tell stories about your family and about burials that way you sound more like a poet than a scholar?" Herbert asked.

"Don't let my father hear you say that."

"I could listen to you tell stories like that for hours."

As they walked around the cleanly swept dust floors of the Islamic burial grounds, Crispin talked about the traditions of the local culture, of the careful preparation, washing, and shrouding of the body that was an important prelude to burial.

Plain domes graced the cemetery. While the graveyard might seem barren and stark to the Western eye, ornaments that are common in Christian burials would be out of place here, where the emphasis is on simplicity and moderation.

"An important part of the final service is prayer for forgiveness for the dead," she said, a bit of melancholy in her voice as it brought to mind her grandmother's funeral in the weeks before she left New York.

She had never been particularly close to her father's mother, a woman who wore her religion like armor. Crispin was surprised when Grandma Leads skipped a generation and left her considerable estate in equal shares to her and Clinton. She had been a widow for decades, and her lady's social circle handled many of the funeral arrangements. Her body was wrapped in a shroud of cashmere and covered in a sheaf of ripe wheat and flowers. Her minister said it was a testament to her life of good works.

"Are you digging again?" Herbert asked.

"Sorry about that," Crispin responded as they circled back to the gate, concluding their tour of the graveyard. "My mind wanders sometimes."

"Occupational hazard?"

"You could say that," Crispin said with a weak grin, rubbing dust from her shoes before getting back in the jeep. As they drove away she told him about her grandmother's funeral.

"It came to mind when we discussed prayers of forgiveness," Crispin said. "I'd always felt that Grandma Leads was so self-assured in her faith that she would never ask for forgiveness, but I was wrong. During her eulogy, her minister said she had asked us to pray for her. Turns out, there was so much about her that I really never knew at all."

Crispin stared out the window and was soon lost in thought. Herbert didn't try to respond, focusing his eyes and his attention on the road ahead.

The second half of the road trip would take them through Asyut. There they planned to take the bridge across the dam to the eastern shore of the Nile, passing from the west bank or west arm of the Ankh to the east, which symbolized life because that is where the sun rises.

Herbert waited until they had crossed the Nile to suggest that they pass the time with a game drawn from their mutual love of mystery novels. "The idea is to take a real-life or contemporary mystery and create a story using the techniques of a famous mystery writer, as in 'What if Dorothy Sayers had Lord Peter Wimsey tackle crop circles?'"

"Or, 'What if Sara Paretsky goes after the fake aliens at Roswell?'"

"Warshawski would never leave Chicago long enough."

"Something Egyptian, perhaps?" Crispin pointed at a group of children in the distance who were leading a herd of donkeys along the side of the road.

"Perfect."

"The Curse of King Tut's Tomb?"

"I'm loving it."

"Now we need a detective," she said.

They considered Agatha Christie, who herself often wrote murder mysteries while seated on the veranda of the Old Cataract Hotel in Aswan.

"How would Agatha write it?" Herbert wondered.

"As a multi-death mystery," surmised Crispin.

"Of course, that's a given."

"Hercule Poirot or Miss Marple?"

"I don't see Miss Marple traveling to Egypt," Herbert pointed out.

"Hercule, then."

"Might be confused with *Death on the Nile*."

Crispin waved as they drew near to the children. Giggles and toothy grins were returned.

"What about Josephine Tey?" The minute Crispin mentioned the writer, considered by many to be one of the best, if not the best, English-language mystery writer of all time, something clicked and they said, simultaneously, "Truth is the daughter of time."

"Too perfect," Crispin said, referencing Tey's masterpiece in which a police detective recuperating in the hospital fights boredom by trying to solve a British historical crime of epic proportions. He asks the question: Were the young princes in the Tower really killed by their uncle King Richard III so he could gain the throne?

"Ms. Josephine's willingness to explore how historical versions of events are often too easily accepted and never really challenged over time is a perfect point of reference for our story involving the fabled Tut Curse," Herbert added.

"As I recall, the deaths attributed to the curse included some workmen and, if you believe the tabloids, even a canary and a dog."

"The dog story was rubbish, but some of the other deaths were all too real." Herbert stretched his right arm above his head and then his left. "The curse theory seemed to take on a life of its own, growing exponentially with each death. Dreadful, really."

Because Herbert had been behind the wheel since they left Cairo Crispin offered to take over some of the driving duties, but Herbert declined.

"I think not. Your recent demonstration of driving talent is not a good recommendation," he said with a laugh.

Crispin swatted his arm with a rolled-up map in retaliation.

"Besides, we'll be there soon," he said, indicating a road sign. He then chronicled the mysterious deaths that legend had attributed to the curse, including two Carnarvons, a nurse, assorted government officials, Egyptologists, and archeologists, as well as the occasional tourist.

"My favorite, if that is the right word, is the story of Aaron Ember, an American Egyptologist," Herbert said. "Perhaps his name was an omen because he died while trying to rescue a manuscript from his burning house."

"What book is worth dying over?" Crispin asked.

"Well phrased. Hold on to your helmet," Herbert chuckled. "It was none other than the fabled *Book of the Dead*."

"I'm impressed. You are a virtual encyclopedia of Mummy Curse trivia."

"Thank you. However, I can't take the credit. I practically grew up with them as bedtime stories since Porchey's death was probably the most infamous of the lot."

"How would Ms. Josephine fit all these together?"

"A crime of passion or revenge, perhaps? No, I think something more devious and complex. A ruse, perhaps, to..."

Crispin was no longer listening. As it often did when she was trying to solve a problem, the idea emerged, fully grown, from the seeds of a single word: ruse. Even as the idea took shape in her subconscious, Crispin felt a ring of truth in it, remembering in that moment an offhanded comment made by Thurman over lunch. They'd been talking about the pressures on Carter when Thurman said, "Good thing the curse came along when it did. Kept the superstitious away."

Crispin realized that Herbert was still in the game so she shook off that line of thought and rejoined him in debate.

"But who could be behind such an insidious plot?" asked Herbert.

"There might be a sleeper in the cast of characters who no one suspects."

"The proverbial butler."

"Or, there are so many motives that it seems that everyone did it as in *Murder on the Orient Express*."

"What do you think our Ms. Josephine would have made of the fact that Howard Carter remained healthy for decades, while those around him died?"

"Suspicious, highly suspicious, my dear Watson," Herbert said, stroking his chin in a campy imitation of Sherlock Holmes.

"Stop, I can't stand it if you start mixing up our detectives."

"Please forgive me but, after all, no less than Arthur Conan Doyle himself blamed the pharaoh's curse for my ancestor's curious death."

"He knew that mayhem covers murders the way sand covers tombs," she said in a half whisper.

Chapter Fourteen

Sophie was in Wimbledon, making good on her promise to Crispin to deliver the gift from Thurman into Ida's hands. The suburb, known for its fabled grass tennis courts, was a forty-minute commute from the center of London on the Underground. Sophie assuaged her annoyance at the time-consuming favor because she planned some serious shopping in the local stores known for their handcrafted knits and wools. Her first stop, however, was Ida's place.

The path to Ida's redbrick house covered in dense ivy was rimmed with flowerbeds still dormant except for the occasional crocus bud. A chill wind blew up a few forgotten leaves from the flowerbed nearest the front stoop as Sophie rang the doorbell installed under the brass pineapple doorknocker. When there was no answer, she assumed that Ida was hard of hearing and vigorously applied the knocker. Still no answer.

Sophie backed off and looked up at the three-story house. Lace curtains were backlit in a warm light of the window in what Sophie supposed was a bedroom, but there was no sign of movement or activity inside. Just as she was considering her next move, a white Scottie jumping up against the inside of the living room window, barking and whining, startling Sophie.

She decided to leave the gift, but since the front stoop offered no hiding place, she looked around for something out of sight. She followed a flagstone path that led to the rear of the house, where she found an unlocked screen door to a covered porch that was home to garden tools, Wellingtons, and a laundry basket. Concluding that Ida would easily find the gift here among frequently used things, Sophie placed it in the laundry basket, carefully covering it with the candy-striped canvas clothespin bag.

As she turned to exit, the door into the kitchen creaked open and the whimpering Scottie dog came hesitantly onto the porch. He crouched and quivered near Sophie's feet.

His paws were bloody.

"Poor little pooch. What happened to you?"

Sophie was a sucker for injured cats or lost dogs. If she found one she always took them to a vet, paid for their care herself, and looked after them until they were adopted into a good home. She knelt over to stroke the little dog and get a look at his paws to see if he needed immediate care.

He fled, wailing, back into the house. Sophie followed. Inside the dark kitchen, she tried to entice the dog to stay put. "Come here, little man."

The Scottie was not cooperating. He would come close, cower near her feet, and quake. The moment she made any attempt to touch him, he would run away from her. Sophie decided that he was trying to get her to follow him. "Smart little man," she cooed.

Sophie wasn't sure what to do. Although her heart told her to follow, the reality of a strange black woman in someone's house in Wimbledon, England, could easily land her in trouble. As if sensing her caution, the Scottie sat at the living room door, cocked his head to one side, and pleaded with his eyes.

"Just one room," Sophie told him, following him in.

Sophie turned on a light and flinched at an unpleasant metallic odor clinging to the air. The dog scampered behind a settee. Sophie looked around the edge of the settee and gasped. "Sweet mother of God."

Ida's body was soaked in dried blood. The Scottie lay with his chin on her chest. The old lady's face was mutilated, a hole where her nose used to be. A scream caught in Sophie's throat when she heard someone behind her.

***

Herbert and Crispin arrived in Luxor late in the afternoon and checked into their rooms at the Old Winter Palace. The fully restored and upgraded lobby of the grand hotel, an island of luxury in the middle of the desert, had been a favorite of Europeans since it opened in 1886. Even Howard Carter had called the Palace home until he built his own place in the Valley after his great discovery. Much of the hotel's iconic history was preserved for tourists in boxed exhibitions and display cases containing turn-of-the-century artifacts.

Crispin showered and changed into a tangerine jersey sundress, adding her mother's butterfly brooch as an afterthought. Because she expected the evening to cool down as the sun set, she draped a cream-colored sweater over her shoulders before meeting Herbert under the grand chandelier in the lobby.

They strolled casually down the sweeping hotel entrance to where a long, sloping staircase opened onto the city esplanade that ran parallel to the Nile. They walked most of the length of the corniche, past dozens of felucca boats with wing-shaped sails that were being docked for the night.

Just as the evening sun was fading over the desert, they arrived at the massive temple complex of Karnak, which is as big as three hundred football fields. In the dimming evening light, centuries of damage to the goat-headed sphinx and dromos that guarded the mile-long promenade to the Temple of Luxor seemed to disappear. On each side of the open esplanade were sad family huts, many of which emitted an odor similar to that of a public bathroom overdue for cleaning. The structures were destined for demolition in service to the relentless excavation of Karnak and Luxor that had occupied archeologists since the 1800s.

"It's as if time is washed away with the light," Herbert said.

"Too bad that it can't take the poverty with it."

"It is only a small step down the path from what Egypt was to what it has become."

"There are probably people who would sacrifice everything to change what they see here," she said.

Herbert and Crispin stopped at the Shari Khaled Ibn el-Walid restaurant, where they dined on lentil soup and grilled filet of Nile carp, served with a lemon butter sauce on a bed of sweet chard. The meal ended with a rich pudding known locally as safar basha.

The conversation on the drive from Cairo had been light-hearted and casual. They talked like old friends, teasing and confiding with no more complicated an agenda than simply enjoying each other's company. As they walked back to the hotel after supper, Crispin sensed the mood between them take a romantic shift. It was subtle at first. Their choices of topic became more intimate, their voices softened, and they used fewer words to communicate.

Instead, they allowed their conversation to lapse into cozy, comfortable silences filled with no more than the sound of each other breathing and their long strides in perfect synchronization. Herbert seemed to walk closer, occasionally brushing her arm with his. Crispin felt herself lean into these moments, welcoming the intimacy.

In a soft voice, Crispin finally said, "I'd like to tell you about my dream. The one on the plane."

Herbert understood that the best response was nonverbal. He said nothing, simply taking her hand in his. How natural and perfect it felt to Crispin. His grip was neither controlling nor indifferent. It was a strong hand, one to help, not to dominate. She liked it.

Their pace slowed as Crispin told him the frightening details of the dream: Ida, the ivy, and the blood. She then explained to Herbert how dreams such as this one had been a constant companion to her since her mother's death. After she'd told him that her mother died in a plane crash that was so fiery there was nothing left of her to bury, Herbert offered his first real response.

"Maybe it was knowing that you were soon to land at the Cairo Airport where you lost your mother so many years ago that triggered morbid thoughts involving a 'mother' figure like Ida."

"That could be, but I think there's more. I can't put my finger on it, but usually these kinds of dreams are warning signs from my subconscious."

Crispin explained that on one level the dream took something from which she normally drew comfort and distorted it to the point where it became the embodiment of terror.

"Tea time with Ida is a chance for shared confidences. In the dream, tea became blood. Life's energy to be sure, but it was clotted, putrefied, fetid. And the ivy was all wrong. On a trivial level the ivy is a symbol of many elite universities in the States. Thus, growth, knowledge, and tradition. The dream turned it into confinement and paralysis."

"I see what you are driving at. What was comfortable became a threat," said Herbert. "You intimated there was more than one level of meaning. What of the other?"

By then they were nearly back to the hotel and Crispin was grateful for the opportunity to suspend the discussion. She didn't want to articulate the sense of cold dread she felt when she remembered the way Ida had transformed into death in her dream.

"Probably nothing. Forgive me, I tend to overanalyze."

Herbert dropped his hand to circle her waist and pulled her close.

"Everyone has the occasional nightmare."

As they approached the rim of the hotel security lights, they stopped. Neither wanted to interrupt the inevitability of where their relationship was going, so they continued without conversation until they were standing at her hotel room door.

"Might I?" asked Herbert.

"Yes."

He traced her cheekbones with his fingertips, pausing to tilt her chin in his direction and completing the motion with a kiss. "A perfect end to a perfect day," he said.

"Has it ended?"

"That is entirely your prerogative."

As he bent to kiss her fingers again she opened her hand and held out her room key.

Chapter Fifteen

The colossus moved.

Crispin was studying two gigantic sandstone statutes of seated guardians representing Amenhotep III that together marked the unofficial entrance to the Valley of the Kings when she was sure the one to the right moved. Then it happened again. The sway was ever so slight, detectable only at the tip of its nemes head cloth. The colossus on the right was the one with the reputation for singing. Because of damage caused by an earthquake in 27 B.C., the wind at night passed through the stones, producing what those who'd heard it through the centuries described as a plaintive murmur.

Herbert had returned to the jeep for a fresh bottle of water. As far as she could tell the scattered tourists standing near the Colossi of Memnon hadn't noticed that anything was amiss with the seated stone giants. Crispin decided not to mention the moving colossus to Herbert. He had a big enough dose of her metaphysical side when she told him about her dream. After their intimacy the previous night she didn't want to challenge their relationship with stories of sentient statues. Perhaps she'd just been in the sun too long. Or, up too late last night?

That morning Crispin and Herbert got up early, returning to the easy banter of friendship with a new level of closeness by the time they'd made the brief stop at the Colossi. Settled back into the jeep, Herbert reached over and looped a strand of Crispin's hair behind her ear and handed her the pith helmet. "We need to protect that noggin," he said with a tenderness Crispin welcomed. They then began their tour of the Valley in earnest, with Crispin keeping the part of the bargain she'd made on the plane by sharing obscure details about death rituals and symbols. There were times she suspected Herbert was humoring her and, like his famous great-great-grandfather, she was satisfied to let people assume he was a mental lightweight.

When they reached Tut's tomb, Crispin could feel her pulse quicken. This is why she'd come to Egypt. Since they'd been in and out of hot tombs for several hours, Crispin and Herbert took a break in the shade of a canvas-covered sitting area where a vendor served bottles of sweet lemonade. The Valley was beginning to fill with tourists. It was a perfect setting for people watching, from a close-knit group of Japanese sporting broad umbrellas and inappropriate shoes to a Norwegian couple with pale skin slowly turning an unpleasant shade of red in the unforgiving sun to a pair of American teens showing off newly purchased, but strangely translated, T-shirts that read: "Njoy Yur Time In Luxor."

Looking across the broad pathway to the well-traveled tombs of Tut and Rameses VI, Crispin was more certain than ever that she was right about the likelihood of a fifth chamber. She'd seen the two tombs before but she studied them with new eyes today. The relationship of the lower walls of Rameses and the backside of the Tut tomb, tucked so completely beneath it, was now obvious in a way that was impossible to ignore.

She couldn't stand the wait any longer and joined the queue for the trip down the fateful stairway that led to the holy of holies, the pharaoh's tomb itself. The entrance, so well lit and manicured for modern tourist traffic, betrayed little of the drama that rattled the world almost a hundred years ago when a water boy found that first carved step and ran to tell everyone. Carter directed the excavation that eventually uncovered the full staircase and the first entrance. In due time, it led them to the long passageway, a second doorway, and its sacred seals, beyond which lay the fabled untouched treasure trove.

Below ground she stood on the raised platform over the original Antechamber point-of-entry of Tut's tomb. From here visitors could see, but not enter, the Annex and the Burial Chamber. The small Annex was about the size of one of the metal storage outbuildings that are so common in the backyards of middle-class neighborhoods in the States. Crispin tried to imagine this empty spot as Carter first saw it, stacked floor to ceiling with the assorted bric-a-brac of ancient Egyptian royal life.

The Burial Chamber, however, was the real tourist draw with its unusual drawings of twelve baboons. The colorful monkeys were some of what was left of the original glory that once cloaked the pharaoh's resting place in layers of protective stone, gold, and mystic meaning. Although the mummy of Tut was still resting in its stone sarcophagus, it was bared of its wrappings and lay naked, stripped of its royal paraphernalia and trappings of divinity. He looked frail, ancient bones without a shred of skin or flesh, on display for anyone with the price of admission.

The ancients had been so reverent in preparation of their young king for the next life, preserving the body through mummification and storing organs in jars, a time-consuming and careful procedure done with exacting care and skill. They had used only the best cloth to wrap him, layer after layer, shrouding him for the afterlife, tucking amulets and treasures in the seams.

His death mask, designed to cover his face, shoulders, and head, was pure gold, as was his first coffin. It weighed more than two hundred pounds and was protected with four goddesses with outstretched wings. The ancients rested this ornate gold coffin inside a wooden coffin covered in gold leaf, inlaid with small pieces of colored glass fitted inside strips of gold. Another, larger wooden coffin was carved and gilded to hold the other two. The triple-nested coffins were then lifted into a massive stone sarcophagus and sealed for all time. They remained there for more than three thousand years.

Then Carter showed up. Away came all of the protection, all of the mystery, all of the sanctity, all of the ritual, layer by layer, until the once-proud king was naked and bare and devoid of dignity, robbed of respect and humanity. Was there ever a man more completely exposed than one stripped through to the bone, denied even a simple loincloth?

She remembered the first time she'd come here with her father and brother. She and Clinton were still in first grade, but the stark nakedness of the boy king moved her brother. He took off his cap and started to unbutton his shirt. He had tears in his eyes, begging their father to please give his clothes to the naked man. In all the decades since Carter opened the tomb, she wondered had anyone ever thought of Tut's humanity the way her brother did that day?

Tut and everything buried with him became just someone's quest for fortune and glory; a mystery to be solved; gold to be mined; fame to be claimed; a carnival show for the curious. "Step on up folks and take a peek."

What about the human being? Who speaks for him? Who protects his dignity, his modesty? The sacred burial ritual practiced with such respect was desecrated first by archeologists and so-called scientists and now by lookie-loos and tourists.

Crispin realized that her cheeks were wet. Who am I to criticize? Am I any different?

"I can't change your fate, young prince, but I can try to add truth to your story," she whispered as she brushed away the tears.

She would have to cut through plenty of red tape to get permission to test her idea about a fifth chamber since it would require some strategic digging, but she was confident that her theory could be proven. "It's got to be there," she said in a low voice.

"What?"

"Oh, nothing," Crispin answered, wondering how long Herbert had been standing behind her. "I was just thinking about the relationship of ancient burial customs across time and culture," she lied.

Crispin told Herbert that the ancient Egyptians had very little interest in their present life.

They saw life on Earth as a transition to the afterlife and, as such, this life was important only in preparation. "That's why their money, time, and talent were directed toward the life to come, instead of this one," she said.

"Seems to me the Pharaohs came out on the long end of that one, convincing the workers to ignore the poverty and squalor they lived in since it was only temporary anyway," Herbert countered.

They were still debating when they arrived at the temple of the only certifiably female Egyptian pharaoh, Queen Hatshepsut.

"After all, Cleopatra doesn't count since she was Greek," said Crispin.

The ceremonial terraced temple had been strategically situated at the base of sharply vertical cliffs the color of over-ripe bananas. They formed an arc as if nature had supplied a three-sided protective wall to cradle the temple.

"Did rather well for herself, I'd say," said Herbert as he took in the porticos that fronted each of the three terraces. The first was lined with sphinx and once had supported living trees. The second had two porticos and rows of colonnades. The third terrace was out of view and led to the inner court.

"The lady built this to legitimize her reign, to elevate her image," Crispin said, with a sweeping hand gesture. "Women have always had to over perform. It takes an exceptional woman to get the recognition that is handed without question to an average male in society."

"Touché," Herbert said with a wink and a smile.

Then the earth began to roll. Even for someone who had never experienced it, the sensation was unmistakable.

"Earthquake!"

Crispin remembered reading somewhere that the safest place in a quake is a doorway. What better place since the temple was mostly portico after portico? Herbert apparently had the same idea. They ran to the relative safety of the nearest portico just before several stones from above crashed near where they had been standing.

On the terrace, some of the tourists hadn't been as quick to act. One lay twitching, the hibiscus print of his shirt weeping red from the gash caused by a flying stone that cut through his chest. Nearby, an old man lay with legs splayed; he was no more than a heap of khaki slacks. Although the quake lasted for only a few moments it seemed longer, subjecting the earth to a combination of quick fire bursts of shaking followed by long rocking motions.

"Make it stop," Crispin begged.

And it did. As quickly as it began, it ended.

All around children were crying and adults, including security guards who had abandoned their posts at the gate, were yelling.

"Stay there," Herbert told Crispin, as he ran to help an old woman who seemed about to faint. She was standing so near the edge of the stair that if she fell, she would tumble to the hard stone platform below.

Crispin refused to remain sheltered with so many people in trouble around her. She crouched near the ground and made her way to the crumpled body of a portly, middle-aged woman with a deep cut on her leg and a head injury. Crispin used the scarf from her pith helmet to make a tourniquet to stop the bleeding. The blistering sun was unforgiving and Crispin knew that the woman would be better off in the shade. She decided to take a chance and move her. It was easier said than done.

Crispin had to convince her muscles that they could and would haul the moaning woman to cover. Her hair was soon wet with sweat and her face flushed from the exertion. She dug her heels into the hard ground for stability and scooted across the ground, hauling the injured woman's weight until they reached the protective shelter of a portico. After propping the woman up out of the sun and giving her a drink of water Crispin sank down to the welcoming coolness of the stone floor.

The momentary satisfaction gave way to the realization that her job had just begun. Other dazed tourists were in need of assistance, so Crispin went back out into the heat, nudging, supporting, and encouraging as many people as she could find to the protection offered by the porticos.

It was an hour later that Crispin realized she'd lost track of Herbert. She found him near the jeep talking to a guard. Other than a flat tire the jeep had survived the quake unscathed. The guard told Herbert that they'd opened the innermost courtyard, the one normally closed to the public, since it offered the best protection until the road cleared and the injured could be safely transported to town.

In the courtyard, a French doctor was already tending to the wounded, and some local villagers were coming on foot from their homes with water and bandages. Tourists from close-by tombs and sites were being evacuated to the makeshift field hospital for care.

Crispin told Herbert she would go there to offer help. With her sweaty hair tied back and her sleeves rolled up, she took up duties serving water to the growing number of injured and frightened tourists. As she moved down the row, ladling water into cups, she nearly dropped the bucket. Sitting along the wall with an expedition that had been caught in the surrounding hills when the quake hit was Laurie Pierce. Next to her was Crispin's father. He was having trouble breathing and his left arm dangled at his side.

Chapter Sixteen

The trip from the Valley to Luxor was brutal. Laurie argued that they should wait for an ambulance. Looking back, Crispin realized she'd said things she probably should regret. She didn't have the energy for regret right now. She knew just enough about medicine to see that her father was in trouble. His breathing had been growing increasingly labored, and the nail beds of his fingertips had begun to turn blue.

Crispin would get her father the medical care he needed even if it meant hand-to-hand combat with Laurie, the police, or anyone else who stood in her way. Herbert had been astute enough not to waste time or energy trying to change Crispin's mind. Instead, he'd helped, first by fixing the tire on the jeep and then by using his contacts to gain them priority passage out of the Valley.

The jeep was crowded, and torn-up streets covered in rubble confounded them. In Luxor, Herbert again ran interference. It wasn't long before Dr. Leads was in the care of a hospital trauma team. A compression injury to his chest was compromising his lungs and his breathing. He'd needed emergency surgery to repair the damage. A few more hours and he wouldn't have survived. Crispin's instincts saved her father's life.

Dr. Leads had been returned to his room for recovery a few hours later. Now that he was safely out of danger and his breathing normal, Laurie left to find something to eat while Crispin kept vigil. Worried that the heavy cast on his broken left arm might cause discomfort, she was trying to nestle it in extra pillows when he stirred.

"It is you," he said in a soft, dry voice, half awake and half asleep. "I thought I was dreaming."

"Yes, it's me," she replied, reaching for his good hand. The tender moment evaporated as he became more alert. His grip tightened as he shook off the effects of the sedative.

His next sentence had all of the authority of a man who is accustomed to being in charge. "Why are you here?"

"I brought you to the hospital after the earthquake."

"Not the hospital. Why are you in Luxor? Why aren't you in London?"

"Ashraf invited me."

Dr. Leads summoned the strength needed to bring himself into a sitting position, pulling his hand from Crispin's in the process.

"Poppycock. I know you better than that. You are here on a wild goose chase. It's that nonsense about a fifth chamber in the Tut tomb," he said.

"Clinton had no right to tell you. It's not a fully developed theory. Just one line of inquiry that I'm pursuing."

"What evidence do you have?"

"That's what I'd like to show you when you are up to it."

Dr. Leads patted his chest as if he was trying to locate something in the inside pocket of a suit jacket. Crispin knew what he was looking for and opened the drawer of a bedside stand to retrieve his glasses. She cleaned each lens with care, as she knew he would if he'd had use of both hands, and gave the glasses to him. Once he was settled, he looked at her with his most intimidating professorial air.

"Summarize."

For this recitation, she felt the need to stand, as if delivering a formal paper in class. There was a white board used by nurses to leave messages so she stood by it, erasing the happy face and contact names and picking up a dry erase marker. She took a few beats to collect her thoughts and then began to set out some of her findings, including the notations on the photos.

"It's curious. When I started, I thought of several possible explanations. After spending hours with original journals and documents at the Griffith and the British Library, I've eliminated all but one," Crispin said. For a moment her enthusiasm of working with her father again made her forget her misgivings so she plunged ahead. "That's why I need what is at the National Museum in Cairo. Ashraf is helping make arrangements."

"Ashraf, of all people, should know better. How did you talk him into helping you?"

"Your daughter can be very persuasive."

It was Herbert who had walked in on the conversation. "Dr. Leads, I am sorry to meet under such stressful circumstances. I am Herbert Van Snyder."

Herbert extended and then withdrew his hand in deference to the cast and IV that hampered Dr. Leads.

"I know who you are. What I don't know is how you are associated with my daughter."

Crispin grabbed the eraser and cleaned the white board, uncertain how much Herbert had heard.

Before she could inject herself into the exchange between the two men, Laurie came in. "Now Daniel, you owe this young man your life," she said, leaning over and kissing Leads.

Crispin didn't know if it was her father's smile in response or Laurie's sweet, soothing tone of voice that she found more irritating.

"My dear, would you and Mr. Van Snyder please excuse me," Leads said to Laurie. "I need a few moments in private with my daughter."

Herbert offered to drive Laurie to the Winter Palace, where she could arrange a room for the night. Laurie objected, but Leads insisted that she go where she could be comfortable. Herbert gave Crispin a hug before he left and said he would check back with her after he'd helped Ms. Pierce get settled.

When they were alone, Dr. Leads turned his full attention on Crispin. "I must be direct."

"Of course. I would expect nothing less."

"Are you still drinking?"

"Oh, please spare me."

"You know why I have to ask."

Dr. Leads started to cough; his head dropped back on his pillow and he closed his eyes. Under other circumstances, Crispin might have objected to his implication, called him unfair, defended herself. But, she'd never seen him so vulnerable and weak.

She was scared. The man resting on the rough sheets of the hospital bed wasn't the robust, invincible man she had grown up with. He wasn't the man who always had the answer to every question. The man who could win every fight; solve every problem; find anything that went missing; fix broken toys; and soothe any injury. She'd grown up under his strict discipline and the shadow of his bigger-than-life reputation, but she'd never doubted his love. When, as an adolescent, she used razor blades to cut herself as a way to cope with emotional pain, it was her father who saw that she received the years of counseling she needed. Crispin understood that it was a commitment to her best interest that drove him even now.

"Drinking like a sailor on shore leave is just another destructive way of coping," he said in a voice that carried none of its usual power.

"I know."

"What are you going to do about it?"

A nurse arrived before Crispin could answer. She checked her patient's vital signs and made notations in his chart. Before leaving she cautioned, "You must not talk so much. Time for you to rest. No more visitors."

Looking at her father, Crispin realized just how much the conversation had cost him. His eyes seemed to sink into dark circles.

"The nurse is right," Crispin said, giving his hand a gentle squeeze.

"I'm not finished with you, young lady."

"I know, but right now, you need to listen to the nurse," she said, removing his glasses and returning them to their leather case. "I'll come back later. I promise you'll have plenty more chances to tell me what you think about my choices."

Crispin kissed him on the cheek. "Love you."

"Love you more."

Herbert was waiting in the hall for her. He told her that he'd received several messages from Ashraf and that the older man wanted her to call as soon as she could.

As they walked away, Crispin saw Laurie enter her father's room.

Herbert insisted on escorting Crispin to a small coffee shop near the hospital for a sandwich and tea. Crispin was too rattled to eat much.

"Now you've met the whole family," Crispin said.

"He cares about you."

"But he doesn't respect me."

"I'm not sure I agree."

"Please don't contradict me. This is the story of my life. You don't know what you're talking about."

Herbert dropped the subject, but when Crispin insisted on returning to her father's hospital room for the night, he tried to talk her out of it.

"You should come back to the hotel with me. You need to rest," he said.

She gave him a look that said it all. "I must call Ashraf. Then I'll spend the night here. Take Dr. Pierce with you. I'm sure she could use a good night's sleep."

***

Ashraf picked up the phone on the second ring.

"You're not an easy young woman to track down," he told Crispin.

"Herbert said you'd been calling."

"How is Daniel? Salma and I have been so worried."

Crispin gave Ashraf a full report on her father's surgery and recovery.

"I am scheduled on the early-bird flight from Cairo to Luxor. What does it look like there?" he said.

"Luxor seems intact. Just a few broken windows and a lot of dust."

Ashraf told her that since airports were scheduled to open again right away, antiquities officials and archeologists from across the globe would descend on the area. They would help to evaluate any potential damage to the temples in Luxor and Karnak and evaluate the structural integrity of the tombs and temples in the Valley. "We'll have to go over everything with, what you call, a fined-toothed comb."

The government was already putting pressure on officials to open up the Valley as soon as possible, but he didn't want to compromise the work. "If the politicians think tourism is suffering now, they have no idea how bad it will be if someone is injured by falling stones or collapsing tunnels," he said.

"It sounds like you have a lot on your plate," Crispin said.

"Yes, but I always have time for my friends. Tell Daniel I will see him soon."

"Don't be surprised if he chews you out for letting me come with you to Cairo."

"You are not to worry about me. I can handle your father."

Ashraf reminded her to touch base with Clinton. "He has called several times. I gave him a brief report after I talked to Herbert, but he will want to hear directly from you."

After he hung up, Ashraf poured himself a drink and offered one to the man sitting in a chair by the window.

The man was Tony.

Just then the phone rang again.

It was Daniel Leads.

Chapter Seventeen

Something was wrong. Dr. Lead's breathing was harsh, rasping. His skin was the color of concrete. A thick, green liquid bubbled on the intake tube of his IV. Crispin jumped up, turned off his IV pump, and pounded the nurse call button.

"Stay with me. Stay with me. Keep breathing."

The nurse was through the door before Crispin could push the call button a second time. One look at the patient was all that the nurse needed before she summoned a crash team.

While the team worked, Crispin explained that she'd fallen asleep in a chair. The swoosh of her backpack awoke her as it slid off her lap. She saw a male nurse with his back to her holding Dr. Leads' IV tube in one hand and a needle in the other. He dropped the needle and exited without a word.

Crispin tried in vain to describe the mystery nurse to security. "I was barely awake and I really only saw his back."

The man from security told Crispin that since she was the only one who saw the male nurse there wasn't much they could do. Before she could grill him further, the doctor who'd been treating her father joined them. "Dr. Leads is resting," the doctor said. "I will have the contents of the syringe analyzed, but from the smell and color I think it is a strong barbiturate."

Crispin was soon left alone with her father and her mounting fears. Whatever was going on wasn't about research and old mysteries anymore. It was much more dangerous. The unthinkable reality had slithered up from her unconscious when she first saw her father at Hatshepsut's Tomb. It grew muscular when she watched from the sidelines while the doctors brought him back to life in the trauma unit in Luxor. It finally took hold and would not let go when they worked to revive him after the attempt on his life. It was like something that obstructs your view when you are trying to watch a movie. At first you pretend it's not there. You lean around it. You tap it on the shoulder and ask it to please step aside. But nothing works. The truth is front and center and must be dealt with. She could no longer ignore her father's mortality.

Of course, she knew at an intellectual level that we are all born with an expiration date. Today had gripped hold of her at an emotional level that was new and painful and frightening. It was a heart thing not a head thing. It reminded her of the double gravestones she had seen in modern cemeteries around her old neighborhood in the States. Even though only one partner had died, the marker was labeled with both names. It was as if the living person was letting the world know, "I'm coming. Watch this space." The image that was now thrust into her brain was a marker engraved, "Daniel Walter Leads, Ph.D. I'm coming. Watch this space." Once imagined, such a bold declaration of mortal certainty can't be unimagined. There was no balm. There was no elixir. She couldn't shake it.

She tucked her hands under her armpits and began to rock back and forth, willing herself to go through a methodical examination of all possible explanations for what she had witnessed. It was important to focus. "Think. Work the problem. What are the possibilities?"

Several came to mind.

Happenstance: a madman was going around pumping drugs into patients in hospitals and just happened to pick her father to prey on tonight. "Preposterous."

Accident: the male nurse made a mistake and brought the sedative to the wrong patient. Now he was afraid to come forward. "Unlikely."

Coincidence: this apparent attempt on her father's life was pure happenstance, an old grudge perhaps, and unrelated to everything that had happened to her in England.

"What would Sherlock Holmes say?"

Cause and effect: something she did, or was about to do, led to the attempt. "But what exactly?"

Flip it around: something Dad did, or was about to do, led to the attempt on him and on me. If this were the case, she knew getting information would be tough. Her dad was famously close-mouthed about his affairs and she wasn't exactly in the mood to cross-examine Laurie. Another problem to solve. Perhaps Carole, his longtime assistant at Cornell, would have answers.

"To what questions?"

If the attacks on her in England were connected to what happened tonight, she was at a loss to see how. Questions ricocheted around her mind. Who knew Dr. Leads was in Luxor? Why give him a strong sedative? What purpose would it serve? Who knew about the fifth chamber? Who would benefit if something slowed her father down? Or, was someone just trying to scare her to call her off the scent?

"What scent? Shit."

Crispin couldn't see how her interest in a decades-old mystery could trigger danger for her or her father. The attempt on his life tripled her sense of urgency and added to her confusion.

The extraordinary things she'd experienced felt like the ubiquitous traffic circles favored by European highway engineers.

Although travelers seemed to merge and exit erratically, if you looked closely you could find a pattern. She needed to find the pattern.

In the 1970s, when he was preparing for the grand traveling exhibition of the Treasures of Tutankhamun, Thomas Hoving said he'd found much of the material that led to his blockbuster exposé stored at the National Museum in Cairo with what he called "junk" about the curse.

"Does that 'junk' hold another secret?"

Discovering the truth meant that Crispin would have to do two things she didn't want to do: she'd have to trust Laurie and she'd have to leave her father.

It only took an hour to set her plan in motion. Thanks to Herbert, her room was still waiting for her at the Winter Palace the next morning, so she was able to bathe and pack. After arranging for a flight to Cairo she tapped on the door to Laurie's room.

She declined Laurie's offer to come in. Standing on the threshold, Crispin launched into an explanation of the attempt on her father's life the night before. She then explained that she had business in Cairo but wouldn't be away long.

"Ashraf will be here soon and he'll help you figure out how to protect Dad. Listen to him and do exactly what he says," Crispin said, as if talking to a teenager who was being left alone for the first time while her parents go out of town for the weekend.

To her credit, Laurie was patient and accepting. "Please trust me. I will protect his life with my own."

Herbert was helping with logistics for the international team being sent to Egypt to assess earthquake damage on historical monuments, tombs, and pyramids. Since he was on his way to the airport to pick up a delegation from London, Crispin was able to hitch a ride with him.

When she had first met Herbert, Crispin had too quickly judged him to be the stereotypical British aristocrat, detached and pampered. Today, Herbert was all business, using his cell phone to field calls, solve problems, and work out logistical details. For decades both the British Museum and New York's Metropolitan Museum had maintained permanent facilities in the Valley. Both were now bringing a variety of equipment for assessing earthquake damage, including high-powered cameras. Under normal circumstances, Crispin would not have relinquished a front row seat to such an epic enterprise. Circumstances were anything but normal.

On the short plane trip from Luxor to Cairo, Crispin sketched out an inventory of her thoughts on two facing sheets of paper. One was devoted to the remaining questions, facts, memories, and fears about her hypothesis regarding a fifth chamber in the Tut tomb. The other list detailed the series of mishaps that had started when she got to London and followed her to Egypt. She drew two columns on each sheet: one for things she knew and one for unanswered questions. The second column on each sheet was longer than the first. The list of unanswered questions grew as she concentrated.

Crispin conceded that her theory about a fifth, never before disclosed chamber in the Tut tomb was a potentially exciting archeological discovery. What it wasn't, as far as she could tell, was a trigger for the kind of mayhem that had visited her and her father.

She arrived in Cairo certain that she would find answers to some of her questions at the Museum. All she got was a bureaucratic tangle of red tape. When Crispin called Ashraf's apartment for help, it was Salma who answered. Salma's relief was evident in her tone more than her words.

"Crispin, tell me about Daniel."

After they'd talked about the earthquake and Dr. Leads' improving condition, Crispin explained the purpose of her call.

"I'm in Cairo at the National Museum. Ashraf told me he'd arrange for me to use the Museum maps and reference work for my project. They say they need to talk to him first."

"Ashraf left for Luxor. Just put the fellow on the line, dear."

After a short conversation in Arabic, the official returned the receiver to Crispin and Salma explained.

"I told him you are an important diplomatic guest and to give you anything you want. I'm sure Ashraf would want you to have full access."

Salma asked Crispin to join her and Ashraf for dinner one night soon, then excused herself since she was running late for a spa appointment. The two old friends said simultaneously, "To hydrate!"

One of Crispin's most enduring memories of her times with Salma was the older woman's insistence on weekly spa rituals to replenish the moisture drained from her body by the dry desert heat of Egypt. It was nothing for Salma to have her hair soaking in a deep jojoba conditioner, her face covered with an enriching collagen masque, and her hands and feet encased in oil and paraffin after receiving a full-body massage with expensive oils.

Salma exited by the front door of the apartment and Tony stepped out from the hallway. He'd been listening.

Chapter Eighteen

Crispin was starting to feel lightheaded and silly. It was the thin air. Her last clear memory was walking down a hall in the Museum basement. Then nothing, until she'd regained consciousness and found herself in what seemed to be a stone box, large enough to move around in, but not large enough to stand up in. She'd learned that painful lesson when she tried to get up and nearly knocked herself out again.

At first wakening she'd known only panic and it caused her to cry out. Her words echoed like screams in a well. They slid, unanswered, down the wall of blackness that surrounded her. She'd crawled around her prison, feeling her way in the dark with her hands. She wasn't able to locate a door, or, for that matter, anything else. Her stomach heaved as she came to understand the truth. She was sealed in.

Each time she sensed herself drifting away she would talk to herself. There was something strangely comforting in the sound of her voice in the empty tomb. The ache in her head made it difficult to concentrate. "Don't worry about the head wound. You'll probably suffocate long before you die of a concussion."

She sensed herself again drifting on the cusp of consciousness so she forced herself to continue the rambling conversation about old lies and new truths.

Her lonely monologue helped Crispin to stay focused as she reached to feel the lump of dried blood on the back of her head. It was disconcerting, not knowing where she was or exactly how she'd gotten there. "A few more whacks to my noggin and I'll need a full-time keeper."

Ultimately, old habits and lifelong training wrestled to retake command. Reason engaged in combat with despair. Reason won.

She concluded that she was probably still in the Museum. Or, at least she hoped so. Devoted primarily to Pharaonic antiquities, the Museum was home not only to the mummies of eleven New Kingdom pharaohs, but also had a large section devoted exclusively to the treasures taken from Tut's tomb. A controlled-access room guarded the gold pieces, including the elegant golden funeral mask inlayed with cornelian, lapis lazuli, quartz, obsidian, turquoise, and colored glass. Although not open to the general public, the basement housed almost as many treasures as the two upper floors.

The Museum, in the heart of Cairo's Liberation Square, had always held a special place in Crispin's heart because it clung to an aspirational time that had long since passed it by. It seemed cluttered, a bit worn out, and decrepit in places as though the government had run out of the money needed for upkeep. The neoclassical, two-story building was chockablock full of beautiful things arranged rather haphazardly without a sense of historical context. In places, the original signage had disappeared and been replaced by paper signs taped to the wall. But still, it held on to its dignity through it all. It put her in mind of her maiden Aunt Tilde's home, a place holding the line on Old World standards and charm. Aunt Tilde's place may have been threadbare, but it was also elegant. The table napkins may have had slightly frayed edges, but at least they were linen.

The teacups may have had a few tiny chips, but they were good English bone china.

Crispin remembered that after the obstinate Museum officials had given her access to the materials that she needed, she'd settled into a small file room in the annex where she could pore over the yellowed news clippings and Hoving's junk about the curse, sorting facts from fantasy. Her unreliable memories suggested that some kind of story was beginning to take shape when she left her work for a short stretch and bathroom break. That was her last clear memory until she woke up entombed.

The realization brought renewed panic that she was only able to control by wrapping her arms around her legs and curling her body into a protective ball. It was as if by taking up as little room as possible she could somehow make the tomb seem larger. For a long time she crouched that way, rocking back and forth and weeping, lost in the incomprehensible.

Crispin concentrated in an effort to piece together everything that had happened since she'd left her father in Luxor. It was just those connections that she'd been searching for in the musty archives before she woke up in the tomb. Sitting in the cold cell she focused one by one on the odd events of the last several weeks, events that she feared her curiosity had set in motion. The idea that had half formed in her mind on the road trip with Herbert was now at the center of her inquiry. The memories and connections came back slowly as if she were meticulously gluing a piece of shattered pottery.

Puzzling about the meaning of butterflies and traps, curses, and boxes, she felt the slightest tickle of a revelation, a lucid moment of near clarity. Then, the connection, so clear for a second, escaped. It was maddening at first, like a movie projector coming in and out of focus, giving her glimpses of random bits of a complicated plot in which she was the star attraction.

After what seemed like an eternity, Crispin was starting to come to the grim realization that this was one problem she might not be able to think her way out of. Whenever she wanted to give up, tenacity barked at her, "Stay focused." A thought would strain at the tip of a half thought and then it was gone again. The only thing that kept her from lapsing fully into unconsciousness was an annoying scraping sound above her head.

I was close. I know I was close, she thought, as she struggled to visualize the content of her handwritten notes, grasping for something to keep her mind active in the overtaking darkness and thinning air. Everything that happened in the hall outside the archives was lost, however. The hall. Then the tomb. Nothing in between.

There it was again: that scraping sound prodding her back to consciousness. "No peace for the dying."

Just when her resolve was a heartbeat shy of despair, a shaft of light suddenly cut through the cell and the dark, blinding her for a moment. It was followed by a familiar face peering in over the edge of the wall.

"Sophie?"

***

In the hours after Sophie found Ida's body she gave new meaning to the concept of "multitasking." Her success was due in part to the competence and support of Sean Thurman. The old man walked in on her just seconds after the gruesome discovery of Ida's corpse. Together, they notified the authorities. Thurman told the police that he'd received an odd call from his old friend the day before. Ida told him that she was excited about a mystery that had been discovered at the Library and asked him to come to London right away. He'd tried her office and been to the house earlier in the day, but hadn't had any success.

It had taken no small dose of both charm and intimidation, but together Thurman and Sophie had convinced the authorities to let her go to Egypt right away so that she could tell Crispin in person about Ida's murder. Since Ida had been dead for at least a day, officials did not consider Sophie a suspect.

What Sophie didn't tell the London police was that Crispin had a way of attracting danger and that whoever killed Ida might be after Crispin. Sophie was cleared to make the trip after an exchange of official calls between Scotland Yard and Inspector Sabri. Not long after police reports of Ida's death were filed at headquarters, Sabri contacted the Yard and became the official Egyptian liaison for the case.

The decision by police authorities to let Sophie, a material witness in a murder case, leave England was conditioned on her agreement to contact Inspector Sabri as soon as she landed in Cairo. As it turned out, there was no need. The Inspector was waiting for her at the airport when she arrived.

As a courtesy, Sabri agreed to allow her to check in at the Mena House before accompanying him to police headquarters. Sabri was surprised to see Crispin in a cab leaving the hotel through one gate just as they drove through the other.

"I thought she was still in Luxor," he said to Sophie.

A check with the doorman confirmed that Crispin was bound for the National Museum. Sophie left her bags and jumped back in the car with the inspector. Unfortunately, the pair lost valuable time when a three-car pileup backed traffic up for miles. Crispin was nowhere to be found when they arrived at the Museum.

The front office explained that Crispin had been given VIP status and left alone in the annex. When Inspector Sabri and

Sophie arrived, the only thing they found was Crispin's backpack. It was on the floor and its contents had been riffled.

While the inspector called security, Sophie went looking for her friend. It might have been instinct, or, maybe, woman's intuition, but she decided to follow a hallway to an underground tunnel connecting the annex to the basement catacombs of the main building. Her gamble paid off when she saw a man with a large birthmark pulling at the handle of a locked door.

"Hey," she'd yelled, planning to ask him if he'd seen Crispin.

Instead of answering, he took off running.

He had no idea that he was dealing with an Olympic hopeful in peak condition, because Sophie overtook him in seconds. She grabbed his collar and with one smooth action wrestled him to the ground, where she pinned him under her knee until Sabri caught up with her.

"He must have put up quite a fight," Sabri said, indicating the cuts and bruises on the man's face and arms.

"Not me," Sophie answered, bending over at the waist to catch her breath. "That's the way he was when I tackled him." She moved out of the way to allow the policeman to handcuff her prisoner.

The man explained in Arabic that he'd run from Sophie because he had just himself been attacked and beaten so he naturally assumed she was an accomplice. He claimed that he knew nothing about Crispin's whereabouts.

While Inspector Sabri led the man away for further questioning, Sophie went with the Museum security police to investigate the locked room. Her heart sank when they opened the door. The walls of the room were lined with dozens of stone sarcophagi with heavy lids. If Crispin were in one of those, they would have to act quickly.

"We're going to need some muscle," she told the guards with her. "Hurry."

While she waited for them to return, Sophie inventoried the room. "We'll need some luck, too," she told herself.

All of the sarcophagi along the right-hand wall had tight-fitting lids. Those lining the left wall were a different story. The lids to most of them were propped on the wall. Only six at the far end had lids in place. Sophie reasoned that if someone decided to put Crispin in one of them, he would choose one with a lid already off. Lifting a lid was no small task since even the smaller ones weighed hundreds of pounds. Why do it twice?

She was right. Museum officials only had to pry the lids off of two before they found Crispin. Whoever attacked Crispin had help since it took three strong men to remove the lid.

Inspector Sabri had insisted they have doctors examine Crispin's injuries, but her head wound, while bloody, turned out to be superficial. The MRI did not indicate a concussion. Doctors sent them home with instructions and cautions along with painkillers. In deference to Crispin's ordeal, Sabri agreed to postpone his questioning. He permitted Sophie and Crispin to return to the Mena House to recuperate as long as they agreed to meet him at his office the next morning at 10:30 a.m. sharp.

***

On the cab ride back to the hotel, Sophie told Crispin how she'd tackled the man with the birthmark and the fight it caused between the Metropolitan Police and Museum Security.

Sophie said she wasn't sure what disconcerted the museum security guards the most: that their important visitor had been attacked or that the Metropolitan Police were involved. The minute Crispin was safe and none the worse for wear, a turf war between the Metropolitan Police and Museum Security broke out in earnest.

"As we left, Inspector Sabri was beginning what some might call an 'intense interrogation' of the man."

"Why can't I remember more?"

"Walk me through what you do remember, leading up to that point. Maybe that will help."

Crispin told Sophie what had happened to her father at the hospital in Luxor. She said that she'd stopped by the hotel before going to the Museum, expecting that the material Sophie was to get from her study carrel along with the package from Georgia would be waiting for her there. When the materials weren't there she decided to go directly to the National Museum.

"Speaking of Georgia, you won't be surprised to know that your precious package was at the Drury Lane flat all right, addressed to me instead of you," Sophie said. "Good thing too since someone pilfered your mail."

"What about the stuff from the Library?"

"Don't worry. I hand-carried everything from London. I cleaned out your research carrel at the Library and brought the whole shebang."

"I'm surprised that whoever's after me didn't get there first."

"Didn't you say that Ida was the only one who knew which carrel you were using?"

"It's a good thing you're backing me up," Crispin said, rubbing the newest bump on her head. "My little gray cells have taken quite a beating."

Crispin confided that it was frustrating to have a chunk of her memory missing. "I have no clear memory of being put in the sarcophagus and only bits and flashes of the rest."

"It'll all come back. Just give it some time."

"I've been pushed, burned, run over, robbed, and buried alive. What else can go wrong?" Crispin asked rhetorically.

Sophie swallowed to clear her mind and her throat. The news about Ida would not be easy to deliver. She took Crispin's hands in hers.

All Crispin could think was that the gesture wasn't typical for Sophie. *She's not a touchy-feely person. What now?*

Chapter Nineteen

"It's like Mariette at Edfu," Crispin mumbled.

Sophie and Crispin were stretched out on oversized cotton towels, enjoying the Mena House sauna after a late evening swim.

"Come again, what did you say?"

Crispin raised up on one elbow and repeated herself. "Mariette at Edfu. It was Dad's way of tackling a conundrum. When you have a big problem, sometimes it helps to look at it piece by piece and then look for the pattern. It's a reference to a French archeologist who reconstructed the Temple at Edfu the way you put together a jigsaw puzzle, piece by careful piece."

The Temple had been no more than rubble when Mariette began work. Many of the original stones from the temple were used in subsequent construction projects. That meant pieces were scattered in buildings and walls throughout the city. Mariette's solution was nothing less than brilliant. He took rubbings of each of the stones and then matched the hieroglyphics, stone to stone, by piecing together the paper pieces. After the puzzle was worked out on paper, it had been relatively easy to plan the reconstruction.

"Sorry I asked," Sophie said, standing and stretching her long legs.

"The story was Dad's way of reminding us that no matter how shattered something looks, how complicated the elements, if there is an answer and you are persistent, you can find it."

"Remind me what we have so far," Sophie said as she leaned back, curling her spine into a graceful backbend stretch that would have been the envy of any gymnast.

While Sophie performed what she jokingly referred to as her "flamingo fandango" by contorting her limber body through the complex series of stretches that preceded her training routine, Crispin went over the scenario the two had constructed. It was based in part on Crispin's site visit to the Valley, in part on what she'd learned at Griffith Institute, and in part on Hoving's narrative about Carter and Carnarvon. As bizarre as it sounded, the story they were constructing about the connection between hidden chambers and the fabled Tut curse fit the facts.

They had mapped out a logical sequence to explain how a fifth chamber at Tut's tomb might have gone unnoticed and unreported. Crispin would need to look at typographical maps to verify certain facts, but she was confident of her conclusions. Following years of frustration and failure excavating in the Valley, Crispin felt certain that Carter had stumbled across an underground storage chamber containing what he assumed was a random cache of forgotten artifacts, some solid gold and silver.

The dry heat of the sauna was losing its appeal so they kept up the discussion while they walked across the hotel's grassy lawn to their room.

"Carter saw a chance to acquire wealth in his own right," Crispin said. "He was obligated by the terms of his agreement with Carnarvon and by Egyptian law to report the find. He didn't. That was his first overt act of deception."

Crispin knew her father would disapprove of the portions of her tale that were the result of educated guesswork. She felt confident that, at first, Carter didn't realize his cache was connected to something much bigger.

"Things were going swimmingly until Carter came across an object imprinted with the cartouche of King Tut," Crispin said. "Although I can't be sure, I think it may have been the infamous lotus head carving."

Some time after the discovery of Tut's tomb, a group of Egyptian officials conducting a routine audit of Carter's work found the delicately painted carving of a life-sized bust of a youthful Tut, emerging from a lotus flower. It was hidden in a wine crate. Carter had never offered a satisfactory explanation for how such a valuable artifact had wound up stored with the groceries.

Crispin speculated that when he'd found the lotus head Carter must have concluded that what he originally thought was a random discovery was actually a chamber to the long-sought tomb of King Tut. "A back door, if you will."

She further suggested that the entrance to his secret find had lacked the requisite royal seals. "It may have been an oversight in the political turmoil that followed the boy king's death," Crispin said. Once he realized what he had, Carter worked on his own, mapping out the likely pattern of Tut's tomb. From that he was able to guess with great precision the location of the actual, formal entrance.

Then Lord Carnarvon dropped a bombshell. He told Carter that he decided to relinquish his commission for rights to excavate in the Valley. Carter must have panicked and that's why he stunned Carnarvon by rashly offering to pay for continuing the work. Ultimately, Carnarvon agreed to underwrite one additional year at the dig. It was time to stage the great discovery so Carter likely paid a young water boy to pretend he had found steps that led to the tomb entrance.

As she unlocked the door to their room, Crispin summarized, "In that decision, Carter set off one of the longest-running butterfly effects in archeology."

"You and your butterflies," Sophie responded, pushing ahead of Crispin to check the room for intruders. When Crispin looked startled, Sophie shrugged. "You can't be too careful."

"That's my problem. I'm never careful."

Crispin's mood deteriorated into guilt when she thought again about Ida and that damn mystery box of files at the Library. She recalled vividly the last conversation she'd had with Ida and the older woman's promise to look for the missing box. Guilt, Crispin's ever-present companion, crawled up from her subconscious and gripped her heart. Maybe Ida's murder had something to do with the box.

Sophie, as if reading her friend's mind, said, "Quit blaming yourself. You didn't kill Ida. There's a crazy bastard on the loose. That's who's to blame. Not you."

"I know you're right. But every action, even a small one, can set in motion an avalanche of unintended consequences."

"Listen to me, it's egotistical to keep thinking your actions are that powerful. You are not responsible for Ida's death. We'll stay on it until we find the bastard, but right now I need a break."

Sophie excused herself for a run, "to get the kinks out and burn a few calories."

"I'll order room service," she told Sophie.

"And don't open that door for anyone else," Sophie cautioned.

"First things first," she told herself. When the charge nurse put her call through to her father's hospital room in Luxor she was pleased that her Dad's voice had all of its familiar strength and command.

"Leads here."

"Hi, Dad. It's Crispin. How are you?"

"Where are you?"

"Mena House. I'll be joining you as soon as I wrap up a few things here."

"I suppose if I told you I'm fine and that you can go back to London you would ignore my wishes."

"I understand that you don't think I'm necessary, but Ashraf and Herbert have asked me to help in the recovery efforts," Crispin replied, adding with a hint of teasing in her voice. "Besides, you have a way of getting into trouble when I'm not around."

"Good night."

"Love you."

"Love you more."

Crispin next placed the room service order, took a shower, and then camped out on her bed surrounded by her research material and notes. Since her rescue from the coffin, Crispin had been fueled by adrenaline and the need to seize hold of the scraps of inspiration that had drifted in and out of her addled brain.

Alone for the first time since hearing the news, she gave herself permission to react fully to Ida's death. Memories of dear, quirky Ida flashed through her mind, what grief counselors called the phenomenon of Life Review. It was the brain's way of cataloguing the loss, of memorizing the important moments of a relationship before they slipped away. Crispin closed her eyes and watched herself and Ida sneaking around the British Library behind Mrs. Powell's back. They laughed over homemade biscuits and tea, debated the value of modern art, shared the pain of lost parents, and told tales of World War II. The scene shifted to lunch with Thurman, to the hand-stitched needlepoint pillow.

Snippets of conversation again laced through Crispin's growing concern that she had been responsible for putting Ida in danger. Why had she told Ida about the box she'd found? Had Ida found it? Was that why she called Thurman? What could have been in the box that would lead someone to murder a kind, old woman? Somehow she needed to fit the pieces together. Like Mariette at Edfu, there had to be an answer.

If her theory were correct, Carter made some serious miscalculations. The worst was his failure to anticipate the limelight, bordering on hysteria, which would follow his discovery. Overnight he went from an obscure archeologist to an international celebrity, and his dig became a must-see stop for elite tourists from around the globe. Nothing in his experience had prepared him for the richness of the find or for the notoriety that came with it. Anyone would have made the same mistake since nothing like it had ever been found before. Or since.

The room service trolley arrived just before Sophie returned, hungry and starved. After a quick bath the two polished off a lavish room-service supper of duck and saffron rice with wine sauce, cubed croquette squash and onions, and pita bread with tahini and hummus.

Crispin played catch-up with Sophie on her notes and her theory. "It is likely that at first Carter was annoyed at the public fascination, fanned by journalists who published reports full of wild stories and superstitions."

"What's a guy to do?" Sophie mocked.

"Right, and the solution may have been the most clever maneuver of all," Crispin said. "It's like what a magician does on stage. The flourish of one hand holding the proverbial bright, shiny object pulls the eye away from what is really going on in the other."

"A diversion?"

"Yes."

"So you are saying that Carter turned to murder to hide his thefts and then invented the curse to hide the murders?"

The bluntness of the statement provoked Crispin to parse her words cautiously, as if she were presenting a conference paper for peer review. "No, I'm not willing to say that Carter was himself a murderer."

"That's all well and good, but there is one huge problem. Herbert's relative, the earl. Wouldn't he have known?"

Crispin mulled it over. She could not accept that Carnarvon knew all along. He would not have been willing to stand by and let the man loot a rich find. "Not necessarily."

"Your problem is you don't want to believe anything negative about the earl because it might reflect on Highfalutin Herb," Sophie chided.

"You're wrong about him."

Sophie wasn't convinced. She didn't like the idea that Herbert was in the vicinity for several of Crispin's "accidents." She reminded Crispin that Herbert had been in the British Museum just before her fall, and that it was because of him that she was in a car alone on a British country road, rather than safe on a train.

Helping herself to a slice of cake topped with cream and crushed pistachios, Sophie added, "Don't forget that he had plenty of time to look through your backpack while you were asleep on the plane. Beside that, aren't you just a little suspicious that he showed up at your door so early the next morning after the fire? I want to know how Herb heard about it so soon. I know I sure didn't tell him."

It was a question Crispin realized she had never asked. She'd just taken it for granted that one of her friends had told Herbert about the fire. "I'm sure there's a logical explanation."

Sophie was mulling over Crispin's evidence from earlier in their discussion. "Tell me again, just how does your theory about what happened in the '20s have one thing to do with that day when all hell broke loose after you dumped that box at the Library?"

"I know, I know. What possible reason would anyone have to want to cover it up now? Why attack me? Why Dad? Why Ida?"

"Like you said, it's like whosit at whatsit."

Crispin pushed the room service trolley into the hall and crawled into bed, pulling the duvet over her head. Even in the dark, Ida and the mystery were with her. It made sense that the danger that began after she discovered the box was connected to Carter's long-buried secret. But, the first time she was threatened was in the British Museum, *before* she found the box. Crispin knew that somehow she must have done something else to attract the attention of Sophie's crazy bastard. But what? She was still trying to sort through missing links and rabbit trails when the mercy of sleep finally blessed her.

***

The next morning, Crispin could tell by the deep, even breathing in the bed next to her that Sophie was still asleep. As she tiptoed to the bathroom Crispin almost laughed at the way the room looked. Before Sophie tucked in for the night she used furniture to barricade both doors of the hotel to prevent intruders. A heavy writing desk braced the doors leading to the veranda, and a chest of drawers blocked access to the hall door.

After she showered and dressed, Crispin braced herself for the thankless task of waking Sophie.

"Sophie girl, you'd better wake up," she called to her, shaking the foot of the bed.

No response.

"Come on, Soph, rise and shine," she said, turning the light on over the bed and opening the curtains to let in the sun.

Still, no response.

"It's after nine," she intoned. "We're going to be late."

From deep in the covers there was movement, so Crispin acted quickly, yanking off the blanket.

Her friend was finally awake, but not happy about it.

As she got up, Sophie signaled the Fifteen-Minute-Rule and stumbled to the bathroom.

***

Crispin ordered coffee, fruit, milk, and scones from room service. She shoved the heavy chest away from the hallway door. Breakfast arrived just as Sophie emerged from the bathroom.

When the two entered the office of Inspector Sabri at police headquarters in central Cairo, the inspector greeted Sophie like an old friend.

"Ladies, I hope that you were able to achieve some rest," Sabri said as he found them comfortable seats in his office and offered a welcome drink of sweet hibiscus tea.

Following an exchange of pleasantries, he handed them a glossy publication folded back to reveal a color picture of a twenty-four-inch statue of Bes, the dwarf god of pleasure. "Does this look familiar to either of you?"

From her expression, Sabri could tell that the photograph in the Sotheby's catalog meant nothing to Sophie. Crispin's face told a different story.

The piece was distinctive in that the smiling figurine of Bes seemed to be dancing with a tambourine. The tambourine was a separate piece made of silver and precious stones, but the god statue was carved from a single piece of translucent alabaster.

Without comment, Crispin flipped through the papers Sophie had brought with her from London and located a photo. It was one of the five enhanced photos Georgia had produced from the negatives Crispin had sent her from the British Library.

"Is this it?" she asked, comparing her photo of her Bes with the one in the booklet.

She then flipped through the catalog and made additional matches with two other distinctive pieces.

One was a delicately carved, solid-gold statue of a pharaoh. Although no more than six inches high, it was perfectly proportioned and the figure was in full stride. The third item was the most unusual piece. It was a necklace, also of gold, set with precious and semiprecious stones including green feldspar, lapis lazuli, and cornelian. Because of the small circumference of the necklace when the clasp was closed, it could only have fit a baby or a very small child.

"This is surpassing strange," Crispin said.

Sabri told them that his officers found the catalog, dog-eared at the photograph of the Bes statute, last night in the rental car of the man they arrested after the attack on Crispin in the National Museum in Cairo.

"He says his name is Karim El-Narsh, but I'm not sure we can trust even that."

After a lengthy interrogation by police, the man with the birthmark had revealed little. A fingerprint analysis had turned up nothing in Cairo police records, but both Interpol and Scotland Yard were combing their files.

"Perhaps now you would like to explain the origin of your photographs?" Sabri asked Crispin.

At first she was unsure where to begin, but Crispin ultimately decided it was best to give a full accounting. She started her narrative with the mess in the British Library, the death at the warehouse, and the mystery box. She told him about her conversations with Thurman regarding the possibility of still yet-to-be reported shenanigans during the Tut excavation and her time spent with archival records from the Carter/Carnarvon dig. Her story ended with her decision to return to Cairo after the attack on her father in the Luxor hospital. The only part of the story she left out was her speculation about the fifth chamber.

Crispin also showed the inspector two additional photographs Georgia had enhanced from negatives. One print was of a solid-gold box, fourteen by eight by six inches. It was crafted in the shape of a sarcophagus and inlaid with gold and lapis both on the surface and the interior. The other photograph depicted an unusual pair of ivory bracelets carved in a continuous circle and then etched, much in the way of scrimshaw or jade.

"Georgia made prints from all twenty-five of the negatives that I sent her, but most were nondescript pottery or household items," Crispin said. "These five, the ones in the catalog and the other two, are unique enough to trace."

Inspector Sabri listened patiently, taking a few notes. After Crispin finished her story, he closed his notepad and with excessive care, then arranged his pen at a perfect ninety-degree angle on top. He sat back in his chair, his hands folded as if in prayer over his mouth, and closed his eyes. Sophie and Crispin looked at each other, confused. After a while, Sabri took a deep breath and seemed to come to a decision, opening his eyes and addressing them.

"I believe you ladies have been forthright with me, and I have decided you likewise deserve an accounting of what I know of these matters."

Sabri told them that the Cairo police had been cooperating with Scotland Yard for months on an undercover investigation of what appeared to be widespread antiquities thefts. Beautiful

Egyptian relics, many of them in almost pristine condition, had been showing up on the auction block.

Initially the police assumed they were nothing more than exceptionally well-crafted fakes. Then scientific tests verified their age. The problem was that these new objects had a limited provenance. The objects appeared to have little or no documented history. This was problematic since a paper trail was one of the most important tools in authenticating such work.

An operative working undercover in London had tipped him off, but that person had been compromised.

"What do you mean, 'compromised'?" Sophie asked.

"You will forgive me, but this is one detail of our work I cannot reveal."

Crispin couldn't say the name that her heart screamed. "Ida."

"I do not want to bore you with my problems. Suffice it to say officials at the Cairo Museum have not welcomed our investigation."

Sabri explained that government antiquities officials, who have the final say on access to historical sites, used their authority to keep his investigators away from active archeological digs. The unfortunate death at Saqqara gave his office a brief opportunity to investigate on site but the access was limited. So far he had been completely shut out at the Bahariya Oasis.

"The newspapers have labeled that find the 'Valley of the Golden Mummies.' They've already unearthed more than two hundred gilded mummies from the Roman era. Let me qualify that, two hundred that we know of," he said. "Officials keep us at arm's length, citing delicate negotiations and international priorities. My policeman's intuition tells me that there is some serious skull digging going on."

Crispin and Sophie looked puzzled.

"I'm sorry, I've used the wrong English expression?"

"Do you mean, 'skullduggery'?" Sophie asked.

"That's it exactly, skullduggery."

Walking around the desk, he leaned against it so that he could make eye contact with Crispin. "We see the connection when items reach the marketplace, but we cannot go to the scene of the crime. Until now. Now there has been divine intervention."

"The earthquake?" Sophie asked.

"I see you understand," he replied with a smile.

***

Sophie and Crispin finished at Inspector Sabri's office and Crispin packed to return to the Valley. Sophie decided to pay a brief visit to Salma.

"Give her a kiss and tell her I'll see her soon," Crispin said.

"I'll catch up with you tomorrow," Sophie promised.

Salma was more than a friend to Sophie. She was like a favorite aunt or surrogate mother. Sophie's mother died in childbirth. Her father, who covered his flaws with a thick layer of charm, was a drug addict who died young.

After the death of her son, Sophie's Egyptian grandmother, Dalila, took on the responsibility of raising the little girl. Sophie often thought that she understood and appreciated Salma most in contrast to her grandmother. Although Salma was Dalila's closest friend, they were nothing alike in values, looks, or priorities. Dalila was wound up in the daily lives of her neighbors and friends, many of whom she nursed when they were sick, cried with when they were sad, and rejoiced with when they were blessed. Salma was acquainted with many, but had few true friends. Her broad circle of casual acquaintances included some young men about whom there were rumors of less-than-platonic relationships.

From her grandmother, Sophie learned how to give and receive unconditional love. From Salma she learned that a complete woman understands the importance of self-love. Not egotistical self-love, but the kind of self-love that stiffens a woman's resolve against destructive criticism, helps her recover from failure, and shields her against men who take but never give.

For all her hedonism, however, Salma had one attribute that was undisputed by friend or foe: she was reliable. If she said she would do something, she did it without reservation or obligation. If she said she would keep a secret, she would take it to the grave. She never betrayed a confidence, at least not knowingly.

Salma had been sharing stories with Sophie for about an hour when she asked if Sophie would accompany her on an errand to a warehouse just outside of town. Ashraf had asked her to deliver some government papers to the owner. "Our young Mr. Dexter was supposed to do it, but he left earlier than expected," Salma said on the drive to the warehouse.

Sophie couldn't believe what she'd heard. "You don't by any chance mean Anthony Dexter from London?"

"Yes, do you know him? He and Ashraf are involved in some exporting work. Such a good-looking young man. And so thoughtful. Ashraf had him to dinner when he arrived in Cairo and we made room for him at our place."

Sophie wanted to ask more, but all she could think was that Tony had been in Egypt for a couple of days and as far as she knew, hadn't said anything to Crispin. Something didn't smell right.

The revelation about Tony paled in comparison to what was waiting at the warehouse.

Chapter Twenty

When Herbert picked up Crispin at the Luxor Airport the next afternoon, he started to greet her with a kiss on the cheek but she pulled back. He hid any confusion he felt. He told her that Dr. Leads was already encamped in one of the visitor's rooms at the expansive, multi-building complex that had been maintained permanently by Metropolitan Museum since the 1920s. Leads had insisted, against doctor's orders, on leaving the hospital.

"You'll also be staying in the main building," Herbert told her. "The room is small but comfortable."

What he didn't tell her was that he'd had to pull strings to get her admitted to the site and that his was the only indoor room available. That morning, he had moved his belongings into one of the tents reserved for local workers so that Crispin could be comfortable.

Much had happened in the short time since she'd left to transform the plateau in front of Hatshepsut's temple. Before the earthquake pummeled the Valley, the area had all the usual trappings of one of the world's foremost tourist destinations: ticket kiosks; parking lots full of buses; and shacks selling souvenirs, chilled juice, and Cadbury candy. And, of course, there had been the ever-present guides, walking backwards in front of eager tourist groups, telling the story of ancient Egypt in every language. Here Japanese. There Italian. Here Russian. There Spanish.

Today, however, the grounds looked like a military campground. The Egyptian government had accepted the offers of New York's Metropolitan Museum and the British Museum to allow their permanent facilities to be converted to the command posts for the operation. The French delegation would concentrate its efforts on sites across the river, including the Luxor Temple and Karnak.

Dozens of tents and canopies dotted the bare ground of the open plateau of the Valley. One of the largest tents was devoted to the work of a group called Engineers for Structural Safety. Like other nongovernmental organizations with a stake in third world affairs, the Engineers had deployed specialists to assess post-earthquake displacement limits of structures. Protected from the unforgiving Egyptian sun by the large canopy, they had efficiently organized their outdoor offices. The Engineers would first calculate the pre-event displacement ratios and then diagram inelastic deformities caused by the earthquake.

There were tents for other specialists as well as for the routine activities of daily life: communications, housing, and hygiene. Some of the larger tents were devoted to keeping workers hydrated and healthy. Truckloads of bottled water had been unloaded, and a first aid station was already seeing patients for sunburns, heatstroke, and other maladies associated with long hours of exposure to conditions at the sites.

Nothing, however, about the transformation was quite as surprising to Crispin as the incongruous sight of men and women buzzing from point to point aboard Segway Human Transporters. The company had airlifted some of the all-terrain machines to the site. They vaguely resembled the two-wheel dollies used by furniture movers, except these dollies ran on powerful electric batteries and were balanced with the aid of a space-age gyroscope. The Segways had already increased the productivity at the site. Not only did the large wheels help workers navigate the sand with speed and ease, but they also were much smoother and lighter than cars and jeeps so no one had to worry about vibrations triggering further damage to delicate subterranean structures.

Although distracted with worry about her father's health and Inspector Sabri's investigation, Crispin couldn't help but grin when Ashraf buzzed up on a Segway. He looked like a schoolboy on his first bike.

"*Sabah el-Kheir,*" he said, dismounting and offering a hand to Crispin as she exited the jeep.

"*Sabah el-Nour,*" she replied. "How's Father?"

"You know Daniel. He ignores his injuries and joins in every discussion," said Ashraf. "To be candid, we are fortunate. His help and counsel have been invaluable."

"I want to pitch in too. As soon as I settle in I'd like you to put me to work."

"There's plenty to do," he replied before wheeling off.

Herbert offered to take Crispin's luggage to her room, but she insisted on handling it herself. Following his directions, she soon located her room on the second floor of the main building. It had minimal furnishings and no private bath, but she was grateful for the soft bed and writing desk. She'd been on expeditions where plumbing was nonexistent and the beds were no more than camp cots. After she unpacked, she went in search of her father since his room was in a separate wing. She tapped softly on the door in case he was taking a nap. She was irritated, but not surprised, that Laurie answered. She almost chastised the older woman for allowing her father to leave the hospital, but swallowed her words. Crispin knew, in fairness, that when Dr. Leads made up his mind, no one could change it.

Laurie was scheduled to meet Dr. Leads in the mess tent and offered to show Crispin the way. While they walked, Laurie filled Crispin in on her father's condition. "You know how Daniel is. He was up and moving the day after you left," Laurie said. "The doctors were surprised at his rapid recovery and that, apparently, he had no lingering effects of the sedative overdose."

When her father joined them for lunch, Crispin had to agree that his recovery was remarkable. Little wonder that his students often called him Indiana Jones, although never to his face. While his skin color still bordered on greenish gray, Leads moved with his usual strength and assurance. If anything, the abrasions and bruises gave him the rugged, tough appearance of a prizefighter. The bitter expression on his face, however, was more than the pain caused by his broken arm and recent chest surgery.

"So here you are," he barked.

"I told you I was asked to help. Besides, you look as if you could use a little rest."

"I do not answer to you, young lady."

"Crispin, Daniel, please—let's enjoy the meal," Laurie interrupted.

Crispin turned on her heel and headed for the buffet, where the cooks had provided heaping platters of grilled lamb, mango slices, sesame rolls, and eggplant fried with spices, olives, and onions. Crispin went straight for the batatis mahshiya. The smell of the potatoes that had been cored, fried, and then stuffed with spicy ground beef triggered memories of when her mother used to pack the special treats so the twins could carry a picnic lunch to their father at archeological digs.

Crispin returned to the table, where her father sat shoulder to shoulder with Laurie, enjoying an intimate conversation. She slid onto a bench across from them, bringing with her a mood of quiet hostility that even the familiar flavors and exotic location couldn't lighten. Seeing Laurie with her father always irritated her. Laurie was ten years younger than Leads and wore her years well. Crispin secretly believed she had help from a plastic surgeon. Laurie was lean and raw-boned, rarely missing her daily workout at the university gym. Today her long black hair was pulled back in a ponytail and she wore little makeup. Her forehead and upper lip were shining with perspiration, but she didn't seem to mind.

Sulking while she ate, Crispin paid little attention to what was going on in the tent until she heard an enthusiastic greeting behind her and turned to see Herbert enter with a group of camp workers. He spent a few minutes with them in what appeared to be a round of good humor and storytelling. When his companions began to eat, he excused himself and walked over to Crispin's table. "Hello, Dr. Leads. Dr. Pierce," he said courteously and then turned to Crispin.

"How is my traveling companion? I trust you are settled," he said, putting a hand on her shoulder in a friendly gesture of camaraderie, nothing more.

"Yes, thank you," she replied more tersely than she intended, especially since her father was glowering at the younger man.

"May I join you?"

"Certainly," Laurie said.

"I wish you had been with me earlier," Herbert said after he took the seat next to Crispin. "Those fellows are full of dark tales, just the kind you'd like," he added, indicating the group of men he'd just left.

"Pray tell," Crispin responded in a lighthearted way.

Turning to Dr. Leads, Herbert asked, "In your time in Egypt did you ever hear of an enigmatic, ancient cult called the Fellowship of Setesh?"

Dr. Leads didn't answer, so Herbert continued his story. "Some say they were heroes, defying the law to protect their ancient culture and burial customs from grave robbers," Herbert said. "Others cast them as nothing more than torturers who used fear to intimidate their opposition and conspiracy to line their pockets."

Clearly enjoying the narrative, Laurie cheerfully interrupted Herbert to ask questions as he spun the tale of the cult's checkered history. Her enthusiasm only served to aggravate Crispin further.

"Laurie, would you please let Herbert tell the story," said Crispin, just brusquely enough that her father reprimanded her for cutting Laurie out of the conversation.

"Crispin didn't mean anything like that, Daniel," said Laurie, but her attempt at peacemaking served only to increase the tension.

"The Setesh required absolute loyalty and could be ruthless in their pledge to protect Egyptian heritage," Herbert said. "Stories of retribution by the Setesh make the Mafia look like amateurs."

According to myth, the cult had a number of hideous methods to punish enemies and keep its members in line. One of the stories involved a linen patch soaked with a foul poison. "The death was relatively quick and quite painful."

"Whatever became of the cult?" Laurie asked.

"It is difficult to say," Herbert responded. "There are those who claim that remnants remain active even today."

"Rubbish, Van Snyder. Pure superstitious bunk," Dr. Leads said, interrupting Herbert as he rose to leave. "You, of all people, should know that such tales are intended for the ignorant and the unsophisticated. Such nonsense has no place where there is serious work to be done."

Crispin, who knew her father's feelings about such historical fantasy tales, thought she detected an extra note of disdain in his voice.

She wondered, is it the story you dislike or is it Herbert?

Local workers usually rested after lunch to avoid the intense midday heat. However, the urgency of the project required that the schedule at this site break with tradition. After the Engineers declared a monument or tomb structurally sound, it still had to be examined by archeologists for signs of aesthetic damage to wall paintings, carvings, or statues. Officials were demanding that the work be completed as soon as feasible. Any delay meant a loss of valuable income that neither the government nor the thousands of Egyptians whose livelihood depended on tourism could afford. They had to be thorough and they had to be fast.

Just as they exited the mess tent, Ashraf rolled up on his Segway to deliver a message.

"Please excuse us. Our colleagues believe they have found some displaced rocks and we need a consult immediately."

Mounting two nearby Segways, Dr. Leads and Herbert buzzed off, leaving Ashraf to make apologies.

"Of course," Laurie said, turning to Crispin. "I need to get back to work, too."

As Laurie walked away, Crispin asked Ashraf what she could do to help. "Give me something useful to do."

There was no shortage of things to do. Crispin went from assignment to assignment all afternoon, diagramming damage to edifices. Without complaint she worked in the heat alongside seasoned archeologists. It felt good to let her mind rest while her body labored. She knew from experience that sometimes the best way to solve a riddle was do something else while the subconscious worked the problem.

That night Crispin sat in her room jotting additional ideas to the evolving scenarios that she and Sophie had developed at the Mena House. She was having little luck making sense of it. The match between the photos in the auction catalog and the negatives she had discovered in London was the first evidence that linked her hypothesis about Carter's duplicity eighty-plus years earlier to modern-day events. Exactly what that link was still eluded her, but she sensed a solution wasn't far off. It was like groping around in a dark room. Shapes were slowly coming into focus but she still couldn't see a coherent pattern.

As she stood to stretch her legs, her feet touched her discarded sandals so she decided to take a walk. Emerging from the front door, she paused to admire the view of dozens of tents across the dessert. Illuminated from within, they made the Valley appear to be covered with Japanese lanterns. Heat still radiated from the sand, giving the illusion that the moon was vibrating gently as if reluctant to complete its ascent. The desert night air was chilly so Crispin pulled her sweater around her and closed the front door. Turning around, she slammed into Herbert, who caught hold of her to keep her from stumbling. He too was out for an evening walk, so they decided to go together.

They walked together the way they had on the cornice in Luxor, their steps synchronizing and their bodies finding a comfortable rhythm. When Crispin's sandal caught on a rough spot and she almost tripped he grabbed her by the waist, and after that they continued their stroll holding hands. When they ultimately circled back to the main building, Herbert told her that family duties would require him to leave soon. His hope was to come back to the Valley as soon as possible. After a brief pause during which he seemed to want to say more, he wished her a good night.

"Aren't you coming in?"

"Camping out in one of the pavilions with some of the fellas," he said with a grin. "Decided to rough it a bit, you see."

Crispin's sweater slipped from one shoulder as she reached to open the heavy front door. Herbert reacted quickly to save it from falling, using both of his hands to settle it back in place and smooth it across her shoulders. Then slowly, imperceptibly at first, he began to stroke her neck. For Crispin the touch was electric. Before she could censor her response, she leaned into his arms and kissed him.

Passion mounted so swiftly that it caught both Crispin and Herbert off guard. He was the first to pull away.

She let her fingers slide down his cheek and across his lips before she turned to go inside. "Thank you."

Across the compound, Dr. Leads stood undetected at the entrance to a work tent, as he watched the intimate silhouettes of Crispin and Herbert.

Chapter Twenty-One

Strapped into a rappelling vest and harness the next day, Crispin was ready to make her descent into a cave. Her job would be to position lights and strobes and hold video cameras for archeologists inspecting the cliffs that embraced Hatshepsut's tomb. She'd volunteered for the assignment since it offered her an opportunity to do something that might help Inspector Sabri.

When they'd met in his office, Sabri explained that his investigation isolated some of the thefts to areas near the cliffs, many of them remote and hard to reach. He had been unable to get permission to send in an expedition since antiquity officials jealously guarded access. Some of the caves had been sealed off for decades. Although he didn't elaborate about the source of his information, Crispin speculated that he had informants in the theft ring.

"Ms. Leads, I need your eyes there," he told her. "If I can find any tangible proof to back up my suspicions, I will be able to get the clearances I need to search the caves."

Crispin was uncertain. "If I see a chance to help, I will," she'd finally told Sabri. "I make no promises."

Now, sitting in a harness, suspended by nothing more than a rope and cable system, Crispin was wondering if she'd made the right choice. "What do I think I'll see down here? A chop shop for antiquities? Ridiculous."

The Engineers had decided that the safest way to examine the caves would be to drop down into the subterranean formations rather than to climb in because it would create less vibration. In addition to an instant visual inspection, teams could then videotape the walls and chambers using high-resolution photographic techniques. Workers had erected a large teepee-like aluminum structure over a cavern and rigged it with a hydraulic lift. Crispin was the first of the team lowered below ground. As she descended, the halogen lights attached to her hardhat and safety vest gave her a sense of omnipotence. The lights illuminated wherever she looked. All else was left in impenetrable darkness.

She'd been at work for two hours when she signaled that she was willing to pull a second shift. Dr. Leads would head up the relief team. Because his left arm was still in a cast, his descent was awkward, causing him to swing too close to Crispin. He almost tangled himself in her cable.

When she tried to help untangle the cable, he pushed away, saying, "I need to do it myself."

Without further acknowledgement of his daughter, Dr. Leads began to record his observations. Suspended by ropes, they worked in relative isolation for the next two hours, interrupted only by the faint hum of equipment and the muffled sound of Dr. Leads speaking quietly into a microphone headset.

Dr. Leads was beginning to show signs that his injuries were causing him to wear out more quickly than usual when Ashraf signaled that it was time for the team to go topside for a rest and a meal. To keep from tangling the complex pulley system of the harness cables, the team exited in reverse order. That meant that Crispin, the first to enter, would be the last to be pulled out.

Free hanging in the leather saddle like a child in a swing, Crispin adjusted her body to take the pressure off her sore thighs. In that moment something above her snapped. She went into a free fall that sent her stomach into her throat and her heart into overdrive. Her safety straps sent her spinning first left and then right as she fell more than fifty feet before she suddenly jerked to a rude stop, hanging like a puppet, legs and arms akimbo. She continued the sickening spin, first one direction and then the other as the harness wound and unwound. When her safety line had caught hold, it rammed into her groin and underarms, causing her to call out in pain.

Above, Dr. Leads held onto Crispin's safety line with his good hand. Alongside him, Ashraf grabbed the line so tightly that the cable burned his palms. Together the two men were able to halt the cable's dangerous sway. Leads yelled into the cave, "Crispin? Crispin? Are you okay?"

When she tried to answer, Crispin realized that the safety vest was compressing her chest, making it hard to scream. It was a pitiful reply that drifted back up from the cave. "A-OK."

"Hold the line, Ashraf," Dr. Leads screamed at his friend, his voice a mixture of fear and urgency. "I'll rig a secondary line."

"Have no fear," Ashraf said. "I have your daughter in my hands."

Just then Herbert came running and grabbed hold of the line.

Below ground the radical twisting of Crispin's harness settled into a fluid swinging motion. Back and forth. Back and forth. Even though she'd had most of the wind knocked out of her, Crispin had somehow managed to hang onto the video camera. The light on her hardhat illuminated what appeared to be signs of recent human activity near a wide space on the cliff wall. The space flickered into the light and then out again into darkness as she rocked back and forth.

She found that by concentrating she could time the swings so that she could take advantage of the intermittent light. She was able to make out discarded photographic film wrappers and a nylon rope. Holding the video camera at an awkward angle and shooting over her shoulder, she did her best to record what she saw.

Before much time passed she felt the vibration of the hydraulic lift begin to pull her to safety. Dr. Leads watched Crispin emerge into the light and give an awkward thumbs-up sign. His mood shifted from relieved to furious while the workers helped unbuckle her from the harness.

After she assured everyone that she was uninjured, her father pulled her aside. "I told you it was too dangerous for you here. I insist that you leave for London at once."

"I will not be dismissed like a child."

"Young lady, you are in no position to…"

Herbert interrupted. "Crispin, I must say, I agree with your father."

Dr. Leads and Crispin responded with one voice, "You have no say in this."

"My mistake," Herbert said with a nod of his head and walked away.

Dr. Leads started to say something to Crispin but she shook her head and turned, limping slightly as she left. He took a step as if to follow her but turned in the opposite direction toward the Met complex.

Ashraf spent a few minutes giving instructions to the crew and was about to catch up with Dr. Leads when one of the workers approached him with the severed cable that once held Crispin's harness. The cable had been cut almost through.

On an impulse born as much of anger as of reason, Crispin stopped at the communications tent. Laurie looked up from her work, surprised to see Crispin. Since the younger woman was clearly not in a talkative mood, Laurie filled the awkward gap. "All of the videos are brought here for streaming," she explained. "We use scanning equipment to mark suspicious areas that need a closer look by the experts in New York or London."

Crispin, still stinging from her father's patronizing attitude, made a quick decision. "Can I use this to catch up on my email?" she asked, pointing to one of several laptop computers open on camp tables.

Crispin feigned aggravation after working for a few minutes, telling Laurie that since she'd been out of touch for so many days, the transmissions had piled up. "There's fifty incoming messages," she said. "Looks like I'll be here a while."

As Crispin had hoped, the others in the tent soon grew accustomed to her presence and ignored what she was doing. No one noticed when, after standing to stretch her back, she covertly inserted and streamed the video she'd just shot in the cave.

"After you've looked at this, call me. We need to talk," was all she wrote in her transmittal email to Inspector Sabri.

"Thanks," Crispin told Laurie over her shoulder as she exited.

She didn't stay long enough to see the smile of appreciation on Laurie's face. It was the kindest thing she'd ever said to Laurie.

Back at the Met, Crispin took a long shower and washed her hair. Bruises blackened her shoulders, armpits, and groin, and her cheeks were scraped and red. In spite of her hat and sunblock, hours in the dessert were taking their toll. She took her time dressing in fresh work clothes, intending to return to the camp and look for something to do. Surely, Ashraf could find her work that was far away from her father and Herbert.

On her way out the door, she heard someone call out her name. A clerk behind the front desk was motioning to her. "Ms. Leads. Ms. Leads, there's an urgent phone call for you."

On the other end of the phone, Crispin heard the voice of an obviously perturbed Sophie.

"Finally. I've been calling your cell since last night. I couldn't make a connection. What have you been up to?"

"Nothing much, just fighting with Dad, spying for the Cairo police, making out with Herbert, and falling down holes," Crispin responded. "Where do you want me to start?"

"Hold that thought just one minute. I want to hear all the gory details of your derring-do, but first let me tell you what I've found."

Sophie gave Crispin a rundown on her impromptu trip to the Cairo warehouse district with Salma to deliver business papers for Ashraf. While Salma flirted with some of the men on the loading dock, Sophie had decided to stroll around the building. She wasn't looking for, or at, anything in particular, just killing time.

"That's when I saw it," she said with emphasis on the last pronoun, followed by a dramatic pause.

"Saw what?"

"A gold box shaped like a sarcophagus. About the size of a breadbox. And, I might say, not just any ol' breadbox shaped like a sarcophagus. It's identical to the one you had in those photos of yours."

"In a warehouse in Cairo? Are you sure?"

"Positive. To be accurate, I should say I saw gold boxes," Sophie said, emphasizing the plural ending to the last noun, clearly amused at her little joke.

Sophie described a side room in the warehouse lined with shipping cartons. Most were sealed, but one of them stood open with the gold sarcophagus just visible in the straw-like excelsior. "I looked it over pretty good and I'm sure it's the same," Sophie said. "Hold on to your parasol. It gets better."

When she'd reached deeper into the shipping carton to see what else was there she'd found another sarcophagus, and then another, and another, and another.

"If I calculated the volume-to-mass ratio correctly, there are at least two hundred of 'em," Sophie said. "And I saw similar sealed shipping cartons lined up on the loading dock, and I'd bet my granny's false teeth that they're also full of gold bread boxes."

Sophie said that she hadn't had time to open the sealed shipping cartons but did notice that each was marked with an inventory number suggesting that the gold boxes were in some of the cartons and that something else, perhaps copies of one of the other artifacts, was packed and ready to be shipped out.

"Shipped out? Where to?"

"I thought you'd never ask," Sophie said. "The labels indicated the shipment was bound for…drum roll please…Suite G-45, 87-135 Brompton Road, Knightsbridge, London. Sound familiar?"

"Knightsbridge? Harrods?"

Just then Crispin noticed that the clerk had been eavesdropping on her side of the conversation. Suddenly self-conscious, she tried to remember what she'd just said.

"Can we finish this later?"

"Someone listening?"

"Yes."

"Then don't talk until I tell you the rest of my news," Sophie said in a conspiratorial tone. "Our old drinking buddy Tony Dexter is here."

"Where?"

"Here, in Cairo. Or at least he was."

While Crispin listened, Sophie told her that according to Salma, he'd arrived about the same time as Crispin and had been staying at Salma and Ashraf's apartment.

In spite of the nosey clerk, Crispin felt she had to risk another question.

"Why?"

"Why what? Why was he staying with Salma and Ashraf or why was he in Cairo in the first place?"

"Both."

"Some kind of business. You know Salma. She didn't ask or seem to care."

Conscious of her friend's lack of privacy on the other end of the line, Sophie offered statements that Crispin could respond to with a simple "yes" or "no."

"Makes you wonder why Ashraf didn't say something, doesn't it?"

"Yes."

"Did you know that Ashraf and Tony were tight?"

"No."

"Do you want to set a time where we can talk and figure out what to do next?"

"Eventually."

"Something you want me to do first?"

"Yes."

"Get a pedicure with Salma?"

"Please."

"Call Inspector Sabri?"

"That's right."

"Should I give him the full skinny on the warehouse?"

"I think that's best."

They continued in the same vein until they had agreed that Sophie would contact Inspector Sabri and Crispin would try to locate a less public place to hold a phone meeting.

That was the quest that took Crispin on a search through the back halls on the main floor of the complex. What she found was a secret that would haunt her for the rest of her life. It would creep into her mind in the early morning and wake her in the night. It would interrupt her when she was thinking about something unconnected and unrelated. Like a petulant child it would demand her attention and require her to think about it again, and again, and again. It would strip joy away from her heart and pull her into melancholy at unexpected times and in unexpected places. What she heard were words that would pound in her subconscious, relentlessly raising the question for which there would never be a satisfactory answer.

"Was it my fault?"

Chapter Twenty-Two

Rounding a corner to a side hall in search of a place for a private phone conversation, Crispin heard her father's voice first. "Cut? What do you mean, cut?"

She started to signal her presence but stopped when she heard Ashraf. "I've tried to warn you time and again that Crispin was in danger. You were too stubborn to listen."

Crispin stood silent, listening from the side hall.

"You know the Fellowship. They will not tolerate interference. Unless you rein her in, Daniel…well, I don't have to remind you. You've seen what they are capable of when they are threatened."

"Melete was never a threat. She was one of them. They had no right to kill her."

It was all Crispin could do to keep from crying out. Untrue. Unimaginable. Unspeakable. The words thundered in her brain, temporarily deafening her until the sound of her father's voice cut through.

"You tell them that if they touch Crispin again, I will expose their operation."

"Think of the cost, Daniel. Your reputation."

"You think I care about that? Tell them I mean what I say."

"I cannot promise that I can control their reaction. If they feel threatened, they will take action, even if it is against one of their own. You've seen it before."

"Stop them, Ashraf, or I will."

"You have to stop Crispin. She is putting her nose where it doesn't belong. She's putting all of us in danger."

Crispin melted to the floor, her legs no longer capable of holding her weight. Her thoughts had no focus or form. They fluttered about her mind like random strips of cellophane caught on barbwire.

"They are not the only ones capable of..." she heard her father tell Ashraf, but the rest of the sentence was lost because the men walked away and were out of range of her hearing.

Time had no meaning for Crispin. All she knew or thought she knew about her mother's death was now no more reliable than a fairy tale. Memories had been erased, leaving only a numb place where feeling should be. What is the truth? What is the lie?

She must have looked either sick or drunk when a cleaning lady came across her sitting on the floor. "Lady. Lady. Are you okay? Lady, should I get a doctor?"

To Crispin's ear the woman's voice seemed muffled and distant and her own reply a bodiless whisper. "No. No. Don't get anyone. I'm...just...give me a moment."

The cleaning lady fetched a wet towel and a glass of cool water.

Although her world no longer made sense, Crispin knew that she must not let anyone know that she'd been there. As the cleaning lady helped her to stand, Crispin convinced her that she was simply lightheaded because of her monthly period. "Please don't tell anyone."

"Our little secret, no?" the cleaning lady agreed, glad to be part of an innocent female deception at the expense of the men who ran the place.

Back in her room, Crispin sat with her head in her hands, unable to move or think clearly. She lost track of time, as if coming out of general anesthesia, until the clerk from the first floor knocked on her door and told her that she had another important phone call.

"Where did you disappear to?" Sophie asked. "I've been working on my end and waiting for you to call back. By the way, before I forget, Inspector Sabri says the video is dynamite."

"Soph, I need to see you."

"What is it? You sound like death. Has something happened?"

"Not now. Can't. Where are you?"

After a few more half sentences, Sophie agreed to meet Crispin at the Cairo airport. From there they would catch a flight to London. Crispin scribbled a brief note telling her father that she was tired of fighting with him and had decided to honor his wishes and return to England. She packed her belongings, taped the note to his bedroom door and left without seeing anyone.

***

Meanwhile in Cairo, Salma, driving a Mini Cooper convertible with the top down, pulled up in front of the metropolitan police station. As she waited, she used the rearview mirror to put on fresh lipstick. Just as she finished, the passenger door opened and the man with the birthmark jumped in. Salma pulled into traffic, leaving bare millimeters between her bumper and the car behind her. She then drove at illegal speeds toward the airport.

***

Sophie packed up, checked out of the Mena House, and met Crispin at the Cairo airport with tickets in hand. The flight from Egypt to England gave Sophie and Crispin time to talk and plan.

Sophie was fully briefed and, uncharacteristically, speechless by the time they landed. They went directly to Salma's flat, where she had cozy guest rooms waiting for them. She told them she'd come to London for a quick shopping excursion and escape from the "craziness" generated back home by the earthquake. As was typical of her, Salma had accepted their request for secrecy without question or apparent curiosity.

"I figured it would be better to go in under the radar and stay away from Drury Lane," Sophie told Crispin after she'd made the arrangements with Salma.

They had two priorities. First, they would attend Ida's funeral. Because of the nature of her death and the subsequent inquest, her funeral services had been delayed. Next on their list was a trip to Harrods to trace the shadowy underworld path of the mass-produced artifacts that Sophie had stumbled across at the warehouse.

"After that?" Sophie had asked.

"I don't know. Something, but I don't know what" was Crispin's only answer.

The next morning Crispin decided to phone the Valley to check on her father. The clerk at the Met front desk said she would send someone to look for him so Crispin was surprised when Ashraf answered instead. He explained that Leads was no longer there. He was under the impression that Crispin had run away with Herbert so he'd gone to Cairo to look for her.

"Herbert? Why would he think I'm with Herbert? Didn't he get my note?"

"When you both disappeared, he assumed you went together. Dr. Pierce tried to convince your father that you had no reason to leave with Herbert, but you know how single-minded your father can be. He would hear nothing of it. Confidentially, I think they had a bit of a row, because she left, too. The driver who took her to the airport said she was returning to New York."

"Where's Dad now?" Crispin asked. Ashraf didn't seem to understand what she was saying because the connection started to fail. The last thing Crispin heard was a jumble of disconnected words. "I…hear…you there? Where…call you?"

Crispin was still focused on the interrupted conversation when she joined Sophie and Salma in everyone's favorite spot, the living room, where floor pillows were piled on a silk carpet next to windows overlooking Kensington Park. The carpet had been especially designed and hand-tied for Salma at a carpet school in Saqqara and was the apartment's one exception to what was otherwise fully westernized décor.

A morning snack of pistachios, figs, and dates was spread out on an antique cotton serving cloth. Crispin eased in next to Sophie, who handed her a cup of coffee and a small plate. Crispin ate without tasting, listened without hearing.

Salma carried the burden of the conversation with stories about the sexy young gardener who had been helping her improve the plantings around her rooftop pool in Heliopolis. "That reminds me," Salma said, addressing Crispin. "Did Ashraf give you the brooch I found?"

"What?" Crispin asked, when she realized the question was intended for her.

"The pin. The butterfly."

"Oh, yes. I'm sorry I didn't thank you. It means a great deal to me. I keep it with me," she said, reaching into her pocket and holding it up.

"May I?" Sophie asked. Crispin handed it to her.

"In fact, it came to me not long after I found Mother's field journal," Crispin said, explaining how she'd found the journal in a box of her mother's belongings stored in her father's attic.

Salma told them that she remembered the box because she and Sophie's grandmother had packed it away and shipped it to the States to save Daniel the pain.

"I don't remember ever seeing any of the things inside," Crispin said. "Dad must have stored it in the attic and forgotten it."

"That would be so like him," Salma said. "To pack it away so that it couldn't hurt him."

Crispin wasn't listening. She was distracted by Sophie, who was holding the brooch to the light, watching how the sun reflecting through the cutwork created a pattern on the wall. Elaborate designs of enamel were imbedded in the gold wings of the brooch. While the clever use of color brought balance to the piece, the regularity was an illusion. The inlayed pieces of enamel were asymmetrical. Even in poor light the intricate spectrum of the pattern shifted from emerald blue to turquoise against the background of Venetian glass, sprinkled with golden foil flecks.

Crispin tilted her head, first to the left and then the right, craning to get a better angle on the image. Then she saw it clearly. It was distinctive, familiar, and unmistakable. Crispin remembered seeing it before. Now she understood.

It was the crescent insignia of the Fellowship of Setesh. She remembered how Herbert had described the ancient symbol when he was telling stories about the Setesh over lunch right after she joined her father and the rest of the earthquake evaluation team in Luxor. When he drew a rough sketch of the symbol, she remembered thinking that it vaguely resembled the universal power symbol or on/off switch on a computer, since it too was an incomplete circle with a slash running through the opening. The angle of the line for the Setesh symbol was more ominous. It suggested a knife-like configuration rotated to a sixty-degree axis at two o'clock. Herbert said some believed that the icon originally represented a dagger through the heart of the world.

Salma was still talking. "I must say, I was surprised when the brooch turned up. I can't remember your mother ever going anywhere without it. I always assumed it went with her, you know, when the plane..." Salma paused to sip her tea, allowing her sentence to die unfinished. "Did you notice the hinge in the middle? It lets the wings go back and forth."

Salma told them that Melete had the brooch manufactured to exact specifications by jewelry artisans in Luxor when the twins were toddlers. She said that's how she knew about the moveable wings.

"Show us," Sophie asked, handing the brooch to Salma.

To free the wings, she held the pin with both hands, gently moving the right wing up and the left down. She then pulled them away from each other and reversed the motion, freeing the wings to flutter on a hidden hinge. As the delicate wings moved, the butterfly changed from a fully open wingspan to upright wings folding almost against each other the way they might look when the butterfly was perched on a twig. The dramatic effect produced a sharply modified profile.

The second she saw the radical change in the shape of the pin, Crispin took the pin from Salma and excused herself, hurrying to her room.

"We understand, dear," Salma called after her.

Crispin pulled her mother's journal from her bag. She lined up the new wingspan profile to the top of the journal where there was a telltale imprint in the soft leather near a hinged clip designed to hold pads of paper. It was not the first time that this innocent little brooch had been in contact with just that spot. As

Crispin played with the wings, moving them gently into different configurations, the hinge mechanism in the brooch ejected a slim, toothpick-size rod. Three grooved brackets popped out around the tiny rod once it was free from the hinge.

She needed no explanation. It matched a small opening in the clip that held paper. It was just below the telltale indentation in the leather that had been made by the wings of the butterfly. It was clear this "key" had been used here many times before.

Before Crispin could insert the key into the spine of the journal, there was a rap on her door. From the other side, Sophie asked to come in. "What are you up to?"

Crispin showed her the key.

No words passed between them as Crispin inserted the key and the mechanism smoothly unlocked the hinge. It popped open easily to reveal a storage pocket that apparently hadn't been opened in years.

Chapter Twenty-Three

Sophie reminded Crispin that they owed a call to Inspector Sabri. Now that she'd learned about her mother and the Fellowship of Setesh, however, Crispin wanted to put as much distance as she could between herself and the law. She'd concocted an elaborate tale about how she'd had to abandon her volunteer work in the desert due to an unexpected academic deadline. Crispin rehearsed her side of the conversation with Sophie and then asked to be left alone. As it turned out, the lie wasn't necessary.

"The Inspector has been expecting your call. He is in the field. I will patch you through to his mobile phone," the police officer at the front desk told her.

Before Crispin could say anything, the inspector took command of the conversation. He was blunt and to the point. "Your father has disappeared."

"What do you mean, disappeared?"

Sabri, who was standing at the opening of an alley near al-Azhar Street in Cairo, told her that Dr. Leads had contacted him asking for a meeting. They'd agreed to meet at the El-Fishawi Café in the celebrated Khan el-Khalili Market. The café was a perfect place for the meeting since it was a haunt for the Cairo literati and political set. Men crowded in to drink potent coffee and enjoy flavored tobacco from water pipes of painted glass.

He told Crispin that when he had arrived a waiter told him that a man fitting Dr. Leads' description had just left. In the face of tough police questions and threats of arrest, the waiter opened up, saying that he had been on his way to Leads' table with mango juice and coffee when two burly men came in. Although Dr. Leads did not appear to want to go, the men forced him into a waiting car. The waiter could give only the barest details about the car and the men. Sabri said he had the waiter under interrogation and expected he would tell them more.

"I am tracking a connection and if I am right, your father is in the hands of those behind the thefts."

A battery of questions erupted in Crispin's mind. Before she could ask them, Sabri dropped the other shoe. "You also need to know that the man we caught in the Museum, the one who attacked you, he has been released from jail."

"How?"

"I don't know how it happened but I promise you that I will find..."

Inspector Sabri wasn't able to finish the sentence. A tall man emerged silent and unseen from behind him. He wore a blue rubber nurse's glove on his right hand and in it was a swatch of fabric that resembled a nicotine patch. Before Sabri was aware of his presence, the tall man pressed the swatch onto the bare skin of the officer's neck just above his shirt collar and held it in place.

On the other end of the line, Crispin heard the policeman's breathing become labored as if his tongue had thickened. It sounded like he had stumbled and collapsed. The panting sounds of struggling breathing came to an end by the time Crispin heard someone else speak. The voice was disguised so that Crispin couldn't tell whether it was a man or woman. The message was clear. "The authorities can no longer help you. We have your father. You have what we want. We will contact you soon about a trade."

The man in the alley switched off the inspector's cell phone and crushed it beneath his heel. He then peeled the glove from his hand, encasing the poison swatch inside and tossing it and the phone into a nearby trashcan. He removed the police investigation file from the inspector's death grip and escaped down the alley.

A stunned Crispin stared at her phone as if the incomprehensible conversation that had ended so abruptly was a transmission from another dimension. She went in search of Sophie and Salma. Crispin's fear trapped language in her throat so when she tried to speak it came out in disjointed, nonsensical syllables. She had to concentrate to regain command so that she could tell them about the conversation and its peculiar end. "I've got to go back, back to Cairo and find Dad."

It took both Sophie and Salma to convince Crispin to stay in London.

"If whoever has your father can get to the police, what do you think you can do?" Sophie implored. "We'll have to wait until you're contacted."

Salma promised that Ashraf would make calls to political and business contacts in Cairo and to friends in the government. "What can be done to find Daniel will be done," she said. "I give you my word."

The mention of Ashraf reminded Crispin that he'd said that Herbert had gone missing as well. "Herbert told me that he was leaving the Valley on family business."

"What business?" Sophie asked.

"I don't remember. I'm not even sure he said. Do you think he has something to do with what has happened?"

Crispin was almost afraid to hear the answer, afraid to find out that her father and Herbert were adversaries in a deadly criminal game.

Looking at her watch, Sophie added, “I hate to say, but if we’re going to make it to Ida’s services we have to leave right away. If you’re up to it.”

***

At the church Crispin was thankful to see that the place was packed. Some of those in attendance were undoubtedly curiosity seekers drawn by the macabre way in which Ida had died. Given the distress on most of the faces, however, Crispin knew the majority were sincere mourners and friends.

Surrounded by people who had admired and loved Ida, Crispin thought again, as she so often had, that it was in the rite of burial that one of humankind’s purest forms of compassion was best articulated. Where else but at such a purposeful gathering could one find so many individuals, strangers really, who were bound to each other for a brief time by communal grief? Crispin doubted that the people in the church that day would ever again have a reason to be together. They represented facets of Ida’s life that, but for her death, would otherwise never make contact. Through this ritual, they had found a place where their personal anguish could be safely released into the embrace of strangers. The full measure of compassion required both offering up one’s own loss to others and taking up a share of their grief.

They took seats at a pew near the middle of the Holy Trinity Church. Crispin noticed Thurman seated up front. The old man acknowledged her with a nod. There were other familiar faces from the British Library and the B.M., including Mrs. Powell, who had stationed herself near Sir Percy. The old peer, looking regal and rigid, was flanked by an equally rigid entourage.

Because she was looking ahead, Crispin didn't notice Tony until he leaned down from behind her and asked if there was room on her row. Sophie squeezed in to make an extra space.

"I thought you might need a friend," he said, reaching to hold Crispin's hand.

Crispin evaded his touch, nodding her head to indicate that the services were beginning.

After the graveside service, everyone huddled in clusters on the church lawn and sidewalks. Crispin was thankful when Thurman joined them. "We've lost a national treasure," he said with a melancholy tone.

Before Crispin could respond, Mrs. Powell walked up. "Good afternoon, Mr. Thurman. Ms. Leads," she said in a formal, stiff tone, acknowledging each with a slight nod. "This is certainly an unfortunate state of affairs. What it will mean for our reputation at the Library, I can only guess."

Crispin started to introduce Sophie, but was interrupted when Thurman excused himself, taking Mrs. Powell by the arm. "There is something I must tell you," he said as they moved out of earshot.

Sophie took advantage of the opening to question Tony. "How'd you like Egypt?" she chided.

Before Tony could answer, Crispin gasped. Across the lawn she saw the man with the birthmark. "That man," she said in a shaking voice. "I think he's the one who attacked me in Cairo."

Just then the man with the birthmark blended into the crowd and dropped out of sight.

"Stay here. I'll find him," Tony said as he ran away.

"The lengths to which some men will go to dodge a question," Sophie said in a lame attempt at humor.

Crispin pulled a shaking hand out of her pocket and showed Sophie an envelope. It hadn't been in her coat when she left Salma's apartment for the funeral. "Let's get out of here. Now!"

***

Sophie and Crispin went to Harrods, but not to shop.

In the years since Egyptian businessman Mohamed al-Fayed bought the House of Fraser Group, parts of Harrods had taken on the ambiance of an overpriced tourist attraction. Boutiques on the first floor slapped the name and logo of the venerable old department store on everything from coffee mugs to T-shirts. One of the most incongruous additions was a garish, shrine-like display evocative of the pharaohs. It had been erected by al-Fayed to honor his son, Dodi, and Princess Diana following their untimely deaths in Paris in 1997.

After Sophie and Crispin made their way through the retail levels to the business offices at the bottom of a discreet stairway, a receptionist directed them to Suite G-45. She told them that it was one of several suites rented to independent business tenants and was not, therefore, directly associated with the store. Like the overpriced souvenirs and clotted cream the tourists snatched up, the mailing address inside the famous retailer was clearly intended to offer a certain air of respectability. When they rented office space at Harrods, by association businesses also rented some of the store's luster.

Suite G-45 was locked. A sign on the door explained a great deal: "Nile Crescent: Importers of Exquisite Antiquities. Sales by Appointment Only."

Anything coming through the Nile Crescent was intended for private sale. There was no shortage of wealthy people around the world who were willing to pay for the privilege of owning a genuine piece of ancient memorabilia. Some private collectors had no scruples and did not bother with standards of international law or restrictions regarding export of historical treasures. Industrial and public buyers, such as museums, were a different story. Not only would they require exhaustive documentation of authenticity, but they would also want proof that what they purchased was legally exported with requisite government approval.

Sophie and Crispin waited near the locked office for more than an hour. When no one came, they left in frustration. They were on a tight schedule. They had another stop to make before their 4:00 p.m. flight to New York City so they added Nile Crescent Imports to their growing list of unanswered questions.

***

More than three hundred kilometers west of Giza in the Bahariya Oasis, Herbert climbed up a ladder leading from an underground excavation. He stopped only long enough to make sure that no one saw him before dashing to the nearby jeep. Driving off, the car accelerated to eighty miles per hour, and then disappeared in a plume of dust. Below ground, a series of perfectly timed explosions punctuated the caverns. The resulting vortex slowly sucked in the top layer of surrounding sand and the caves began to silently fill. Soon the entrance was obscured. Before long it was if the entrance had never been there.

Chapter Twenty-Four

Late that evening Georgia was dancing around her New York City apartment, listening to Willie Nelson on her iPod while blowing on her wet fingernails. That's why she didn't hear the doorbell until it chimed during the momentary silence between songs.

"Hold your horses. Can't you wait?" she yelled as her visitor switched to impatient banging. The banging continued as Georgia ignored the peephole and fumbled with an assortment of deadbolts and locks. When she finally managed to get the door open, she let out a screech that could be heard two floors away.

Sophie's fist was in midair, ready to deliver another blow to the door, and a sheepish Crispin was grinning behind her. "It's about time," Sophie snarled playfully as she gave Georgia a hug.

Although the three college roommates hadn't been together in some time, they easily returned to a familiar routine. Georgia offered to call for a delivery from a neighborhood deli. Her friends were too hungry to wait. Instead, they gathered around the dining table to nibble on leftover Chinese takeout from Georgia's nearly bare refrigerator.

"Catch me up," Georgia said.

At first Georgia interrupted them with questions. As Sophie and Crispin filled in the story, she grew quiet. Their narrative arced to a dramatic climax when Crispin told her about opening her mother's journal to find postage-stamp-sized sheets of microfilm.

"We could tell by holding the film up to the light that while it had a few photographs it was mostly pages of a manuscript."

Sophie interrupted, "The details were impossible to make out."

After Ida's funeral and the unsuccessful trip to Harrods, they'd gone in search of a public library with a microfilm reader. In the age of digital documentation, it took several stops to find a reader that would accommodate the outdated film technology. When they were finally able to read the microfilm it contained a bombshell.

Some of the microfilm sheets were Melete's simple journal entries and daily observations that did no more than reinforce things that Crispin already knew, or thought she knew, about her mother. Melete had fallen in love with the people and the culture of Egypt. She was at home in the casual surroundings and adopted the local mode of dress, favoring loose cottons and open-toe shoes.

"In places her descriptions were poetic," Crispin said. "Especially when she wrote about walking barefoot, comparing the feel of the hot, dusty sand pressing against her feet to that of a mother's touch."

"I love it," Georgia said. "Can you read me some?"

Crispin shuffled some of the papers and then found a passage she liked: "Tonight, I was captivated by the sky again. I felt as if I could escape into the pure blackness of it. The starlight designs of the night are a kind of divinity. I can see the hand of God writ large against a canvas of limitless size, color, and form. When I stand beneath these constellations I feel one with the ancient civilization and those who stood on this very sand and looked at these same stars and constructed from them a purpose for life and a life after death."

"She may never have read the work of Carl Sagan, but when she wrote about the stars, her observations that they gave precious meaning to the smallness and fragility of earth in the great, infinite span of all that you could see sounded very much like the musing of an astrophysicist," Crispin said.

Reading her mother's words reminded Crispin of how much she had lost that day on the tarmac, the sensitive and passionate woman she never got to know.

What she didn't say, couldn't say, was how surprised and disappointed she was to find almost no mention of herself or her brother in her mother's writings. It was as if Melete's love for Egypt had left little room for them.

Trained as an artist, Melete threw herself into all aspects of daily Egyptian life and donated untold hours as a volunteer at local hospitals, schools, and charities. Her early journal entries were hopeful and full of her love for life. As the years passed, however, an increasing emotional turbulence began to seep into the entries.

The pages of microfilm were, however, much more than musings about life in Egypt. Melete had secretly pieced together a detailed history of theft and murder by the infamous Fellowship of Setesh. Crispin had no idea when or why Melete's research into the Fellowship began. From the details in her notes it was clear that she had been at it for some time. "Mother documented illegal activities, working her way from her time back through time, decade by decade," Crispin said.

Melete's notes got as far as a few years before the Carter era. Her narrative ended only days before her sudden death. It was clear that Melete, like Crispin, believed there were serious, unresolved questions surrounding the artifacts from Tut's tomb.

And, more to the point, her mother was closing in on proof that there was a connection to the Setesh.

"It's ironic that I worked forward in history from Carter and Carnarvon and mother worked backward from her own contemporaries into the past," Crispin said.

If Melete's work was read in conjunction with Crispin's, the story was nearly complete. The microfilm photographs that accompanied Melete's narrative were of cunning Egyptian objects that she said had recently been auctioned or sold. Only one had a cartouche connecting it directly to Tut. That's why Melete had gone to London, to consult with someone at the Egyptian collection. Her airplane had crashed on her return flight to Cairo.

The timing of Melete's investigation had been fortuitous. It came at the same time that there was increasing international "Tutmania" in the mid-1970s as the result of a decision by the Arab Republic of Egypt to pay homage to the American Revolution Bicentennial by mounting a spectacular tour of Tut artifacts in the States. The traveling exhibition included some of the most splendid gold objects from the boy king's tomb. At about that same time Thomas Hoving, then director of New York's Metropolitan Museum of Art, was writing his exposé. Ultimately, his bestseller would insinuate that Carter had systematically hidden precious objects from authorities.

"Mother's work goes much further, however, and shows that the few items Hoving documented were just a drop in the proverbial bucket."

After reading her mother's story, Crispin now fully understood parts of the conversation she'd overheard between her father and Ashraf. Her mother's research had been a threat to the Setesh and she'd paid dearly for it.

"And now they have Dad, too," Crispin said. "If they want Mother's evidence, I'll give it to them."

They were so caught up in their discussion that everyone jumped when Georgia's purse suddenly rang. When Georgia answered her cell phone, she looked from Sophie to Crispin, momentarily confused. "Herbert," she mouthed as she tried to hand the phone to Crispin.

Crispin vigorously signaled that she didn't want to talk to Herbert, so Sophie took the phone from Georgia and hung up without so much as a "goodbye."

Sophie reached out and turned Georgia's cell phone off when it rang again, circumventing incoming calls. When Georgia objected, Crispin explained that everyone she'd met in London, especially Herbert and Tony, was under suspicion.

Sophie reminded Georgia that according to Melete's narrative, both men were ideal recruits for the Fellowship of Setesh. Herbert's family reputation, if not its very fortune, depended on preserving the carefully crafted history of the Tut discovery. In fact, Melete had written about several run-ins with Herbert's father and her suspicions that he knew more than he let on about the purloined artifacts from the 1920s.

Then there was Tony, who perfectly fit the profile of the archetypical Setesh recruit. He was bright and ambitious but from a poor family. Like Carter before him, he yearned to fit in with his high-society acquaintances.

Crispin didn't seem to be listening. She was thinking about Herbert's call. "Georgia," she said. "Give me your phone."

Before they could ask her what she was doing, Crispin turned it on and called up the menu of recently received calls. The last incoming call had a 212 area code. Herbert was in the city.

***

Is it possible to be too tired to sleep? Crispin wondered as she walked the floor of Georgia's apartment that night. She made an effort to be quiet because Sophie was sleeping on the pullout sofa in the living room. She envied her friend's ability to go to sleep anytime, anywhere. Sophie told her that she'd inherited the talent from her father, who was notorious for sleeping on the job.

"For me, it's like a light switch. When it's time to sleep, I just flip the switch," Sophie said. "Waking up, now, that's a different story."

Crispin was just settling into a chair by the window and wrapping herself in a blanket when her phone rang. Fortunately, she was able to grab it on the first ring. Her relief on hearing Clinton's voice was short-lived. He was calling from a bay island off the coast of Honduras, where he was stranded. Roatan was in the middle of a storm of biblical proportions. Not only was the local airport closed, but the ferry from La Ceiba was also riding out the gale on the mainland. All oceangoing vessels, whether large or small, had been anchored away from the shore.

"Crisp, I'm still trying, but it doesn't look good," he told her. "Tell me what's going on."

Talking in hushed whispers so as not to disturb her friends, Crispin answered questions and filled her brother in on her plans for the next morning. All she knew from her father's abductors was that she would be contacted during an auction at Sotheby's. The note told her when to report to Sotheby's. She'd found the instructions in an envelope in her pocket when she left Ida's funeral. Someone had slipped it into her overcoat.

"Any ideas about who gave you the envelope?" he asked.

"No, there are too many possibilities."

Clinton listened without interruption as Crispin told him about Ida's funeral until she mentioned the man with the birthmark.

"Describe him again. What did you say he looked like?"

Crispin described the man, who was taller than her brother and had long, black hair.

"I'm guessing he is of Middle Eastern descent," she said. "What made him distinctive was the port-wine mark that nearly covered his forehead."

"It may seem crazy but that sounds a lot like Tarek."

"Tarek, of course. My God, I think you're right. I knew there was something familiar, but I couldn't put my finger on it."

Tarek Hilmy was the son of one of the Mediterranean Gang and a childhood playmate. Although Tarek was four years older, Clinton was his friend during the time their families were together in Egypt. Some of the other boys made fun of Tarek because of his birthmark. Clinton never seemed to notice it. Shortly after Melete's death, Dr. Leads returned to the United States with the twins. The last time the families had talked was a few years later when they heard that Tarek's father had been killed in an accident at an archeological site in Iraq and his mother was planning to move the children to England. After that, the Gang lost contact with the Hilmy family. Clinton and Crispin tried to think of all the possible explanations for why their childhood friend would suddenly turn up in Cairo and try to hurt Crispin.

"Our problem is we don't have sufficient facts on which to base a conclusion," the ever-practical Clinton said.

***

The next day, seated in the aisle of a back row in the auditorium at Sotheby's with Sophie and Georgia, Crispin was finding it hard to concentrate as she waited for word of her father. She jerked every time someone walked by. The sorry state of her jangled nerves was exacerbated by the fact that she'd spent most of the previous night awake.

In an effort to stay focused, Crispin began to flip through the auction catalog. The cover looked identical to the one that Inspector Sabri found in Tarek's car when he was arrested in Cairo. Inside was a startling difference. The three pieces that matched Crispin's negatives from the British Museum—the alabaster statue of Bes, the delicate statue of gold, and the infant's inlaid necklace—were no longer featured in the catalog. Someone had pulled them from the sale.

There had to be some kind a connection between Dr. Leads' abduction and the change in the auction inventory. For the life of her, Crispin couldn't figure out what that connection could be. Now she was mentally kicking herself for spending so little time investigating the export designation for the warehouse items when she and Sophie visited Harrods after Ida's funeral. It was just possible, Crispin thought, that the three pieces had been pulled from the auction because of some shadow on their authenticity or a paperwork snafu. It was impossible to know for certain.

The auction seemed to take forever. At another time, Crispin might have found the wrangling and price competition for the various objects interesting, even exciting, but today it was all just one big distraction. Even Georgia, the consummate shopper, seemed disinterested. After two hours, the auction was winding down and they had received no word or attempt by anyone to contact them.

Glancing to her left Crispin saw Sophie shrug and mouth a question. "What now?"

The note given to Crispin at Ida's funeral had been explicit: they could expect further instructions at the auction. The auction was over and nothing.

"Let's go," she told her friends.

They were on the way out the door when one of the assistant auctioneers approached them. "Ms. Leads?"

"That's me."

"This is for you," he said, handing her an embossed envelope of eggshell vellum.

Crispin's hand shook as she accepted it from him. She struggled to tear open the envelope. Sophie took it from her and opened it. After reading the contents, she looked at her friends. "Anyone in the mood for a party?"

Chapter Twenty-Five

It felt peculiar to be dressed in evening wear and nursing a cocktail in a room full of art patrons, financiers, socialites, and politicians. The note handed to them at Sotheby's was an invitation to an after-hours party at the Metropolitan Museum of Art to celebrate the premiere of a new exhibition. Across the embossed invitation someone had written: "Bring what we want and you will get what you came for." So, a fancy-dress gala is exactly where Crispin and her friends found themselves that night.

Caterers had converted the Great Hall into a setting appropriate for a lavish party. Potted palms with their trunks wrapped in tiny white lights defined the edges of the party rooms and flowering plants-ringed bases of the Greek and Roman statues. Tables along windows facing Fifth Avenue were crowded with serving platters and chafing dishes. Nestled among them were towering flower arrangements of cymbidium orchids, white tea roses, arabesque calla lilies, and hydrangeas. Sprays of tiny lavender orchids spilled over the edges of ersatz urns. A string quartet supplied background music as tuxedoed wait staff passed trays and freshened drinks.

Crispin was dressed in a knee-length black organza cocktail dress with a swing skirt. The neckline flattered her décolletage because it scooped over her shoulders to cap sleeves. She'd borrowed the Viktor & Rolf from Georgia. Sophie had borrowed a bright red Rochas bustier with a formfitting mini that emphasized her long legs, and Georgia wore a rust and chocolate cocktail dress by Carolina Herrera.

As she scanned the crowd in expectation that every person who smiled in her direction was the contact person, Crispin nervously fingered her mother's butterfly brooch. It was a lifeline tethering her to her mission. Time after time she was disappointed or embarrassed when she made quizzical eye contact that either confused or flattered an art patron.

They must think I'm a flirt or, worse, a fool, Crispin thought.

Sophie tried to calm her friend, handing her a small plate of fruit and canapés. "Here, you can at least pretend to eat."

"Thanks," Crispin said, taking the plate. "At least it gives me something to do with my hands."

In a hushed, more encouraging tone, Sophie whispered, "Hang in there. It's almost over."

Georgia joined them, breathless and excited. "I was just visiting with one of my daddy's old friends from back home and you'll never guess who he said he met tonight," she said. "Guess."

"Please, Georgia, I'm in no mood to play guessing games," Sophie snapped.

"Bless his heart, he told me just now that he'd met an 'honest-to-goodness' British earl," Georgia said. "The heir to the estate of no less than, are you ready?"

"Georgia, I'm not in the mood," Sophie interrupted.

"Lord Carnarvon, his own self!"

"Herbert?" Crispin asked.

"As I live and breathe."

Before Crispin could fully absorb Georgia's news, Sophie caught sight of a familiar face across the room.

"It looks like the gang's all here," she said, indicating a small cluster of partygoers who stood near the edge of a row of palm trees that partially blocked the way that led to the café on the southern side of the Museum. The caterers had left just enough room between palms so they could service the party tables from the kitchen.

Behind the palms, almost hidden, Crispin saw what Sophie saw: Tony. He was engaged in an animated conversation with a man she didn't recognize. Before Crispin could react, however, the crowd movement obscured him from view. When Crispin could again see the side hall, the pair had disappeared.

"I can't stand this waiting," Crispin said as she moved toward the opening in the palms. "Let's see if we can find them."

"Georgia, find Herbert and don't let him out of your sight," Sophie ordered while following Crispin.

Ducking behind the palms, Crispin found the hall that led through the dimly lit Rockefeller Wing. For reasons she couldn't fully explain to herself, she felt the need to hide her presence. She moved through the hall with caution, taking refuge behind a display of fifteen-foot Amat memorial poles from New Guinea.

There was a surreal feeling to the night. City streetlights reflected through the yawning southern windows, creating wedges of light and shadows. The effect was as if she were trapped inside a Cubist painting with its monochrome palette of blacks, whites, and grays.

That's when Crispin saw Tony and the stranger emerge from a shadow only to turn down a back hall and into the two-story gallery of European art that hugged the eastern courts. Crispin was so absorbed watching them that she was startled and nearly yelled out when Sophie tapped her shoulder. Sophie, who had been only a few steps behind, put her finger to her lips, signaling for silence.

They tailed the men through the ornate and decorative European arts collection until they reached the adjoining gallery, where a delicate, wood-carved choir screen separated the paintings from displays of weaponry. The men had disappeared. Crispin and Sophie paused only for a second, considering which direction to go, when Crispin felt, more than heard, something moving above them on the second-story loft that rimmed the gallery. Before she could react, a battle-axe flew at them, landing only inches from her feet. It was from one of the wall displays.

Crispin and Sophie took refuge between two armored horses as an onslaught of polished swords, spears, helmets, and miscellaneous unidentified flying metal objects rained from above. Fortunately, the armor that covered the mannequin horses and their riders, engineered to guard gallant knights in battle, did its job again, protecting the two as they huddled out of danger.

As quickly as it had begun, the attack stopped. Taking a deep breath, Crispin and Sophie cautiously revealed themselves. There was no sign of who was responsible for the attack. The floor around them was littered with antique weaponry, some of which was damaged and bent.

"This way," Crispin said softly, gambling on the instinct that told her that the pair they had been following would continue on course through the eastern hall rather than double back toward the party.

Passing through an open-air courtyard that led to the American Wing, Sophie and Crispin found themselves in a side hall where they again had to make a choice: go up a long staircase or turn right into the Sackler Wing, where the Temple of Dendur stood.

Before Crispin and Sophie could make up their minds, fate intervened. Down the stairs came two men, one more than six feet tall. Both looked as if they had serious disregard for government warnings against the dangers of steroids. They each had a firm grip on Dr. Leads, propelling him along between them. Leads' eyes had the dull and out-of-focus stare of someone who had been drugged. Normally impeccable, he looked dirty and disheveled, his hair a tangled mess and his face long overdue for a shave. Even the cast on his left arm was filthy and cracked.

Crispin wanted to run to her father, but Sophie held her back. They were no match for the men one on one. They would need the element of surprise.

***

Meanwhile, Georgia did as instructed, returning to her father's friends. They gave her a good description of Herbert and, at their suggestion, she began her search near the front entrance. She recognized Herbert the instant she saw him. It was the cut of his Savile Row, hand-tailored tuxedo that, to a clotheshorse like Georgia, made him easy to spot.

Crispin and Sophie are right, she thought. *You are beautiful.*

Herbert moved through the crowd, avoiding with tact an elderly matron who approached him and making his way with care to the edge of the crowd near the main entrance. He glanced around and then slipped into a darkened corridor that led past the gift shop and reception area and down the back hallway.

Pit stop? Georgia wondered as she followed him.

She saw Herbert step into a freight elevator. She watched the lighted panel above the door to see which floor he stopped at and then, determined not to lose her prey, Georgia bounded down the nearby stairs to the ground floor gallery that housed the Met's renowned Costume Institute Collection.

At the sight of the room packed with glass cases displaying Dior, Chanel, Versace, Gaultier, Valentino, and Schiaparelli gowns, she whispered under her breath, "Get thee behind me, Satan. My Southern Baptist mama would say, 'To covet is to sin.'" Before she could get her bearings, one of the tuxedoed mannequins materialized behind her, grabbing both her arms in a firm grip. "Who are you and why are you following me?" the figure whispered in her ear.

"Why, I am Karen Claudia Marie Farris of the Savannah Farrises. You are, I believe, Herbert Van Snyder III, are you not?" she answered without fear.

"Crispin's friend?"

"One and the same," Georgia replied, turning and offering her hand. "You can call me 'Georgia.' Everyone does."

***

An entire wing with pyramidal glass walls had been added to the Met to accommodate the Temple of Dendur when it was transplanted to New York from Upper Nubia. Construction of a second Aswan Dam had doomed the Temple's original home as Lake Nasser inundated the Nubian homeland. Built in 15 BC to honor the goddess Isis, Dendur had been taken apart stone by stone and installed in New York City in 1978. Many experts considered it one of the finest temples in all of Egypt.

The man nearest the Temple seemed to be counting stones while his burly companion held Dr. Leads.

"What's he doing?" Crispin whispered to Sophie. Before her friend could answer, a section of the Temple's support wall slowly began to rise like a window opening. It stopped at the man's shoulder height, so he had to stoop to enter. The man behind him pushed Dr. Leads through the opening before it began to quickly slide back into place. It all happened so fast that Sophie and Crispin only caught a quick peek at a steep stairway into the bowels of the Museum before the panel closed shut.

"Holy shit," Sophie mouthed.

Before Sophie and Crispin could react, Herbert came in through the opposite entrance to the gallery and they again ducked for cover.

"I told Georgia to keep an eye on him," an irritated Sophie whispered.

Herbert confidently mimicked the wall taps of the abductors, counted stones, and then pressed in at just the right place, causing the opening to again appear. Like the men before him, Herbert ducked and disappeared below ground. Although Sophie and Crispin sprinted from their hiding place, they were too late.

"Damn it to hell," said Sophie. Crispin wasted no time. She'd watched Herbert and now, searching for the right combination, tried to imitate his exact sequence of taps on the stones.

***

Below ground, Herbert entered a stony chamber whose walls buttressed inward to a roughhewn granite floor. The architectural optical illusion produced the sensation that if any of the low ceiling's metal girders shifted by even a millimeter, the walls would careen in upon each other like a Chinese lantern after the string has been released.

Thin rectangular gaps strategically located in the stonework permitted wedges of diffused light from above to cast diagonal shafts along the length of the twenty-five by thirty-foot chamber. The room was empty save for two stainless steel tables set up in the middle of the space alongside each other. The addition of leather straps with Velcro fasteners was the only thing that distinguished these tables from the sort of embalming tables found in mortuaries.

Dr. Leads was gagged and strapped down on the table to the left. Both ankles and his uninjured wrist were tied fast. His broken left arm was pulled taut into an awkward and obviously painful position and secured with extra bandages.

Herbert ran to Leads and removed the gag.

Leads mumbled; the words were ill formed and painful because his lips and tongue were numb and parched from the damage inflicted by his captors.

As Herbert started to undo the restraints, he recognized the sarcasm of a familiar voice over his shoulder. "Welcome, Sir Herbert. We've been expecting you," Tony said as he entered through a door to one side of the stairs.

The two Egyptians who had forced Dr. Leads below ground were with Tony. They wasted no time overpowering Herbert. One grabbed his ankles and the other his shoulders, lifting him like a corpse onto the second table and then strapping him down.

"What a shame that your fancy tux is getting all mussed," Tony said, running his fingers down the lapel of Herbert's jacket.

He dismissed the two Egyptian thugs, who exited the way they had entered.

Giving the straps around Herbert's ankles another pull to make sure they were especially tight, Tony continued to taunt Herbert. "I realize these are not the kind of accommodations you are accustomed to, my Lord, but we'll do our best to make your stay, shall I say, memorable."

Tony turned his attention to Dr. Leads. "Foolish man. You broke faith with us when you went to the police. With the help of your daughter, we will recover."

"Crispin is in London. She...," Leads said with a cough.

"No," Herbert said. "She's here."

"Van Snyder, you fool," Leads said.

"Now, now, gentlemen, no recriminations, please," Tony said. "We've been playing with Crispin and her roommate, but they're quite the little soldiers. Full of surprises. You should know that by now, Dr. Leads."

Moving to stand at the foot of the table where Dr. Leads lay, Tony unrolled a canvas cloth and began arranging instruments, as a doctor might before an autopsy. "I have something here you can appreciate," Tony said as he held up two instruments.

"You're a little old to play with toys, aren't you, Tony?" Herbert said with a bravado that only seemed to infuriate Tony.

"Hold your tongue, Van Snyder, or you will get us both killed," Dr. Leads mumbled, his voice horse and dry.

The largest of the ancient implements was about the length of a chef's knife except the blade was thinner and curved, giving it the look of a scythe. It was especially designed for use by ancient Egyptian embalmers to disembowel corpses for mummification. The smaller tool was similar to a thin knitting or crochet needle. Its shaft ended in a sharp bend that resembled a Victorian buttonhook. Although half the size of the first, it was equally dangerous since the ancients designed it to be inserted through a corpse's nose to remove the brains. Both instruments appeared to have been refurbished, their edges honed to a like-new sharpness.

"To my immense satisfaction, I have found this one to be quite effective," Tony said, fingering the nose hook.

"Ida?" Herbert spat back, throwing his weight against the restraints to no avail. "What kind of sadist are you, Dexter?"

"Ida Fowler? Thurman's friend?" Leads asked.

"What a man. You must have felt incredibly brave to torture an eighty-year-old woman," Herbert added, making no effort to hide his disdain.

Unwilling, or unable, to contain his fury, Tony attacked. Bound fast to the table, Herbert was defenseless as Tony's fists rained down on him, unleashing all the pent-up anger and resentment that had accumulated against the privileged and rich since boyhood. Herbert became the surrogate for a lifetime Tony had spent pressing his nose against a window where he didn't feel welcome.

"Can't you see, Van Snyder, he's only brave when his opponent is weak or helpless," Leads mocked.

"Shut up! Shut up! Shut up!" Tony yelled with the fury of a schoolyard bully, stuffing linen into both of the men's mouths before kicking the table with his boot and storming out of the room.

He wasn't gone long. When he returned the rage had dissipated. His tantrum had had the effect of calming Tony, much like a spigot on a steam kettle. Any heat that remained was evident only in a slight flush in his cheeks. His eyes were ice. He had a black ink pen in his hand. Opening Dr. Leads' shirt, Tony marked his chest down the middle with the pen.

"I want to get this just right," Tony sneered as he raised the scythe-like disemboweling tool.

Chapter Twenty-Six

A museum guard monitoring a bank of security cameras in another part of the Met spotted Sophie and Crispin tapping around on the wall of the Temple of Dendur. The guard reached to set off an alarm, when Tarek Hilmy stepped up behind him and flashed a set of official credentials. Hilmy ordered the guard not to activate the alarm and instead tripped a switch, causing the hidden panel on the Temple of Dendur to open.

Having failed twice before to be quick enough, Crispin was ready to sprint the moment the panel rose to shoulder level. She stooped to clear the opening and bolted for the stairs.

A more cautious Sophie hesitated. "No way. Too easy," Sophie said to the empty space where Crispin had been standing. Taking a few seconds to kick off her heels and look around, Sophie followed, barefoot.

Halfway down, Crispin slowed her pace and tiptoed forward with greater stealth, uncertain about what lay ahead. At the bottom, she warily peered into the subterranean chamber. In the diffused light she saw Herbert and her father, bound and gagged. They could see her at the foot of the stairs and she could see them. The gags in their mouths prevented them from talking. Their eyes carried a frantic warning. Instead of rushing in, she stood her ground for a moment, immobilized.

Tony, who'd heard the sound of Crispin's heels on the granite, was ready to ambush her from a hiding place behind the stairway. When he lunged at her with the scythe above his head ready to strike, he cast a shadow against the cold stone floor. It gave Crispin just enough warning to dodge out of harm's way.

Before Tony could react to Crispin's evasive maneuver, Sophie arrived, ramming him with her shoulder. Sophie's momentum knocked both of them off their feet. As they clutched and rolled, Sophie pulled Tony close to her, kicking him with her feet and then jamming her knee into his scrotum with the full force of her powerful legs.

"God damned bitch," Tony grunted as he clutched Sophie's scarlet bustier and pulled her to her feet.

The tight-fitting corset allowed him to hold her at arm's length. Restricted in this way, Sophie was not able to hit back but was able to dodge the sharp blade of the scythe. Until she wasn't. The blade made contact, slashing Sophie's upper arm to the bone. As she clutched her wound, Tony threw her to the ground and jumped astride her, raising the scythe above his head to deliver the coup de grâce.

From behind, Crispin grabbed the long handle of the scythe and leaned back onto her heels, applying the strength of her whole body to keep Tony from using the barbaric instrument. For one fleeting moment, Crispin thought she was winning the wrestling match. Then Tony, who still held Sophie with his left hand, simply let go of his end of the scythe. The sudden release sent Crispin flying backwards and crashing against the wall. In the force of the fall, the scythe flew from her hand, slid across the floor, and came to rest under the table where Herbert lay.

With both hands now free, Tony repeatedly bashed an already bleeding Sophie with his fists until a vicious blow to the side of her jaw knocked her out.

Before Crispin could regain her bearings from where she lay stunned on the floor, Tony grabbed her by the throat with both of his hands, lifting her until her feet were off the ground. The excruciating pain that accompanied the slow constriction of her windpipe caused Crispin to panic and dig at Tony's hands with her fingernails. Denied oxygen, Crispin weakened and her grip began to loosen against her will.

Just then, Crispin spotted Ashraf over Tony's shoulder. The two Egyptian men who had abducted her father were behind him. Without uttering a word, Ashraf signaled instructions to the taller man, who covered the distance to Tony with a few broad steps. He took hold of Tony and with a single, expertly executed twist broke Tony's neck.

Tony's grip eased and Crispin, fighting for air, dropped to the floor, her legs too weak to support her. She imagined that Tony's eyes pleaded with her to save him just before the glint of mortality failed him and a place surpassing hope of salvation claimed his soul.

"Thank God, Ashraf...," she whispered when her voice returned, but she swallowed the rest of her sentence when Ashraf picked up the nose hook from the instrument roll where it rested at Lead's feet and brandished it before her father.

"A cunning piece of work, Daniel, don't you think?" Ashraf said. He then muttered a few words in Arabic to the second man, who reacted with surprising speed. He pulled Crispin from the floor and roughly pushed her forward so that she was positioned between the heads of the two tables.

"Now, my dear Crispin," Ashraf said in a cold, certain tone that she'd never before heard in his voice. "You have something that I want."

Struggling to regain her normal breath, Crispin surveyed the scene before her and felt fear and uncertainty melt away. It was replaced by clarity. The feeling was more than the product of simple anger or even hatred. It was deeper than either, and, ultimately, more dangerous. What Crispin felt was a kind of courage that came not from the foolhardy disregard for danger, but rather from a determination to go on in spite of it. On any other day, all that had happened in Egypt and London, the relentless assault to her body and soul, might have sent her into an emotional collapse. Not today. Her friend lay bleeding. Her father was threatened. Herbert was in danger. Lives depended on her. There was no time for sitting in the corner. There was only one direction. Forward.

Sophie's blood, which continued to seep from her wounded arm onto her bodice, soon saturated the fabric and trickled into a puddle on the floor. "I need to check on Sophie," Crispin said, smoothing out her dress.

"Give us a moment to tidy up," Ashraf ordered. At Ashraf's signal, his men lifted Tony's body and carried it out.

From the way they were positioned, Crispin, who had moved over between the two tables, could see Herbert's right hand but Ashraf, on the other side of Dr. Leads, could not. Although he couldn't speak, Herbert clutched his right hand several times and then made subtle stabbing motions. Crispin understood what he wanted.

"At least let me take the gag from Dad's mouth," she said. "He's having trouble breathing."

"Remove the gag? After all these years, you finally have what you have wished for: his undivided attention," Ashraf mocked. "We have a bit of time until my men return so, Crispin, this is your chance to astound him with your brilliance."

"You mean my research?"

"Your 'investigation' might be a better term," he said, growing cynical. "You have caused a great deal of trouble by sticking your pretty little nose where it doesn't belong. Now, tell us how you worked it out. Dazzle us, Crispin."

Trying not to let the old man's mocking rattle her, Crispin began her explanation with the facts and suppositions that she and Sophie had worked out about what had happened in the 1920s when Carter first discovered the fifth chamber and kept it a secret.

"Why do you think he did that?" Ashraf asked.

"Even though Lord Carnarvon respected Carter and considered him a friend, it's easy to imagine Carter's jealousy and resentment—always around rich people but never having any money himself," Crispin said.

"So like our poor Mr. Dexter," Ashraf smirked in false sympathy.

Crispin looked away from Herbert, knowing that what she would say next might hurt him.

"Maybe Carter justified his actions as a reward, or unpaid commission, for all his fieldwork in the hot sun while his patron sipped tea in the comfort of his country estate."

"Carter toiled while Carnarvon played," Ashraf taunted.

During her soliloquy, Crispin had paced up and down as if giving a university lecture, moving back and forth, using her hands in broad gestures, often seeming to speak to an invisible audience. In the process she managed to use her foot to nudge the scythe out from under the table so that it was within her reach but out of sight to Ashraf.

Herbert followed her every move.

Crispin worked her explanation up to the connection to the curse.

"The old newspaper clippings about the curse were most useful in identifying possible murders," she said. "I figure there were perhaps a dozen, maybe more."

"Maybe more?" Ashraf asked.

Looking up at Ashraf, Crispin detected a fleeting look in his eyes as if he thought he'd trapped her.

"Maybe your daddy can help you," he said, pulling the gag from Dr. Leads' mouth.

"Ashraf, I swear I will..." Leads said.

"Save the macho threats, Daniel. It is beneath you," Ashraf said. "Our girl has shown great resourcefulness. Now you must do something she would never expect from you and reward her with information. Yes?"

Crispin dropped her hands to her side so they came to rest unobtrusively near Herbert's.

"My daughter knows how I feel about her," Dr. Leads reacted defensively.

"Not because of anything you've ever said," Ashraf responded. "Now is your chance for redemption."

"Crispin, your mother was, well, she was so idealistic that she..."

"Joined the Fellowship of Setesh?"

"How did you find out?" her father asked, clearly surprised.

"You told me, but you didn't mean to. It's..."

"Never mind how you know, just tell us what you know," Ashraf interrupted.

"I learned a lot from Mother's journal. You see, she kept copious notes...," Crispin said, her thoughts becoming jumbled as she worked out of sight to free the straps that were holding down Herbert's right wrist. She was finding it difficult to maintain a coherent narrative.

Dr. Leads could see what she was trying to do and helped by taking up the threads of the story. "Your mother was not motivated by greed. She loved Egypt and its people."

By the time Melete had joined the underground group, Dr. Leads explained, the Setesh had been rendered nearly impotent, reduced by an internal power struggle. "Her natural leadership skills were invaluable given the void she found there," Dr. Leads said. "She earned the trust of others and rose quickly in the ranks. Since she was trained as a scholar, she naturally documented everything."

"The microfilm?" Crispin asked.

"All these years I felt safe because I believed that her journal was destroyed in the airplane crash," Ashraf said.

"Until I found it in the attic."

"Surely now you understand its importance," Ashraf said.

Dr. Leads stepped in to again run verbal interference. "Tell me, Ashraf, when did you first side with the criminals?"

"From the beginning, Daniel. I was never able to resist the money."

"And the power."

"You and the others were so easy to deceive. Good ol', fat, dim-witted Ashraf; harmless, silly Ashraf. I had you all fooled. Even Salma."

"All except Melete," Leads said with a sense of pride.

With Ashraf fully engaged by her father, Crispin was able to work on the straps around Herbert's wrist.

"Mother!" Crispin screamed with sufficient volume that it masked the noise as she undid the Velcro.

Ashraf accepted the outburst as simple female hysteria, telling Crispin, "The truth is hard, is it not?"

"That's why they took her out of the game," Leads said with a slight tremble in his voice.

"They did more than that, Daniel. They made of her an example to the price of disloyalty. They made her a martyr."

Her eyes wet with tears, Crispin took a single step that brought her next to her father. She leaned over and brushed his forehead with her hand, as a mother might when checking a child's temperature.

"Love you," he whispered, in a tone with more genuine emotion than she'd ever heard in their rote family salutation.

Over the years it had become more perfunctory than meaningful and for a moment she didn't respond, so he repeated it. "Love you."

"Love you more," she answered, cradling his hand in both of hers.

Ashraf seemed to lose interest. "No more delays. Where is the microfilm?"

"Here," Crispin said, shaking the flared skirt of her cocktail dress.

"How ingenious. Now if you please," Ashraf said.

Crispin at first teetered from one foot to the other, trying to rip her hem. Still wearing her suede evening pumps, she was having trouble maintaining her balance. "I'll need to sit," she said, dropping to the floor, her skirt billowing around her and covering the scythe.

Seated on the cold floor, Crispin carefully removed the delicate microfilm packets from where she and her friends had basted them safely into her hem. She then used the camouflage provided by her full skirt to retrieve the scythe and, as she stood, slipped it out of sight along the edge of the table under Herbert's arm.

Crispin reached across her father to hand the microfilm packets to Ashraf, who held them a moment before slipping them into the inside pocket of his jacket.

"Fair trade," Crispin said, careful to obstruct Ashraf's view of Herbert behind her. "You have the film, now let us go."

"Surely, you're not so naive," Ashraf said as he picked up the nose hook.

"I'm surprised at you, Ashraf," Dr. Leads said. "You usually don't do your own dirty work."

"How well you know me, my old friend," Ashraf scoffed. He pointed to his two men, who had silently returned and were awaiting instructions. Ashraf said a few words in Arabic and handed the nose hook to the larger man, gesturing to the other man to remain where he was.

"Now, my dear, to prove that I am not totally without sympathy, I have a reward for you," Ashraf said to Crispin. "You get to decide who will suffer a mummy's fate. Will it be your father, or, dare I say it, your lover?"

Crispin, who had rested her foot on the rocker switch that locked the wheels of the gurney where Herbert lay, pushed down, releasing the brake and then, with all the force she could muster, sent the metal table rolling across the slick floor. "Here's my answer," she shouted in defiance.

Her bold action set the room into motion the way pinball machines release energy, each action generating an equivalent reaction. Herbert, astride the flying gurney and armed with the scythe, had already freed his other hand. Though his ankles were still bound, he was still able to lean over the edge as the table rammed into the larger man, cutting deeply into the arteries of his neck with the sharp blade. The man's face turned from swarthy to a pale shade of green as he gripped at the wound and collapsed, his knees crushing into the hard floor.

The nose hook fell from the injured man's hand and slid across the room to where Sophie was lying. As the table with Herbert bounced against the opening to the stairs and slid into the nearby wall, Crispin worked to release the straps that held her father's wrist and ankles.

Herbert, still holding onto the scythe, removed his remaining restraints. His feet were numb because the bindings were so tight that they cut off his circulation. When he tried to stand he stumbled to the floor.

"You are a pathetic bunch," Ashraf said, recovering from his surprise at the sudden reversal of action. Then with a laugh that sounded like a campy villain from the early days of the talkies, he deliberately crushed Herbert's hand under his boot, forcing him to release the scythe.

Crispin finished pulling at the restraints that held her father.

Before Herbert could recover it, the second of Ashraf's thugs took action and scooped up the scythe. He then grabbed Crispin by the shoulder, brandishing it in front of her eyes.

"You wouldn't want him to blind her, now would you?" Ashraf said to Herbert, who was now on his feet. "Step back." Herbert froze in place.

Dr. Leads, now free, was enraged, as only a father can be when his child is in mortal danger. *"Monstrum horrendum,"* Dr. Leads proclaimed as if invoking a final judgment on his former friend's soul. He then threw himself at the man holding his daughter.

For Crispin the next few seconds seemed elastic, warping into unnatural time. She lived and felt the intensity of each motion and action as her father grabbed her out of harm's way. She was fully present in the moment. Her senses of smell, sight, and touch were hypersensitive. She felt her father's grip on her arm, down to the individual pressure of each finger of his hand. She smelled a lingering hint of his favorite aftershave and could read each gold flake in his eyes.

Dr. Leads' momentum was so powerful that it propelled him forward, where he took the full thrust of the vicious weapon in his abdomen. Momentarily bewildered by the unexpected quantity of blood, the man yanked hard at the scythe. Whether intentional or accidental, in that act, the curve of the scythe scooped first upwards into Leads' heart and then scraped downwards against the inside of his ribs, cutting through his lungs.

Ashraf didn't see Sophie, who'd regained consciousness and had been pulling herself across the floor with the nose hook in her hand. From the floor she gave a painful push, slashing Ashraf on his Achilles tendon. His leg crumpled and he dropped to the floor in pain just as Herbert jumped at him. Sophie, Herbert, and Ashraf were in a heap wrestling on the floor when a police SWAT team stormed in.

Only a step or two behind the authorities, Georgia let out a scream when she saw Crispin and her father. It was an extraordinary sort of scream, the kind that gained momentum as it traveled into the upper octaves, where it wavered like the rattling discharge of a Gatling gun and then trembled off the hard walls, absorbing all ambient sound in its path.

The room was left still and unnaturally quiet as if in frozen witness to the unfolding tragedy. Crispin cradled her father's body in the folds of her blood-soaked dress, her hands pressing into the cavities in his chest and abdomen, a futile attempt to hold life in place where it had already drained away.

Chapter Twenty-Seven

The media were having a field day. The headline in the *New York Post* screamed: "Cocktails. Curses. Corpses: Met Gala Turns Bloody."

Even the staid *Times* was pulling out all the stops with supplements to the page one, hard news coverage about the deaths and resulting police investigation. One sidebar featured interviews with luminaries who had attended the party. A think piece focused on the potential impact of the deaths on the Met's reputation. The third article, carried in the Business section, speculated about the connection to Sotheby's and how this tragedy, when coupled with other recent scandals, could further weaken the financial stability of the auction world.

Although the news crawl on CNN claimed "Police Question Carnarvon Heir," Herbert volunteered to handle the first round of official questions about the bloodshed at one of the world's most distinguished museums.

With Herbert's diplomatic status and pedigree, the New York City cops handled him with kid gloves as they conducted an extensive interview at headquarters. Herbert was forthcoming in his explanation, even arranging, with a well-placed phone call, to have Scotland Yard's investigative files opened to the New York police without question. The London detectives said that Herbert had been working with them and with Egyptian officials and asked that he be afforded the same courtesies as an officer of the law.

Herbert told them that he had been drawn into the investigation because of his connections with the archeological community. His role grew over time as he continued to find more evidence that the illegal sale of artifacts by Ashraf Rashad and his underground organization had a long and shameful history.

"Bit of an amateur detective, you see," Herbert said.

From the look on the face of Sergeant Phil Carson, the younger of the two policemen, Herbert gathered that the story he was telling sounded like some well-worn plot out of a dime store paperback. The older detective, who had introduced himself as Thomas Fuller, however, was inscrutable. His expression suggested that in his twenty years on the force he'd heard stranger tales than this one about hidden tombs, mummy's curses, and ancient cults.

Near the end of Herbert's story, a uniformed female officer tapped on the door and said that there was a gentleman there to see them. Tarek Hilmy was behind her.

"This is an associate of mine," Herbert said, introducing him to the two policemen.

"We've been expecting you," Detective Fuller said, standing, shaking the new arrival's hand and offering him a place to sit. He then explained to his confused young colleague that Mr. Hilmy was an undercover agent for Scotland Yard.

"I understand that the Yard first began to suspect Anthony Dexter in connection with the suspicious death of a worker involved in digitizing files for the British Library," Fuller explained. "Isn't that right?"

"He was sloppy with that one so we put a tail on him," Hilmy said. "Dexter was responsible for at least two attempts on Crispin Leads' life. I couldn't find proof, but he was our primary suspect in a fire at her London flat."

"She unknowingly came into possession of something that could incriminate the Setesh and, at first, I think Dexter was just trying to scare her," Herbert said. "But he found out that she doesn't scare so easily."

"That's right. His attacks ultimately turned deadly," Hilmy explained. "I did my best to help her in Cairo, at the National Museum, when Dexter locked her in a tomb, but he got the drop on me. Had a couple of ruffians with him. Since I was flying undercover, I couldn't let on to local authorities."

"Why kill Crispin before he got what he wanted from her? It makes no sense," Sergeant Carson asked.

"Rashad claims that over time Dexter became increasingly resentful and unreliable and his methods unnecessarily cruel. He says that Dexter especially resented Crispin and Herbert because they represented everything he didn't have—privilege and wealth," Detective Fuller said.

"It sounds like Ashraf is spinning quite a tale," Herbert said.

Fuller smiled in agreement. "He and his lawyer paint a colorful scenario. Unfortunately for Rashad, the two men he employed are ready to strike a deal with the district attorney to turn state's evidence. They're hired mercenaries, with no loyalty to the Fellowship."

Detective Fuller asked Hilmy to fill in some of the details about Rashad's illegal enterprise.

Hilmy explained that Rashad had to accelerate his scheme when a great discovery was made in the mid-1990s in the Bahariya Oasis in western Egypt. That's when archeologists found what has been referred to in the popular media as the Valley of the Golden Mummies. It is believed to contain hundreds of mummies, many of them with gilded masks and waistcoats. The excitement about the find meant that archeologists would be swarming in. Spreading excavations at the Oasis threatened to come uncomfortably close to the hiding places used by the Setesh for artifacts they were moving onto the black market. Rashad had to move quickly.

"Inevitably, he got careless," Herbert said.

"Over the years he had been careful not to move too many objects through Nile Crescent Imports at once, since a sudden surge of new artifacts might cause suspicion. The change in circumstances in the Valley of the Golden Mummies upset his timetable and what he feared came to pass," Hilmy said. "The Yard is closing down that operation as we speak."

"Is there much gold left in the desert?" Detective Fuller asked.

"Oh, I should think it's fairly well disposed of by now," Herbert answered.

After two hours of intense questioning, Herbert, whose face bore testimony to his ordeal the night before, was beginning to tire.

"Why don't we continue this tomorrow since we have some other people to interview today," Detective Fuller said.

"I am happy to stay as long as I am needed," Hilmy added.

"Before you go, I have one final question," Sergeant Carson said to Herbert. "Can you explain the secret chamber below the Temple of Dendur?"

"I only recently learned of it myself," Herbert said. He told them that the Sackler Wing was built during times of great uncertainty and political turmoil domestically and abroad. Met officials, worried about civil unrest and the strains of the Cold War, built the secret chamber as a holding place where museum treasures could be moved quickly to underground safety should it become necessary.

"It was never really needed and soon fell into disuse," he said. "Through their political connections the Setesh learned the serial code combination to the access panel and used it for the occasional rendezvous."

"Good enough," Detective Fuller said, standing to indicate the interview was over.

Chapter Twenty-Eight

An old metal drum behind the Leads' home in Ithaca was spitting fire into the early morning light. Clinton had dragged the metal drum—used every fall to burn leaves—out of the garden shed and stood huddled over it while Crispin fueled the furnace with maps, charts, and tablets covered in handwritten notes and data. She pulled notebook after notebook from the box she'd had shipped from London.

Crispin fed the fire blindly until every piece of research from her long hours of work in Luxor, Cairo, and London was consumed in the flames. Small scraps of burning paper danced in the air around the barrel for a few moments before floating to the ground as their flame burned out. Soon the ground around the maple tree, still wet with the last residue of winter ice, was littered with paper ghosts and Crispin's hair was sprinkled with ash.

Melete's journal was at the bottom of the box.

"Crisp, are you sure?" Clinton asked.

"It's part of the curse. We have to burn it."

She held it for a moment before adding it to the fire.

Then she poured the remnants of a whiskey bottle on the fire. The sudden addition of alcohol to the hot embers caused a blue flame to leap from the fire, almost scalding Crispin's face.

Clinton grabbed her away from danger, but she didn't seem to notice. She was numb and detached.

"It ends here," she said, her voice filled with self-recrimination.

No more running. No more chasing answers, Crispin thought as she buried her hands in the sleeves of her sweater to cover the new scars on her wrists.

***

Herbert looked surprised to see Sophie open the door to the Leads' family home. She was standing next to a wheelchair, holding onto the handles. When she wobbled, he grabbed her elbow.

"Whoa, there."

"Damn it. I've got to get back in shape."

After he helped settle her into the seat padded with sheep's wool, Herbert offered to come back at a better time.

"Sit, Herb," she ordered. She used her feet to roll back inside to the living room, where a fire burned in the hearth and books and newspapers were scattered on the floor.

"Yes, madam," he said with a mock salute, pulling up a straight-back chair so he could sit close to her.

Sophie sipped juice through a straw and collected her thoughts. "I think I might owe you an apology," she said, finally.

"Not necessary."

"I figured you for a troublemaker."

"Apology accepted," Herbert responded, grinning.

The self-effacing response caused Sophie to smile for the first time since she'd been released from the hospital. The smile deteriorated as she cradled her bruised jaw. "Ouch. They say it's only a hairline fracture, but it still hurts like hell."

Gingerly drinking more juice, Sophie asked Herbert to tell her about his interview with the police, adding that they were expecting a follow-up visit from NYPD. "Detective Fuller, I think," Sophie said.

"Where is Crispin?" Herbert asked.

"Upstairs."

"I'm here."

The voice came from the staircase. Crispin, dressed in wrinkled pajamas and her father's oversized bathrobe, joined them. Her hair was pulled back in a loose ponytail but haphazard tufts of hair poked out of the rubber band. Her eyes were red and swollen.

Herbert stood up when she came into the room and walked toward her as if to greet her with a hug. But she shook him off and curled up in a wingback chair, pulling a hand-pieced quilt over her legs.

"Clinton's gone into The City with Georgia to help Aunt Tilde make arrangements," she said. "We're going to bury Dad at Woodlawn next to Grandma and Grandpa Leads."

Crispin pointed to some of the newspapers on the floor. "I see you're a big hero now," she said, her words wrapped in bitterness that she made no attempt to mask.

"Newspapers are not always a reliable source for facts," Herbert said. "But, then, you know that."

"Tell me about Ashraf."

"Are you sure?" Sophie asked.

"I'm not a child."

"Ashraf is wanted for crimes on three continents," Herbert answered. "First, however, he must answer for his part in the deaths of Tony and your father."

Crispin dug her nails into the palms of her hands. "What did he tell the police?"

Herbert spoke slowly. "He's hired a first-class attorney. They claim that it's all a big misunderstanding. He's playing up his own injuries and claiming that Dr. Leads was his good friend, his death a tragic accident. As far as Dexter, Ashraf is spinning a fantasy. He insists that Dexter had become a crazed psychopath who attacked you and Dr. Leads. Ashraf says he arrived just in time to save your life and that Dexter was killed when he fought back."

"Disgusting," Sophie said.

"Tortured logic to be sure," Herbert said.

"What about the thugs who were with Ashraf at the Met?" Sophie asked. "They're the killers. They are the ones who kidnapped Dr. Leads."

"I understand they are cooperating with authorities to avoid extradition," Herbert said. "But…"

Crispin dabbed her eyes with a tissue. "They're hired guns. Who will be believed? Ashraf or the thugs?"

"Crispin, you and Clinton must know that his fictionalized version won't hold up in court. I will testify. You will tell them your side of the story."

"You have more faith in the system than I do," she answered.

"What about Salma?" Sophie asked.

"They are questioning her but from evidence so far she didn't have a clue about Ashraf's criminal operations," Herbert said.

"That sounds like our Salma," Sophie said with a grin.

"How much did you tell them about the Fellowship?" Crispin asked.

He gave them a quick summary of the most recent underground activities of the Fellowship and ongoing investigations in Cairo and London.

"How about the old stuff, from the excavation of the Tut tomb?" Sophie asked.

"You tell me," Herbert said.

Crispin's voice had a mechanical quality as she told the story of her work, part detective, part historian, weeding through the old news clippings and records about the various deaths that had been attributed to the curse. From the earliest days, Crispin said, traditionalists in the Fellowship of Setesh were sworn to protect Egyptian heritage, so they had reason to fear the international interest that Tut was generating.

"It was one thing for the Setesh Fellowship to manage a handful of archeologists, directing them away from the rich hordes beneath the sand," she said. "Carter's discovery of the Tut tomb changed everything. It meant that every armchair archeologist in the world would descend on the Valley in numbers the Setesh could neither monitor nor control."

"In other words, Carter wanted to protect his secret and they wanted to protect their ancient relics," Herbert said. "Common needs make for uncommon bedfellows."

Sophie said, "The confusion and fear generated by the curse provided a plausible public explanation for a series of gruesome deaths that plagued the Tut worksite."

"I came to believe that Carter was so desperate to keep his secret that he was willing to form an alliance with people who had questionable morals and few qualms about bending the rules," Crispin explained.

"Is it possible his alliance goes back even further?" Herbert asked.

"The goods in the fifth chamber?" Sophie asked.

"I agree," Crispin said. "It is little wonder that the records were doctored to hide the fifth chamber since Carter had systematically ransacked it early on, when he thought he had simply stumbled onto a rich cache."

"Before he made the connection to Tut," Sophie added.

"He was looking for a partner to move the artifacts to the black market," Crispin said. "Enter the Setesh."

"Then, when he figured out what he actually had, the curse came in handy," Herbert said.

"Carter undoubtedly confided in someone he trusted about the fifth chamber and it was that person who introduced him to the Setesh Fellowship."

"Do you have a name?" Herbert asked Crispin.

"I came up with several candidates, but no solid evidence. It was likely someone young and impressionable since that's the type of person who was attracted to the Fellowship. Carter could easily convince others that he had lofty motives and was only trying to protect the artifacts from unscrupulous and greedy archeologists and corrupt government officials."

"If I might add, my ancestor was highly suspicious when Carter said he would pay for the dig out of his own pocket. It was not in character," Herbert said. Carnarvon had quietly made inquiries into Carter's affairs. His business contacts in banks in Great Britain and Egypt established that Carter was making substantial deposits into his normally thin accounts.

"Before the old boy could confront Carter, a water boy stumbled onto some hidden steps, and the rest, as they say, is history," Herbert said. "At first everyone's attention was diverted by the sheer wonder of the unprecedented find. Eventually, though, Porchey had the chance to ask Carter directly, 'Have you told me everything?'"

"That fits," Crispin said. "Carter was starting to worry that Carnarvon was growing suspicious."

"Then Porchey became sick and died and the 'curse' was born," Herbert said.

"It was a perfect marriage of need and circumstance. I have a high level of confidence that at least twelve deaths attributed to the curse can be linked in some way to the Fellowship," Crispin said.

Much of it is, of course, speculative, Crispin explained. For instance, there is the case of the young water boy who had helped stage the original discovery.

"I found a brief news write-up about a cave-in that killed five workers," she said. "As is typical, the papers were more interested in the deaths of English and American notables than of humble natives. Their ordinary lives were simply too insignificant to receive widespread media attention."

She said that she probably wouldn't have made the connection, except that the Arabic news clipping was stored with all the others about the curse. It wasn't until the third paragraph of the news story that one of the five who died was identified as the ill-fated water boy. With each death the fear of the curse grew, something the Setesh found increasingly useful. So when anyone became suspicious or panicked, it was easy to dispose of him while simultaneously adding to the aura of the curse.

"A nice bit of detective work. Will you be able to provide the authorities with your evidence?" Herbert asked.

Crispin turned her head toward the window. Raindrops speckled the glass. "It's all gone now."

"I see. It is unlikely that much about these matters will ever come to light now," he told her.

Still gazing out the window, Crispin said, "So when you briefed the police you didn't tell them about Carter?"

"They didn't ask," he replied.

"Convenient," Sophie said.

"What about the information in your mother's journal? The more recent documents?" Herbert asked. "The police may ask about that since it fills in a consequential time period when the Fellowship split into competing wings. One wing led by Ashraf was corrupted and sold off antiquities. But the other exists to protect the heritage of the ancients."

"I burned it all," Crispin said, rubbing her temples, a warning sign that Sophie recognized as the precursor of a migraine.

"Do you need your meds?" Sophie asked.

"I already took something. It'll be okay," Crispin replied.

"So, you don't think the police will question us about the old stuff," Sophie asked.

"They will have their hands full dealing with what happened at the Met, not to mention two deaths in England and the murder of a policeman in Cairo," Herbert answered.

"Don't forget Madu, the dismembered man, at Saqqara," Crispin said. "His family deserves justice, too."

"And, there's the matter of the Ashraf's international antiquities fraud that goes back decades," Herbert added. "Locating, authenticating, and repatriating the pieces will take years."

"We may be able to fill in some blanks for them on that one," Sophie said, telling him about her discovery at the warehouse in Cairo.

"At first we didn't understand why so many duplicates were made but then I thought of Poe's infamous purloined letter. Sometimes, the best hiding place can be right out in the open. The real artifacts, hidden among fakes, would never be questioned by authorities."

Crispin leaned back, resting her head on the back of the chair, and studied Herbert for a long time before she spoke again. "Why didn't you tell me about your connection to Scotland Yard? Didn't you trust me?"

The sound of a car pulling into the driveway diverted Crispin's attention.

"That must be Detective Fuller," Sophie said.

Herbert stood to leave.

"Answer me," Crispin asked Herbert again. "Didn't you trust me?"

"That's a fair question. All I can say is that I've never lied to you but I am not in a position to tell you everything. At least not right now. Can you accept that answer?"

The doorbell rang.

"Herb, I withdraw my apology. You really are an ass," Sophie said, rolling herself toward the door.

Herbert followed her. When he opened the door, they greeted Detective Fuller and invited him in. Fuller shook rain off his hat and extended his hand.

"Ms. Nessim, Van Snyder. I'm here to speak in private with Ms. Leads."

***

"How did you ferret out the connections to Tut?" Detective Fuller asked Crispin.

Still wrapped in her father's robe, Crispin was aware of a sensation that was both frightening and strangely familiar. It had started when she pressed her hand to the wound in her father's chest in a futile attempt to keep his life from draining away. Her circuits misfired, disconnecting her emotional self from reality. After that she could see herself going through the motions of life but not really present in it.

She watched as the ambulances took her father and Sophie away. She let Georgia help her with the police that horrible night. She observed herself make that impossible phone call to Clinton with the news and waited for his arrival home in Ithaca. All of the things that needed to be done were done, but it seemed that someone else was doing them. For just a moment when Herbert arrived early today she felt a momentary reconnection within herself, but it had drifted away. Now, she sat before the fire, answering questions in a voice that she knew was hers but sounded like that of a stranger.

Detective Fuller had seen this phenomenon before, so he repeated his question. "How did you ferret out the connections to Tut?"

Crispin answered, "Ida Fowler and Sean Thurman, with their encyclopedic knowledge of Egyptian artifacts, were invaluable resources."

"Right, it was Ms. Fowler who found the first hard evidence of the illegal sell-off."

"So, Ida was the first to recognize its significance?"

"What do you know about it?"

Crispin explained, "I stumbled upon the evidence in long-forgotten files that likely would have remained lost except for the decision by the British Library to digitize its archival files."

"What else can you tell me?"

Crispin tried to look at Fuller, but her focus shifted left to the bookshelf and then to the carpet.

"The sordid tale," she said, "had its beginning during the original Tut excavation when the world was suddenly fascinated by sensational stories in the international media about a mummy's curse. I believe the diversion gave the Fellowship of Setesh the opportunity it needed to undertake an archeological relocation of historic proportions. A rich cache of unbelievable treasures was moved from the Valley of the Kings to the Bahariya Oasis, where it remained safely hidden away."

Almost as an afterthought she added, "The poor Egyptian press. They were never taken seriously even when they dutifully reported stories told by local villagers, who said they had witnessed surplus military biplanes from the Great War leaving the Valley laden with treasures."

"What else do you know about this Fellowship?" Fuller asked.

"Things remained stable until the 1970s," Crispin said, then patiently explained that some members of the Fellowship had wanted to maintain only their ancient mission of protection and preservation of the dead. Others wanted to use the wealth that had been secreted in the Bahariya Oasis for more than fifty years to benefit the living. They believed that some of the ancient artifacts, judiciously managed, could help the poor in Egypt, especially the Nubians, who had been displaced by the building of the High Dam at Aswan.

Fuller interrupted, "So, the resulting turmoil and power struggle gave Ashraf Rashad the opportunity he needed. He played both sides against the middle, convincing the warring factions that he was with them. In reality he was only in it for himself."

Crispin cinched tight her hatred of the man who caused the death of her parents.

She slowly rolled out the last of her theory. "After he gained power, his first act was to ravage the cult's ancient holdings. Some items were easy to dispose of since they were gold and could be melted into untraceable ingots. Unique or unusually beautiful pieces were sold on the black market."

"Do you have proof?"

She made herself look directly at Detective Fuller. "Not one shred of hard evidence."

"Let me know if any turns up," he said as he stood and walked toward the door. "You take care, Ms. Leads. I'll let myself out."

After Sophie heard the front door close she rejoined Crispin and they sat together without speaking as the logs in the fireplace slowly burned to ash.

Chapter Twenty-Nine

Crispin felt as though she were watching from somewhere just above the aging gray tombstones and fresh gray grief. Death and loss had left her mind and body disconnected. She looked down as the frigid wind floated through the open-sided tent, lifting the mourners' coats like raven parasails.

The minister was reading from the Apostle Paul's first epistle to the Corinthians: "For this corruptible must put on incorruption, and this mortal must put on immortality."

As if it finally grew weary of the separation, Crispin's mind recorded her body's far-off response. At first it was just the salty sting of tears.

"Then shall be brought to pass the saying that is written, Death is swallowed up in victory."

Then it was a tremor. And, finally, her voice, a mere whisper. "Can you forgive me?"

Clinton saw the tears and felt the tremor. He could hear the soft question, although he was afraid to answer. Afraid, because he was uncertain whether the question, so soft and yet so clear, was meant for him or for their father, whom the pallbearers were now lowering into the grave.

Crispin's mind now felt what her body felt, the heaviness that comes after hours of weeping, and of longing to undo time, to settle on a different course. A safer course. A less costly course.

On cue, she took up a handful of dirt but held onto it, as if reluctant to let go.

As she squeezed the clump of earth until it stained her gloves, Clinton cupped her hand in his. His touch eased the strain from her grip, and they were able to release the dirt into the open grave together, a gesture of final parting.

Crispin responded, releasing a soft sigh as her mind gave up the final safety of distance. She heard and saw and felt the minister recite the all-too-familiar passage that signaled the end of the service.

"O death, where is thy sting? O grave, where is thy victory?"

***

Neither Clinton nor Crispin saw the black limousine parked out of sight just beyond the funeral tent. It seemed to hover there, exhaust fumes cloaking it in haze. The limousine pulled out of the Jerome Avenue Gate and slowly made its way toward Manhattan, snaking easily through traffic before pulling up to an Art Deco office tower two blocks off Central Park East.

Three passengers exited the limousine, entered the building through double doors, and rode the elevator up to an elegant conference room that formed the centerpiece of the penthouse. Inside was a twenty-foot table engraved with the crescent symbol of the Fellowship of Setesh. Among the faces around the table were some that Crispin would have recognized: Tarek Hilmy, Mrs. Powell, Sean Thurman, Detective Thomas Fuller of the NYPD, and Michael, the bartender from the Pump & Duck.

The first of the passengers from the limousine to join them was Laurie Pierce, followed by Salma. After they took their places at the table, the last person from the limousine entered the room. Out of respect, everyone stood as Herbert entered. He walked to the head of the table and introduced Salma and Laurie as the newest members of the Setesh leadership.

"Given recent events we are indeed fortunate that our organization will have the benefit of two such experts dedicated to our continued mission to preserve ancient cultural heritage across the globe," he said, as a servant backed out of the double doors, closing them behind him. "We have a full agenda. Let us begin."

The End

What's next for Crispin? Turn the page for a taste of our heroine's third adventure in the Crispin Leads Mystery Series BLOSSOM

Blossom: A Crispin Leads Mystery

New Mexico, 2006

Crispin saw the note sticking out of the neck of an empty Glenfiddich whiskey bottle when she unlocked her office door. Someone had cleaned everything off her desk and positioned the bottle dead center.

"Not again," she mumbled as she tossed her briefcase onto a sagging wingback chair in the corner. She plopped down at her desk and studied the bottle for a minute before pulling the note out of the bottle and unrolling it.

The message was a silly rhyme on construction paper with words assembled from mismatched letters cut out of magazine and newspaper ads: "Who's to say you've gone away? Time to come out and play."

Whoever was messing with her wasn't very creative or original. When she tossed the bottle in her trashcan, she heard something rattle. She retrieved the bottle and shook it. There was definitely something inside. She held the bottle up to the light but couldn't make it out through the opaque green glass.

She turned it upside down and shook it like a ketchup bottle. After a few unsuccessful shakes, she dislodged the prize.

It was a tiny, lead Scottie dog, one of the original game tokens from a Monopoly set.

Crispin dug around in her purse to locate a key to the bottom drawer of her desk. She pulled out a shoebox and smoothed out the note, adding it to the others that had been left for her over the past six weeks.

She toyed with the tiny Scottie dog, rolling it around with her fingertips before tossing it in next to the growing stash of tacky trinkets that had accompanied the earlier notes: a miniature plastic snow globe with a nun inside, a pencil case shaped like a sarcophagus, a package of Gillette single-edge razor blades, the letter tiles D, N, and A from a Scrabble game, and a cellophane bag of multicolor Glitterati wrappers. No mints. Just wrappers.

There was a knock at her door just as she locked the desk drawer again. Her first grad student of the day was arriving for office hours with Professor Leads.

Thank You
For Buying *Digging Up the Dead*

If you enjoyed reading *Digging up the Dead* as much as we enjoyed writing it, please consider:

- ✦ Writing a review on Amazon.
- ✦ Telling your friends on Facebook and Twitter about *Digging Up the Dead: A Crispin Leads Mystery.*
- ✦ Donating a copy to your community library.
- ✦ Letting your local independent bookstore know about our book.
- ✦ Nominating *Digging Up the Dead* as a read for your book group.
- ✦ Making sure your name is on our mailing list so you receive information about future Crispin Leads adventures. Go to www.meredithlee.net or send an email to 39starswrite@gmail.com.
- ✦ Reading the award-winning first book in the series, *Shrouded: A Crispin Leads Mystery.*

Meredith Lee
(aka Dixie Lee Evatt and Sue Meredith Cleveland)

About the Authors

Meredith Lee is the pen name for the Austin-based writing team of Dixie Lee Evatt and Sue Meredith Cleveland. Meredith Lee is a woman who has no age, no future, and no past, unless Dixie and Sue give it to her. As such, she will not get older, get sick, or make mistakes, unless they allow it. She doesn't have to do laundry, clean toilets, have mammograms, or worry about the latest styles. They can give her any experience they want to from their life or withhold them. She can travel or stay at home. She can have sex or be celibate. She can get drunk and wake up without a hangover. Dixie and Sue are her all-powerful Wizards of Oz. In that way she is like the characters in their stories. She shares with those characters a special ethereal otherness apart from Dixie and Sue. They invented her and they own her, body and soul. But unlike their story characters they gave her a real, substantive, tangible, authentic piece of themselves—their middle names.

The first two installments of the Crispin Leads Mystery Series, *Shrouded* and *Digging Up the Dead*, were back-to-back finalists in the 2017 and 2018 Writers' League of Texas manuscript contests.

A former political reporter for the *Austin American-Statesman*, Dixie later taught at the S.I. Newhouse School of Public Communication at Syracuse University. While there she published a book, along with colleagues, on the communication practices of small organizations, *Thinking Big. Staying Small.*

Sue is an award-winning artist who has worked in multiple media including oil, watercolor, and fiber. Her earliest publications include articles advocating childbirth education and humanizing hospital care. *One Slip Over the Line*, Sue's work-in-progress Young Adult novel, was a 2015 finalist in the Cynthia Leitich Smith Writing Mentor Award. Sue's essays, literary memoir pieces, and short stories have been featured in award-winning literary journals, magazines, and blogs.

When Dixie and Sue teamed up to write fiction, they sold a screenplay treatment to a Hollywood producer. Although the movie was never made, they used the seed money to found Thirty*Nine*Stars, their publishing company. They also wrote a second screenplay based on the life of a Waco schoolteacher who was imprisoned during World War I because of his work with early radio broadcasting. That screenplay, *Wireless*, was a finalist for the Chesterfield Writer's Film Project in 2003.

In 2017, IngramSpark recognized Thirty*Nine*Stars with their Ignite Rising Star Award, which recognizes authors who have demonstrated a savvy approach to their self-publishing journeys.

More biographic information can be found at
www.meredithlee.net.

Acknowledgements

We wish to thank all of those who helped make this story possible.

First, we owe a great deal to Lovespell Entertainment and to the editors, agents, authors and readers who guided our work along the way, especially: Ken Sherman, Aviva Layton, Minna Proctor, Katherine Moore, David Aretha, and Laurie Hunt.

A novel like this wouldn't have been possible without on-site research in Egypt. Therefore, we are especially grateful for the expertise of Dr. Salma Ghanem, Dean of the College of Communication at DePaul University, for her insights about Egyptian culture and for the hospitality of Mr. and Mrs. Hassam Hafez and their daughter, Nihal Hafez, during a research trip to Cairo. In travels through Saqqara, Luxor, and the Valley of Kings, the instruction of two local guides, Dalia Wassim and Abdul-Wahab-Abou-Eldagag, helped to bring an authenticity to these pages for which we are eternally grateful.

We also owe gratitude to our team of experts: our tech super hero, Thomas Payne; our financial wizards, Terry Bleier Paul and Justin Moore; our cover artist, Elizabeth Mackey; two smart ladies who generously shared their legal wisdom, Manning Wolfe and Melynda Nuss; and our magical photographer, Sam

Bond, who made us comfortable during a photo shoot at the Texas State Cemetery.

Writing can sometimes be a lonely and singular undertaking, but we always had the support of a broad community of talented writers, including those who are part of Joy of Revision; Pen & Fork; Sisters in Crime; Write Submit Support; Mystery Writers of America; and Writers' League of Texas.

We especially want to thank the following individuals who selflessly offered valuable critique and support: Michael Noll, Becka Oliver, Beth Sample, Carol Dawson, Gina Springer Shirley, Betty Bewley, Rodney Sprott, Linda Robin, Rosemary Hook, Sherry Lowry, Dr. Jack Swanzy, Gogi Hale, Lisa Mann, Diana Baker, Paige Bonnivier Hassall, Mary Hale Etheredge, Kathy Waller, Bethany Hegedus, Claire Campbell, Gloria Amescua, Erin Sewall, Nancy Miller Barton, Rebekah Ann Manley, Michelle Howell Miller, Carolyn Ruppert Lucas, Jessamine Dana, June Ann Hartman, Erin Lee Golden, Linda R. Rivera, Sue Adamson, and Norris Atkins.

We were encouraged by many reviewers, readers, and book groups who read the first book in this series, *Shrouded,* and told us that they wanted to see more Crispin Leads adventures. For all of you who sent us notes, reviewed our book, and invited us to your book clubs, we can never thank you enough for your encouragement and kind words. You kept us writing! We also want to thank one of Austin's true treasures, its legendary independent bookstore, Book People, and the support of its staff, including especially Michael McCarthy, Scott Montgomery, and Abby Fennewald.

Finally, but most especially, we are grateful to our family and friends who have patiently supported us through this long, sometimes rocky, but always happy creative process: Chevis Cleveland, Patricia Hewitt, Jennifer Hallisay, Todd and Michelle Hewitt, Taya and Sed Keller, Brenda and Joe Buck, Crispin and

Paul Ruiz, Claudine and T.H. Stone, Scott and Emily Cleveland, Charlotte and Mikeal Clayton, Shane Cleveland, Rebecca, David, Isabella and Vincent Palmisano, John and Connie Cleveland, Peggy Pate, Sandra and Jeff Ransom, Emilia and Ashlynn Keller, Earl and Jean Wright, Suzanne Belser, Kathryn Roberts, Johnnie and DeDe DeMoss, Rosemary Sullivan, Jean and Jess Elliott, Lynda and Jack Bertram, Jane Hickie, Don and Nicki Beth Jones, Bob and Deanna Glasgow, Nancy and Steve Moore, Cathy Fryer, Connie Sherley, Nancy Jo Spaulding, Nancy Rogers, Hilda Valencia, Elva Schultz, Mary Alice Hearn, Ilze Aviks, Kati Bachman, and Ingrid Iverson.

Look everyone, we finished the sequel to *Shrouded*!

Shrouded: A Crispin Leads Mystery.

By Meredith Lee.

Meredith Lee, a pen name for Dixie Lee Evatt and Sue Meredith Cleveland, has crafted an exceptionally engaging mystery that begins as Crispin Leads, a young NYU graduate student, is newly arrived in Rome, where she has been awarded a Vatican grant to pursue a research project. Shortly after her arrival, a murder occurs in the Vatican offices where Crispin is to meet with a bishop to discuss her research. It's not long before another murder occurs, which soon leads Crispin and her friend Roberto to discover connections between the deaths and the Shroud of Turin.

As the well-paced narrative moves from Rome to Turin, from Spain to Paris, the plot delivers numerous twists and surprises, and the author richly describes each locale, including specific landmarks and foods unique to the regions. Even better, the characters are well developed and engaging; Crispin is a vulnerable, intelligent young woman, while Roberto provides a calming presence. He also has a secret that raises questions about his motives. Readers will eagerly await Crispin's return in future stories to watch her methodical—and absorbing—deductive skills in action. -BlueInk Review

CPSIA information can be obtained
at www.ICGtesting.com
Printed in the USA
LVHW080427161118
596833LV00004BA/169/P

9 780999 223321